CHAINED HEART

SLATER SIBLINGS SERIES #2

MISSY WALKER

Cover Design: @germancreative

Editor: Swish Design & Editing

For Liv. You are strong, wild and independent. Nobody can ever change that.

I

JULIUS

Today is different.

The boardroom is where I've been numerous times before. However, I am unusually on edge.

As the door shuts, I sit at the head of the table with my brother staring me down at the other end. I may get fired from my own company or who knows what else. I need to think of another solution, and I need to do it quickly. Unfortunately, I've been up all night, and nothing has come to me. Unlike the billion-dollar ideas I had when starting Slater Corp. with my brother, I have nothing, well, nothing viable anyway.

No pleasantries are exchanged with the board members, as everyone knows we're down to business.

"Right. Let's get down to it then," Jacob Jones, my right-hand man and confidant, leads the meeting.

He is a friend and a foe, exactly the person you want on your board. Beside him are Hector and Phillip, both men who held prestigious positions before sitting on the Slater Corp. Board. Opposite those are another three men. Then three more men sit between my brother and I, all serving on the board for a decade or longer.

I steeple my hands in front of me, ready for the onslaught. "What you did has fucked things up, Slater," Jacob says.

"I understand as such, and I've been working to try and fix it," I reply, my tone resolute. He knows no one else can get away with talking to me like that. Still, I don't like his fucking tone.

"Fix the media storm surrounding your dick in a senator's fiancée's pussy."

I pin him a stare, but Jacob just stares me down.

"You don't have to be so crass," my brother and joint CEO, Vincent, interjects.

"You pay me to tell the truth. As soon as the news broke yesterday, our shares plummeted nine percent, wiping hundreds of millions of dollars off our share price. And they are still falling. Do you really think the media will stop?"

I stare at my brother, already knowing the answer. They want blood, and I'm the fucking bait. Vincent shoots me a sharp look before adding, "No, they will not stop."

"Then we don't have another choice, Julius. You've tied our hands. I think you know how this is going to go. We need to vote," Jacob announces. "For Slater Corp. to survive, you have to step down as CEO effective immediately unless you can tell me another way."

My nostrils flare. I had to go and sink my cock in a pretty pussy that was not mine. I blame my fucking father for this entire mess. But what the fuck did I expect? I knew this was coming.

I sit tall in my leather armchair and address the board. "I built this company with my brother, forged from our own hands. I will not let my indiscretion ruin what we have built. Do what you must. I accept the result."

Vincent stares at me. He must think I'm such a disappointment. Here we thought I'd be the one to settle down first, never him. But he is practically married, living with the love of his life, Rosie West, while I fuck myself into a black hole.

Jacob inhales sharply before speaking. "All in favor of Julius Slater stepping down effective immediately. Raise your hand."

I'm not shy, so I'll look them dead in the eye. I know why they are doing this, I know it, but I can't do anything but hate them all at the same time.

Jacob raises his hand almost immediately, followed by Hector and Phillip. They point to the sky like a dead straight arrow. My eyes fall around where the three men sitting opposite do the same. Then all eyes fall on my brother, Vincent, who is opposite me.

"Vincent. The vote needs to be unanimous," Jacob states, pushing for his decision.

"Sorry, brother," Vincent says, his tone clipped, but he pauses, his palm flat on the table. "But there is another way."

I stare at him in confusion. I've thought about all the ways I can keep my company, all leading to a dead end and none of which have made any difference to the media torrent coming down on us.

"What is it?" Jacob asks impatiently.

"You won't like it, brother. But it *will* work."

2

ISABELLA

"**N**o honey, don't do that, please!" Fox pulls on my arm, biting it as I drop him off at the shitty daycare I can barely afford.

"Momma, don't leave me," he screams as I try to pull him off me. His sharp incisors dig into me, and I squeal as I pull him off.

"Fox, please," I holler, but I'm being polite. I really can't handle the stares of the childcare workers this morning. I'm late for work and desperate to have my son dropped off, which is just around the corner from work.

"Momma, don't go," he cries out, tears in my eyes.

Bitch face number one stares at me as I try to disengage from my four-year-old son.

"You know there are other childcare centers not far from here. I'm sure he'd feel more comfortable there."

"No, it's fine," I say, feeling his teeth release my skin and the burning sensation it leaves.

"He's just settling in."

The other woman pipes up. She's tall, thin, and has

4

wiry glasses that sit atop her pointy nose. "He's been here for six months now."

"Look," I say, exasperated, and they widen their eyes. My son is special, the most important person in the world to me. The last place I want him to be is here, but between custody battles, legal fees, and rent in this city, I'm forced to put him in care where I doubt there's enough care at all. "He's just had a disruptive morning, is all," I say, calming myself with a steady breath.

Maybe if you ungrateful women gave a shit about the kids in your care, they would actually want to come here.

They all titter as I extricate myself from my screaming child. As soon as I'm in the clear, my son throws his drink bottle, sending it skidding across the linoleum floor.

That's a regular occurrence too.

"Go and pick it up now, Fox," Rachel, one of the women, says and points her finger at him, aggressively close to his pint-size face.

I shoot her a stare, but right now, I don't have any other option but to keep him here. I lower my gaze to my son as he clings to my leg. "Everything will be okay, sweetheart. I will see you tonight."

He reluctantly peels off me, his eyes like pools of sadness. My heart is ripped from my chest as I turn around and push the rickety door open.

Things have to get better, don't they? Whenever Fox returns from his father's, his outbursts escalate at drop-off. Today is the first time he has bitten me to try and prevent my leaving. Between this and the pressures of custody, something has to give.

I step onto the sidewalk and walk the three blocks to Slater Corp. The more I walk, the more pain I feel from the stress weighing me down. I try to push it away, but the excruciating memory of my ex's hands on me haunts me even when I'm awake.

"The fucking kid," he says, pushing him out of his hold and into my room. Fox falls forward, tumbling onto the carpet in our one-bedroom condo in Queens.

"You're over two hours late!" I shriek. "I was worried sick!"

Locked in a fierce gaze, a surge of hatred courses between us. His eyes pierce into mine, drilling deep into my soul, while I, in turn, meet his gaze head-on.

I hate this.

One week on, one week off custody with our son. I will bleed every last dollar to fight him for full custody.

"You're always fucking judging me. What gives you the right, Bella?"

"He's my son. How dare you," I accuse, and he steps closer. A putrid combination of tobacco and alcohol assaults my senses, the noxious odor striking the base of my nose like a physical blow, instantly twisting my stomach in disgust. "You're drinking with Fox in your care?" My tone brims with assertiveness.

"It's none of your fucking business what I do. You're not my wife anymore." The bitterness in his words is unmistakable.

"It may not be my business anymore, but it damn well concerns our child."

"I'm away for the next few weeks, so you'll have him all to yourself. So what if I wanted to spend more time with my son?"

"Do you mean more time drinking?" I counter.

His eyes narrow, filled with defiance, as he struggles to find a winning reply.

As the thought crosses my mind, an opportunity presents itself. If I can discreetly record this moment without him realizing it, it could serve as valuable evidence for my custody case.

My lawyer's advice echoes in my mind, urging me to gather any possible dirt that could strengthen my position. This might be my only chance.

With determination, I shift my focus to my son, Fox, who remains blissfully unaware of the commotion caused by his father. In a swift and fluid motion, I gently turn away, reaching around to embrace Fox, ensuring he feels the comfort and protection of my presence.

As I hold Fox close, I notice his small hands grasping his Lego bricks nearby. It's the perfect moment to discreetly retrieve my phone and gather evidence that could help safeguard my son's well-being. Carefully and without drawing attention, I retrieve the phone from my pocket, silently activating the video recording function.

Positioning the phone beside Fox, I shield it from Travis's view with my body, ensuring the phone remains hidden. With a calm and composed demeanor, I engage Fox in clicking Lego bricks together, joining in his innocent play.

"What the fuck?" I hear Travis's voice exclaim, his words filled with surprise and anger. In my peripheral vision, I detect his arm reaching toward my phone.

Fuck.

He's too quick as he grasps it before I do, then, in an instant, a firm hand clasps the nape of my neck, asserting control over my movements. With a swift and forceful motion, his palm strikes my cheek, delivering a sharp, stinging blow that leaves me momentarily disoriented, pain radiating across my face.

Like an explosive impact, my eye throbs with searing pain as if it could burst out of my face. The intensity forces me to crumble to the floor, instinctively clutching my injured cheek.

"Fox, go lock yourself in the bathroom," I whisper to him in a firm voice. I hold my cheek, trying to bury the insufferable pain this man has inflicted upon me.

Fox's obedience is routine. He's seen this many times before, so he does as I tell him, but not without looking back at me first.

With a nod of acknowledgment toward Fox, I summon every ounce of strength to rise to my feet, each movement laced with pain.

"Get out," I demand.

I can't even look at the man I was once married to.

"You fucked up here. See what you make me do?" he growls out, attempting to deflect responsibility for his violent outburst.

"Please, just go, Travis," I plead, my voice on the brink of collapse as an immediate headache pulsates through my head.

His words slice through the air, laced with a venomous threat that sends a shiver down my spine. "Don't even think about going to the police, or you know what's coming." He sneers, his voice dripping with malice.

The weight of his words clings to my burning skin, leaving a bitter taste of potent toxicity. The insidiousness of his threat hangs heavily in the air as he reminds me of his family's power to potentially tear our son away from me for good.

"Get out!" I scream louder this time, unable to contain my rage.

"You watch your mouth, Bella. You might not be my wife anymore, but I will take him away from you forever if you fuck with me like that again."

"I'm sorry," I say, just wanting him to leave. I can't bear to think what my life would be like without Fox in it.

And my ex has the means to do just that.

I shake off the searing memory of last night and walk into Slater Corp. my face covered for the most part. As much as I want to take the day off, I can't. Not with the scandal involving my boss and CEO, Julius Slater, breaking in the media last week. He needs me now more than ever, and I can't show up because I have a bruising mark across my cheek I can hide with makeup.

Security tosses me a nod as I swipe my card, traversing across the onyx marble-clad foyer and ascending into the elevator to the fortieth floor. This building never ceases to amaze me, nor the achievements of Julius and his brother Vincent, who until recently held the CEO post in the London office.

I put aside my things as I arrive at my desk. Julius isn't anywhere to be seen, but Vincent's booming voice is coming from his office.

Silence follows, and the next thing I see is Vincent flinging open his office door and striding toward Julius's. I'm so pleased he's stayed here and not returned to London to run that office. He's been needed here more than ever before, especially since the scandal erupted a week ago that embroiled my boss in an affair with a senator's much younger fiancée.

In the past month or two, I've sensed a change in Julius. Something isn't right, but I can't quite grasp what it is. But it's not like I'd ask. Our personal lives remain strictly off-limits in our interactions. Julius maintains a professional boundary, and I respect that.

But Julius's broad shoulders and deep blue eyes are seriously something else. I can't help but be drawn in whenever I catch a glimpse. I know the deal—we keep things professional, so I admire from afar without crossing any lines.

Except for that one time, late in his office. Drained from another fight with my ex, Julius returned from a late lunch tipsy and flirtatious, and I reveled in the much-needed attention. His lips brushed mine then he pulled back in alarm, apologetic and vowing never again to touch me that way.

"Good morning, Bella," Vincent greets me with his usual warm tone. It's funny how everyone seems to call me Bella, except for my own boss.

"Morning, Vincent."

As he walks past my desk, I sense his sudden pause and make a conscious effort to angle my face down, hoping to hide the welt on my cheek. Yet, out of the corner of my eye, I catch Vincent looking at me curiously, his gaze lingering for a moment longer than usual.

"What on earth happened?" Vincent's concern is evident in his voice as he takes in my bruised face.

I quickly dismiss it, trying to downplay the situation. "It's nothing. Is everything okay with you?" I divert the attention, aware of how Vincent has softened since his relationship with Rosie.

Unfortunately, Vincent doesn't let it go easily and leans across from my desk, his expression firm. "It's not nothing, is it?" he presses, refusing to accept my dismissive response.

The weight of his persistence reminds me this isn't the first time he has questioned me. My excuses are wearing thin, and I feel the need to deflect the conversation. I shuffle some papers across my desk, feigning engrossment in my work, anything to avoid the topic at hand.

"Is Julius inside?" he asks, shifting the conversation, and a wave of relief washes over me as he changes the topic.

"No, he hasn't arrived yet," I reply, grateful for the shift in focus.

"Good. Follow me. I want to talk to you in my office," he directs, and my heart sinks.

The nerves coil within me as I slowly rise from my seat.

"Is everything okay?" I meekly offer, trying to match his stride as we walk together.

"No, everything isn't okay," he responds firmly, extending his arm to open the door to his office.

I step ahead, entering his office, and the door thuds shut behind me, intensifying my anxiety. Swallowing the lump in my throat, I sit in the armchair across from his desk.

"Oh," I weakly reply, feeling the intensity of the situation pressing upon me. The thought of losing this job is inconceivable, especially now. With legal bills piling up and custody battles consuming my life, I struggle to stay afloat, surviving on a diet of instant noodles just to keep my head above water.

It's not that they don't pay me well. They do. But the overwhelming burden of legal expenses to secure custody of my son is taking its toll.

Vincent settles down across from me, his expression serious. "Bella, I can't stand idly by while you come to work with a different bruise every few weeks."

With my face lowered, tears well up, threatening to spill. The weight of my perceived failure presses upon me, suffocating my spirit. For too long, I've endured his abuse. "Oh," I whisper, feeling a mix of shame and despair wash over me.

"Is your ex-husband doing this?" Vincent probes, his voice laced with concern.

A lump forms in my throat like a grainy mound of sand. Shame and self-blame consume me as I grapple with the overwhelming emotions. It's as if I bear the weight of responsibility for the ongoing abuse.

If only I had been stronger and had found the courage to walk away from him sooner, maybe none of this would be happening now—the custody battles, his escalating drinking, and the relentless cycle of abuse that continues even after leaving him.

But fear grips me. I'm terrified to admit the truth to Vincent, to expose the reality of my situation. Admitting it to him would make it real, validating the pain and torment I have endured.

"What you tell me will stay between us, Bella."

"You promise?"

"I promise." Vincent's reassurance cuts through my fears, offering a glimmer of hope and support.

"Yes," I manage to utter, the words almost bursting out on an exhale. "It's Travis."

He leans forward, his fingers steeped together in a thoughtful gesture. "Tell me everything," he encourages, and the floodgates open as I begin to speak.

Words pour out of me, carried by emotions I didn't realize were waiting to be released. It's cathartic in ways I couldn't have anticipated.

At that moment, I realize I haven't truly discussed my ordeal and the daily trauma I live with, with anyone except for my best friend, Harley. She's the one who knows and has been there for me through it all. But beyond her, it's been a secret I've carried alone, the trauma I've locked away in the depths of my heart for fear of it taking over.

3

JULIUS

Thanks to his intervention, the board's plan to fire me from my own company has been halted, and I can't help but feel both gratitude and curiosity.

I meet my brother's gaze, taking in his presence as he sits across from me. I'm all ears, leaning in, eager to hear what he has in store. But something about his demeanor has me on edge like he's holding back a card I haven't seen yet.

What could he possibly be thinking that hasn't already crossed my mind?

"Well, what is it, Vincent?" Jacob's impatience seeps into his voice, fueling my own anticipation.

"It's an arrangement of sorts," Vincent responds, and I lean forward, my eyes fixed on him, waiting for further explanation.

"Go on," I snap out, my impatience betraying me.

Vincent's words hit me like a jolt of electricity. "I want you to marry Bella," he states, and for a moment, I question if I heard him correctly. The weight of the stares shifts from Vincent to me, intensifying the gravity of the situation.

"My secretary?" I seek clarification, my disbelief evident.

"Yes," Vincent affirms, his tone steady.

I can feel my blood boil with anger and confusion. "And why the fuck would I do that?"

"Because your marriage will blow this entire mess away," Vincent explains, his voice firm.

I shake my head, resolute in my response. "No, it won't," I assert, refusing to let this proposed solution cloud my judgment.

"Wait, hear him out," one of the board members interjects, their curiosity piqued. "Where are you going with this, Vincent? It's certainly an unconventional proposal."

Vincent takes a moment to gather his thoughts before responding. "Bella is a single mom and deserves stability and security in her life. By marrying her, you'll be seen as a compassionate and caring individual, willingly taking on the role of a father figure to her son. It will help reshape the narrative the press has painted of you from a philandering playboy and homewrecker to someone who is capable of genuine care and compassion."

The room falls into stunned silence as his words sink in.

As the weight of the proposal hangs heavy in the air, I find myself unable to contain my laughter. The sheer absurdity of it all seems to echo through the room, but it's met with a chilling silence—not a single chuckle or smirk in response. The atmosphere becomes so still that even the sound of a pin dropping would be deafening.

"He may have something here, Julius," one of the board members remarks, their tone contemplative and firm.

The unexpected support for Vincent's proposition catches me off guard. My laughter fades as I realize there might be more to this idea than meets the eye. Uncertainty washes over me as I consider the potential implications and outcomes of such a drastic arrangement.

"You can continue working here while Isabella moves in. A quick courthouse marriage will sweep this entire scandal with the senator's fiancée under the rug," Jacob states, piecing it together like a well-formed jigsaw puzzle.

Vincent's gaze holds firm as he responds, "Yes, that's the general idea. It would provide a way to put this entire ordeal behind you."

I shake my head, struggling to comprehend the gravity of the proposal. "Have you even spoken to Isabella about this? Have you considered her feelings in all of this?"

Vincent's expression wavers slightly. "Not entirely, but I have a feeling she would be open to the idea."

I scoff, my incredulity mounting. "Come on, you can't be serious," I exclaim, my voice laced with astonishment and frustration. "Isabella has been my dedicated secretary for the past four years, loyal to a fault. She's not the type to enter into a fake marriage, especially not for me." The thought of Isabella willingly agreeing to such a proposition feels like a betrayal of the trust and camaraderie we have built over the years.

"You let me worry about that part," he says, and now the cogs are turning in my brain.

What does he know about my pretty secretary that I don't?

"You know, this could work." Jacob is deep in thought as he ponders the idea. "Get her to agree, Vincent, and I think this could be a viable option. The *only* option," he quickly corrects.

The media would backflip so hard at the story we could spin. With all the late nights, the work trips, and the time spent together, this story could actually work.

"And how about the senator's fiancée I just fucked? If I

was so dedicated to my secretary, why would I fuck Grace?"

"Because you thought Isabella was going back to her ex-husband," one of the suits interjects. "You were distraught, did a stupid thing. We can get PR to spin it in a way that makes you look like the poor heartbroken man that thought the love of his life was leaving him to go back to her ex-husband."

"Jesus fuck. Listen to you all. You sound like a regular *Bold and the Beautiful* soap opera."

"It's the only option if you want to keep your job here," Vincent says, cutting through the clatter of fireworks going off in my brain.

"What's it going to be, Julius?" Jacob asks as all eyes turn to me.

Sure, Isabella is undeniably stunning with her long brown hair, porcelain skin, and those captivating powder-blue eyes. But let me make one thing clear. There has never been any room for romance between us, except for that one drunken kiss late one night in my office that we never, *ever*, speak of.

Our relationship has always been strictly professional.

I've always maintained a deep admiration for her from a distance, appreciating her beauty and dedication to her work, but entertaining any romantic notions? No way. It's just not something I would dare to consider. I mean, she has a kid, for fuck's sake.

"As long as after everything settles down, we can get a divorce."

"Of course." There seems to be a unanimous vote in favor of this, which appeases me.

"Fine," I utter in disbelief at my own words. But this company is my everything, and I will be damned to give it all up because my dick went wayward.

"Now get it done," Jacob says firmly over his wiry glasses perched atop the bridge of his nose.

I'm walking, my body numb, and Vincent is beside me as we move out of the boardroom. "It's for the best. You'll see," he says.

As I turn toward my brother, confusion and disbelief etch across my face, I speak my truth. "Forgive me, brother, but I just can't see it at all right now."

He lets out a sigh, his expression a blend of frustration and determination. Tilting his head forward, he forces my gaze to meet his. Reluctantly, I shift my focus and find myself locking eyes with Isabella. She stands there, her dark brown hair pulled up in a high bun, dressed in her usual professional attire of a blouse and skirt. But something catches my attention—a mark on her face that wasn't there before, a stark contrast to her usual flawless appearance.

"Good morning, Mr. Slater," she says brightly.

"Isabella, hello."

"Let's talk in your office, Julius," Vincent says. "Join us, Bella," he adds, and I briskly walk past her inside my office.

Vincent and Isabella sit beside one another as I curl behind my desk and slide into the seat. I'm grateful I am still here. However, I can't shake off the lingering sense of unease. This unexpected turn of events is something else entirely, something I hadn't envisioned or anticipated.

As I lift my gaze, I meet Isabella's piercing blue eyes. Her gaze has a sense of readiness, an unspoken understanding that she is here to carry out my instructions.

Isabella has always been the epitome of professionalism, the perfect secretary.

"The board has suggested that the only way I can retain my position here is by marrying you, Isabella."

Isabella lets out a bark of laughter. Unblinking, I stare

straight back at her. Her eyes widen as she realizes this is no joke then she shifts her gaze toward Vincent. I can't help but feel a sense of unease.

What have they been discussing?

The tension in the room becomes palpable as their unspoken conversation hangs in the air, leaving me uncertain about what has transpired between them.

Vincent takes a deep breath, his voice steady as he addresses Isabella directly, "Isabella, I truly believe that by marrying my brother, you can help alleviate the scandal surrounding the company and secure a stable future for you and your son."

Isabella's eyes widen in surprise, her hands tightly gripping the armrests of her chair. "Wait, what?" she blurts out, her voice filled with disbelief. The shock in her reaction mirrors my own confusion.

"That's what I said," I reply, flattening my hands across the table.

"Listen, brother, you have to put this scandal behind you if you want your position here, and Bella, by agreeing to this marriage of convenience, you can secure the funds to fight for full custody."

Full custody?

How does my brother know so much about Isabella's personal life? It puts me on edge that he's aware of things I don't know about her.

"But I don't love you." Her words are raw and genuine, hanging in the air with tangible weight.

I can't help but let out a bitter laugh, the irony of the situation not lost on me. "Don't worry, Isabella, the feeling's mutual," I retort, a tinge of bitterness coloring my voice.

"This is a marriage of convenience, purely for the sake

of appearances. There won't be any love involved," Vincent asserts, his gaze shifting between the two of us. "Once the scandal has blown over, you can proceed with a swift divorce. However, to make it believable, it would be best to wait at least one year."

Isabella's eyes flicker with uncertainty and apprehension as she questions the next steps. "And what happens after the divorce?"

I interject, my tone laced with a hint of frustration. "Then we go back to how things were here."

The last thing I want is to be tied to my secretary in a marriage, even if it is just for show. Couldn't they have found another candidate? Someone more suitable? Isabella is nice and all, with a pretty face and a kind heart, but that's where it ends, *except for the slight mishap in my office with her a few months ago.* I quickly push that thought aside. This is merely a solution to a problem.

Isabella's voice cuts through the tension, her words brimming with a newfound frankness. "And do you think we can?" she questions, her gaze steady.

"Of course, why not?" I counter, rubbing the nape of my neck in frustration. "Look, I don't want to do this either," I say, leveling with her.

Vincent turns to me, his expression serious. "You heard what the board said. It's either take steps to fix your image or face the consequences of being fired."

"And I'm supposed to be the pity case just because I'm a single mom?" Isabella interjects, her voice tinged with frustration but also a hint of resignation.

Her words hit us like a sudden jolt, exposing the brutal truth of the situation. It's a rare moment of vulnerability from Isabella, revealing the unfair expectations and sacrifices thrust upon her. In all honesty, I can't help but feel that this burden falls more heavily on my shoulders.

"It's not as simple as that," Vincent assures her, though we both know that it is.

She lets out a heavy exhale. "So my son and I are just meant to live with you?"

"No," I respond quickly, and Vincent stares at me.

"This needs to be done the right way if it is to be believable. There's no way the media will buy that you're married and not living together. You can have a quick engagement, and next week we will go down to the courthouse and make it official," my brother so kindly explains like we have no other choice.

"Where would I sleep?" she asks, her voice laced with concern.

"I have four bedrooms and a study. You choose," I say. "Although away from me is preferable."

"Okay," she says meekly, and I notice her shift in her seat uncomfortably.

"So, it's settled. Isabella, take the day off today to get things sorted."

"No, that's not necessary," she says, loyal to a fault.

"You haven't had a day off since starting here," I say. "If you can't juggle this, I can have my housekeeper fetch your things. Where is it you live?"

"Again, not necessary. I can get them this evening..."

"Well, if you'll excuse me." Vincent stands and motions toward the door. "I have more fires to put out and some good news to share with the board and public relations. This will all work out," Vincent says to both of us. "You'll see." He looks at us then walks out, leaving her staring at the floor.

"I should go—" she says, but I cut her off.

"I don't want this as much as you, Isabella," I say, trying to reassure her. She tilts her somber eyes to meet mine, and her once-veiled professionalism slips as I see a sadness lurking underneath, catching me off guard. "I don't mean it like that. You're a beautiful woman, Isabella. I'm not the marrying type. Hell, I'm not the relationship type, yet I'm doing this because I'm backed into a corner. If I want to stay at the company Vincent and I built from the ground up, this is the only way. My company is my life, ingrained in my blood, and I'm nothing without it."

"The truth is, I don't have a choice either if I want to secure the life for my son that he deserves."

I should press her here, but I don't. We are strictly business, and I swore I would never look at her that way again.

She's not my problem.

Her ex-husband and her kid, again, not my problem.

I've made that clear by never asking her about her personal life, and she has adhered to the boundaries I've set in the workplace since she started with me four years ago.

"Then it's settled," I say, determined to shift my focus back to work.

There are pressing matters that demand my attention, and dwelling on the intricacies of this unconventional proposal won't help resolve them.

"Great. I'll move in tomorrow after work," Isabella declares, rising from her chair and smoothing her skirt as she turns to exit.

I find myself momentarily captivated by her figure as she walks toward the door. The idea of her becoming my wife feels surreal, almost absurd.

"Oh." She turns suddenly, catching me off guard. I quickly avert my gaze, but she squints at me as if sensing something. "What's your address?"

4

ISABELLA

Even though the dust has barely settled on our new arrangement, I find myself exiting the subway and walking to his fancy Park Avenue address. My son, Fox, is beside me.

I know this will confuse him, but I still don't know what or how I will tell him I have a new husband. He's four. He understands somewhat, but with new surroundings and a new face that isn't his father, I cringe and squeeze his hand as I look down at the address in my hands.

The scent of nearby vendor hot dogs fills my nostrils, distracting me. I haven't even eaten since breakfast. Between another busy day at work, going home, and packing my entire life up, well, as much as I could take in three suitcases, I hadn't had time to eat.

"Momma, please!" Fox tugs on my hand as we walk past the street vendor.

"Are you hungry, sweetheart?" I ask, stopping and staring down at him.

My boy is so handsome, with his huge blue eyes and smooth skin. His short hair dusts across his eyes as the wind sweeps past, and I ruffle my hands through it as he nods at the man behind the stand.

"Well, I guess," I say, standing upright. I only managed to give him some chips while I was packing, so the poor boy would be hungry. The last thing I want is for him to go to our new place hungry and expecting food.

"What can I get you?" the man with curly black hair asks over the steaming pots.

"A hot dog, please," I say. "With cheese and ketchup."

"Lots of ketchup," Fox adds with a toothy grin.

"Of course, little man," the street vendor says with a smile. He has a kind heart, a warmth emanating from him. It's pretty clear he is a father himself.

"Are you coming or going?" he says, taking in the suitcases beside me.

I glance at the second-hand suitcases. "Ah, coming, I guess?"

"We're moving to number thirty, fuck avenue."

"*Park* Avenue!" I correct, and the vendor lets out a bark of laughter.

"May as well be called Fuck Avenue with all the..."

I raise my brow.

"Not that you are..."

"Uh-huh."

He hands me the hot dog, and I give him some change. "Thank you," I say.

"Miss, I didn't mean..."

"I know, it's fine."

"Number thirty Park Avenue is a well-known address around here... and you, Miss, just look so normal, is all I meant to say."

I hand Fox the hot dog and smile at the vendor. "Have a nice evening, sir," I say as I throw the bag over my shoulder and curl my fingers around the handle of the wheeled suitcase, dragging it behind me.

"Mmm, this is so good, Mommy," Fox exclaims with a big grin, taking a big bite of the hot dog.

Pushing aside my fears, no matter how stubborn they may be, I choose to embrace this moment. Seeing my son happy, healthy, and safe brings a surge of warmth to my heart. If marrying Julius Slater is what it takes to ensure his continued well-being, then I'm willing to make that sacrifice.

I smile down at my son as we stroll in the balmy evening. A man in a suit passes us, his blue eyes raking over me. *Blue eyes.*

Julius's are darker, and the way he looked at me that night, my body warms as I think back. I haven't let myself think about the time we shared a few months back in his office.

My mind is preoccupied with my unpleasant encounter with my ex-husband earlier in the day as I continue working at my desk. The wounds from our altercation are still fresh, and I long for a distraction, something to lift my spirits.

Suddenly, Julius stumbles into the office, clearly a little tipsy from his lunch-turned-dinner meeting. My eyes widen in surprise as I watch him scan the room, a mischievous smile forming on his lips when he spots me still diligently working.

"Well, well, well, look who's ssstill here," he slurs playfully, his voice carrying a charming tone I haven't heard from him before.

I raise an eyebrow, caught off guard by his unexpected behavior. This is the first time I've seen this side of Julius, and it's oddly captivating. The timing couldn't be more perfect, considering the emotional rollercoaster I've been on today.

As I get up and smooth my skirt, his eyes drag down, and I feel a fire burn within me at his gaze. "Do you have a moment to go through your schedule for tomorrow?" I ask.

His eyes snap up to meet mine, and I muster a small nervous smile.

"Of course," he says, his smile teasingly broad and reserved only for me.

Damn, this playboy side the media talks about, how can any woman resist him?

I step into his office, closing the door behind us, the sound echoing with a weighty finality. It's an ordinary act we've done countless times before, but tonight, there's an undercurrent of excitement coursing through me.

No. I forcefully push those feelings away, refusing to let them distract me.

Julius settles into his chair, and his eyes beckon me to sit beside him. It's a position I've never occupied during our meetings, and the invitation stirs a mix of nerves and something else within me. I swallow hard, the pounding of my heart reverberating in my ears as his gaze tracks my every move. He watches me like a predator eyeing its prey.

"I assume the lunch went well?" I manage to ask, my voice slightly shaky, trying to distract myself and regain control.

"Indeed, Isabella," he responds with a mischievous grin, his words dripping with a tantalizing undertone. "But I must say, finding you still here is the highlight of my day."

My brows furrow in confusion, caught off guard by his comment. "What?"

Julius leans in closer, invading my personal space with an intensity that sends shivers down my spine. My breath hitches as his gaze locks onto mine, holding me captive. "You are stun-

ningly beautiful," he whispers, his warm breath grazing my cheek.

The electric current between us crackles with tension, and I forget how to breathe for a moment.

"Julius, you're drunk," I assert, my voice trembling with caution and a desire I have no right feeling.

A smirk curls on his lips as his eyes hungrily trace the outline of mine, his proximity creating an intoxicating whirlwind. The air thickens with an undeniable charge, and his hand knots at the back of my head, drawing me toward him, our lips finding each other in a searing kiss.

The kiss lands like an electric jolt, wiping my mind clean of any other thought. Julius's lips, warm and firm, press into mine, the lingering taste of scotch between us. His touch makes my heart pound and my skin tingle, and as my hands find their way to his neck, it's as if I'm truly alive in this singular moment.

Suddenly, his door flies open, and we both pull away from one another in a rush.

"Hope I'm not interrupting," Vincent says as he looks between us.

Oh fuck. Fuckity fuck.

"Of course not," Julius replies, and I quickly launch out of my chair, exiting the office.

Shit. What the hell was that?

Confusion rattles me, but I know it's best to just blame the alcohol and move on.

Fox's voice pulls me to the present, and I stare down at him and realize we're here.

"Momma, why are we stopping?"

We stand in front of the towering skyscraper, mesmerized by its grandeur. The large gold digits and the luxurious red carpet beneath the impressive awning make it clear that this place is beyond anything I've ever encountered. Awe and apprehension fill me as I take a deep breath.

"We're here, sweetheart."

Approaching the doorman, I introduce myself, "I'm Isabella Moore, here to see Julius Slater."

The doorman's eyes scan me and my son, his doubt evident as he takes note of Fox's ketchup-stained T-shirt and the remaining hotdog he's holding. "Is he expecting you?" he asks, his tone laced with skepticism.

"Yes," I reply firmly, determined to assert my purpose despite the suspicion.

"Of course, please let me help you with your luggage." He smiles broadly.

"Thank you," I say, holding onto my son's hand and walking inside as he keeps the door open for me.

The foyer is gold and black, mimicking the opulence of the Slater headquarters.

"Ms. Moore, Mr. Slater is expecting you," a man greets me from behind the marble front desk and smiles warmly.

"Hello, little man," he says as he lowers to Fox's level. "I'm Franklin, the concierge here at thirty."

"You look funny," Fox says, pointing at his burgundy hat that matches his tie.

"Fox," I interject with a nervous smile.

"My son thinks I look funny too." He chuckles, amusement evident in his voice. "Come on, let me guide you to Mr. Slater's floor. We can't keep him waiting."

"Who is Mr. Slater?" Fox's innocent question hangs in the air, demanding an answer.

Franklin's gaze flickers between Fox and me, his curiosity palpable.

I quickly think on my feet, searching for a response that

won't divulge too much. "He's the man I mentioned earlier, the one we'll be staying with for a little while," I explain, my voice laced with cautious uncertainty.

Taking charge, I guide Fox toward the elevator, determined to distract him from further inquiries about the man I'm reluctantly moving in with.

Franklin leads the way, his stride confident as he speaks. "Mr. Slater resides on the top floor, the penthouse," he informs us with a bright smile.

"Thank you," I murmur, my nerves tingling with anticipation, yet I can't deny the apprehension building.

As the elevator ascends smoothly, I crouch down to Fox, who is devouring his hotdog.

Somehow he has managed to make a mess with ketchup smeared all over his moss-green T-shirt. I quickly grab a tissue from my pocket and moisten it with a lick, attempting to blot away the cascading ketchup stains that resemble a snaking pattern down his side.

"Momma..." Fox whines, pushing me away in frustration.

"Fox, please," I plead, trying to clean the stains, but my efforts only seem to aggravate him further.

In an instant, he lets out a high-pitched shriek, and I reluctantly withdraw. The last thing I need is for him to be irritable just as we step out of the elevator.

"Okay, okay, darling. Remember your manners, just like I taught you, all right?" I remind Fox, who is gently rubbing his tired eyes.

"*Paw Patrol*," he exclaims with enthusiasm. "I want to watch *Paw Patrol*." His voice echoes in the elevator just as the doors slide open.

Quickly, I rise to my feet, discreetly tucking away the used tissue into my pocket.

"Ms. Moore, I'm Paola, Mr. Slater's housekeeper," a poised woman introduces herself, her impeccable attire contrasting with my disheveled appearance. "And who is this little mister?"

"Oh, hello," I greet her, feeling self-conscious. I must look like a mess compared to her. "This is Fox, my son."

"Lovely to meet you, Fox," Paola says warmly, extending her hand and crouching to his level.

Fox glances at me, then at her hand, and unexpectedly slaps it away. My face flushes with embarrassment, and I quickly step in. "Fox! I'm so sorry. He's just exhausted. It's been a long day of work and daycare."

Paola rises gracefully, her smile slightly forced. "Of course, dear. Let me show you to your quarters. Mr. Slater is in the study."

I nod gratefully, eager to escape the awkwardness of the moment and follow Paola as she leads us inside.

As I step inside, the foyer opens into a surprisingly vibrant and cozy space, defying the expectations I had of Julius's typically professional and controlled demeanor. Polished oak floors adorned with plush rugs create a warm and inviting atmosphere. A large sitting area catches my eye, adjacent to a well-equipped kitchen. However, it's the breathtaking view straight ahead that truly captivates me. Floor-to-ceiling windows showcase the sprawling beauty of Manhattan, leaving me momentarily speechless.

"Wow, Momma! Look," Fox exclaims with sheer excitement, his hands pressed against the pristine glass, spreading his tiny fingers wide.

"Fox," I scold gently, my eyes widening in awe. "Wow," I whisper, as no words can adequately describe the grandeur before us. The living room alone is larger than our entire rental apartment in Queens.

Paola's voice breaks the spell. "Welcome to your new home, Ms. Moore."

I instinctively move closer to my son, wrapping a protective arm around his shoulder while offering a shy smile to the housekeeper. I wonder what has been said about our situation to the staff and those within Julius's social circles. It feels like entering uncharted territory.

Suddenly, footsteps echo through the room, and Julius appears in view. He's still dressed in his suit from earlier, though slightly disheveled. His navy-fitted pants hug his strong thighs, and the powder blue shirt clings to his defined arms. His tie is absent, and the top buttons of his shirt are undone. Even his usually immaculate hair falls slightly across his eyebrow and sweeps across his blue eyes. My heart skips a beat as I take in his undeniably handsome appearance.

"Mr. Slater, I didn't want to disturb you, sir, as you mentioned being busy. But your guests have arrived," Paola informs him, her voice respectful yet concerned.

Julius's gaze shifts to Fox, and the horror on his face is undeniable. His smile fades as he takes in the ketchup stains on the luxurious rug beneath us.

"Is that ketchup on my thirty-thousand-dollar rug?" he utters in disbelief, his voice steeped in frustration.

My eyes drop to the eggshell-tone rug beneath us, where a glaring red splatter of ketchup mocks me. It's like a bullseye, drawing attention to my blunder. Panic sets in as I immediately pull out the tissue from my pocket, attempting to blot the mark and only making it worse.

"Stop," Julius and Paola say simultaneously, their voices commanding and forceful.

The sound reverberates through the room, causing Fox to drop his hot dog and burst into tears. My heart sinks at the sight of his distress, and I quickly leap into action, wrapping my arms around him and pulling him close.

Julius's hand goes to his forehead, clearly feeling the weight of the situation. I can see the strain in his expression, mirroring my feelings of embarrassment and regret.

"Don't worry. I will take care of this," he says, exhaling heavily as the reality of the situation sinks in.

Paola swiftly steps in, assuming control of the situation. "Ms. Moore, let me show you and Fox to your rooms. I'll have someone clean this up," she offers, giving me a reassuring smile in an attempt to alleviate my embarrassment.

"Thank you, Paola," I say gratefully, relieved to have her understanding and assistance.

We follow her through the expansive penthouse as she leads us to a beautifully appointed bedroom with a large, inviting bed with Fox still sniffling beside me.

"This is your room." She turns and smiles. "And this here is Master Fox's room."

He bursts open the door forgetting about his tears. "My own room!" He squeals in delight.

"But, of course," Paola says, smiling.

Stepping inside Fox's room, I take it all in. It's simply decorated with a rug and bed in the middle, a perfect haven for Fox. It's beautiful but not a four-year-old boy's room. Not at all like Fox's room at home, full of color, writing on the walls, and toys strewn across the floor.

"I'll have someone bring up your luggage. Please make yourselves at home. If you need anything, just let me know," Paola warmly announces.

"Thank you, Paola. We really appreciate it," I reply, my voice filled with gratitude and relief.

As she departs, I take a deep breath, attempting to process the whirlwind of emotions and fatigue weighing heavily on me. I turn to Fox, who is already exploring his new space, his eyes wide with excitement, but I can see the exhaustion.

"We'll be okay, sweetheart," I assure him, though I'm not entirely convinced. "We'll make this work."

Just then, Julius appears in the doorway, his expression tight. "So, you're Fox," he says in a grim tone. He holds out his hand, and Fox, being Fox, fist-bumps him.

I let out a nervous laugh. "I'm sorry about your rug. Can I arrange for it to be dry-cleaned for you? I don't want you to be out of pocket."

"Isabella, that is not necessary. Let's ensure Fox is seated when he's eating next." He raises his eyes at Fox, and Fox wipes away his tears, rubbing his eyes.

"If it's okay with you, Mr. Slater, I think Fox is tired, and I would like to put him to sleep."

"At seven o'clock?" he asks, dumbfounded.

God, this man has no idea when it comes to kids.

"Yes, that's his bedtime," I explain, "Or, at least, a bedtime I consistently attempt to maintain."

Reacting to my announcement, Fox propels himself onto the bed as if it were a spring-free trampoline, beginning to jump with surprising vigor. His exhaustion seems to evaporate instantly, replaced with a sudden burst of energy.

"Good God, this child is a monkey," he exclaims, observing Fox's hyperactivity with a blend of shock and amusement.

"Yes, well, kids, you know..." I offer, trying to minimize the chaos.

"Little man, we don't jump on the furniture," Mr. Slater asserts firmly.

"But it's so fun," Fox cries out in protest, and I quickly cross the room, plucking him off the bed and into my arms.

"Come on, time for bed," I coo, holding him close. "Say goodnight to Mr.—"

"Julius. You can both call me Julius here," he interrupts, and I glance at him in surprise.

"Julius," I repeat, the name tasting strange on my tongue. He has always been Mr. Slater to me—my employer, nothing more.

"Goodnight, Jules Monster," Fox exclaims, and I can't help but cringe at the error.

Julius lets out a sigh, his patience apparently stretched thin. "It's Ju. Lee. Us," he enunciates, sounding out each syllable. But by now, Fox is curling his arms tightly around my neck and, with unexpected strength, pulling me down onto the bed with him.

When I finally pull free, Julius is gone.

What the hell have I got myself into?

It's after ten. I've unpacked, and now Fox is finally asleep after I read not one but four books to him after our luggage arrived.

Quietly, I step out of my room, suddenly aware of the gnawing hunger in my stomach. The house is steeped in silence, prompting me to wonder if Julius has called it a night. As I tread down the hall, I take note of the layout.

A guest room and bathroom are opposite our rooms, then adjacent to that is the study. Briefly, I peer inside. A mahogany desk commands the space, its surface a chaotic mix of stacked documents and a computer in sleep mode.

There's a set of grand double doors next to the office. Which I guess must be Julius's room. My curiosity goes a bit wild as the questions race in my mind.

What does the room look like? How plush is his bed? What would he look like all curled up in it, or taking a shower... naked.

Suddenly, a growl from my stomach cuts through these thoughts like a hot knife through butter, reminding me not only of the meal I've missed but also of the need to keep it professional with Julius. With my stomach acting as my compass, I head toward the kitchen, eager to whip up a quick sandwich before bed.

"He's some kid you got there." I spin on my heel and find Julius in the armchair near the fireplace, working on his laptop.

His eyes hover on the gap between my T-shirt and jeans. He hasn't seen me in anything other than formal blacks, blouses, and stockings.

He's staring because this is rare. Unusual to see me like this, right?

"You scared me," I say as he peers over his laptop screen.

"Sorry, that was not my intention."

He closes the laptop before getting up and walking over to me. He's large, and I feel meek beside his six-foot-four frame. The scent of his aftershave coasts by my senses, and I try to ignore the warmth of heat spreading through my blood.

"Sorry about the rug," I say again. "Not the first impression I was hoping for."

He laughs and looks over at it. "Paola has it sorted."

"I can see that. She's a wonder." I marvel at where the stain once was. You wouldn't even know it was there anymore.

He stares at me, unmoving, and I can see how having me here would be strange.

"Um... can I just help myself? I haven't had dinner," I ask rather sheepishly.

He brushes past me, and I smell the familiar scent of him, woody and dark tones that make me clench.

"This is your house now. Help yourself." He opens the refrigerator, full to the brim with fresh fruit, juices, smoothies, quiches, and smoked meats.

"On the stove are dinner leftovers in the blue casserole dish, or grab anything you want in here."

"Thank you," I say as I lift the lid on the casserole dish on the stove, the scent making my mouth water. My stomach makes an incredibly loud noise, and I blush with embarrassment as it fills the quiet space.

He lets out a laugh. "Eat something, Isabella, before you faint on me."

"Plates are here," he offers, and I blindly turn, falling against him.

"Shit, sorry," I say as he catches me from landing flat on my face.

He sets me straight back up, his hand not leaving my elbow as he tips my chin up to his.

"Hopefully, my housekeeper, Paola, can alleviate some of the stress your little one brings on you."

"He isn't a stress," I grit out defiantly, trying to push aside the scattering of goose bumps from Julius's touch.

"He's a tornado with limbs," Julius says matter-of-factly. He is still holding my chin, and I notice my breathing curl into my throat.

"He is very energetic. All boys are at that age," I say, his blue eyes darkening as something swirls between us.

"I guess we should lay some ground rules," he states, removing his hand abruptly and skirting around the kitchen to sit on a chair.

Slowly, I move, grabbing a plate and serving myself some casserole, ignoring my flagrantly overzealous mind and the lingering warmth from his touch.

"That's probably a good idea," I agree.

"We have to keep up this charade for one year, Isabella. We will not let this interrupt our working relationship or jeopardize it in any way. I value you as my secretary and have since you joined the company. Work must come first above all else."

"Of course, Mr. Sl—" I stop, correcting myself. "Julius," I agree, coming to sit beside him.

"We will need to be seen in public together for the media to buy this story. So social events, galas, dinners, you will accompany me."

"I'm not sure that's always possible with Fox," I reply as I dig some meat and carrots onto my fork and pop them in my mouth. The flavors are heavenly, and I immediately dig in for more.

"What is the arrangement you have with your ex-husband?" Julius asks as he watches me eat intently.

"Fox is with me for a few weeks until Travis returns from a work trip. Then it's back to normal. I have a week on, and so does he. For now."

"For now?" I inquire, and she looks at me, surprised. Because I never ask her anything personal, nor do I delve further than necessary. "Never mind," I say, not wanting to delve into anything but a working contractual relationship. It's none of my business, nor do I want to make it. "I will ask Paola to arrange for a babysitter if you have Fox on an evening of an event."

"I would like to make sure that Fox likes them, so I will need to meet them. I'm not just handing my son over to anyone."

"Nor would I expect you to," he says sternly.

"And what about other romantic partners during our agreement..." He lets the sentence dangle in the silence.

"Pardon?" I ask, blindsided by the thought that he might entertain the idea of seeing someone else concurrently. But considering we aren't romantically involved, it does fall into place. He is, after all, the most sought-after billionaire bachelor in Manhattan.

"I believe we shouldn't engage with others in that way," he proposes to my instant relief. "At least until this controversy subsides."

I exhale a breath I didn't realize I was holding in. "I don't really have the bandwidth for a partner anyway," I confess. "And honestly, dating is the last thing on my mind," I add, the echo of my ex's betrayal still ringing loud in my ears. The prospect of trusting another man seems distant, if not impossible. "I'm never dating again if I have any say about it," I mumble to myself, not meaning for him to hear.

"Is that so?" he questions, an unreadable expression on his face. I stop eating, meeting his gaze. "Never say never, Isabella."

5

JULIUS

The vision of my secretary almost makes it impossible to ignore the blood rushing to my groin.

Yes.

My secretary.

But sleep evades me at the sight of Isabella in light-washed jeans fitted around her waist and a T-shirt that lightly brushes her porcelain skin. Her dark brown hair is loose, a stark contrast to her polished, tight bun at work each day.

She devoured her meat like a carnivore beside me tonight with me watching on, uncertain about this whole arrangement.

Her kid, for starters, is a wrecking ball. A year with him and my penthouse will be akin to the Roman ruins. I make a mental note to ask Paola to raise the Van Gogh and Pollock artwork higher and out of reach.

Eventually, I drift off, but I'm awoken by screaming. It's coming from down the hall—the kid's room.

Christ, what the fuck is wrong?

I jump out of bed, flinging the sheets off. It's still dark as I throw open my doors and walk down the hallway. I find Isabella in his room, crouched beside him, stroking Fox's head. She doesn't see me, so I make myself scarce, but not before watching her with him for a moment longer.

The way she strokes his head tenderly, the love she pours into soothing her child.

So much love.

I swallow at the jarring sight, suddenly insanely jealous of mother and son before me. Sent off to boarding school at a young age, I never had that love with either parent. I watch on in wonder and awe. Her touch calms him almost immediately, and she seems to know exactly what he needs. She's so patient and kind. It's another side of her I never knew existed.

Once he drifts off the sleep, she gets up and tiptoes out of the room, closing it behind her. It's then she sees me in the shadows.

"Jesus!" She jumps in fright as the door clicks shut. "Sorry, Julius. I didn't mean to wake you."

"Is he all right?" I ask, concern lacing my voice.

"Yes, just a nightmare." Her gaze dips to my bare chest. Wearing nothing but low-slung sweats, I stand just in front of her, taking her in.

She's wearing satin pajamas. The camisole has thin straps and tapers down into a V where the outline of her ample breasts shows.

Fuck me.

Who knew that hid under her uniform of a blouse and skirt?

Awkwardness seeps between us like that day my brother walked in on us in my office.

That day I buried so deep in my mind and cast away like the mistake it was.

Business and pleasure should never intersect. I've lived by this code for as long as I can remember.

"I'm glad he's doing all right," I tell her, distancing myself slightly. "I'll see you in a few hours."

Her response is a muted "Yes." As the dark night starts giving way to dawn, I watch her retreat into her room.

With an exhalation, I turn my back and return to my room, where sleep remains stubbornly out of reach. My efforts to erase her image, dressed in silky pajamas, only fan the blazing embers of desire into a sharper, brighter flame.

I give up on sleep and retreat to my office, deciding that plowing into my work is the only way to stop thinking about her. But as soon as the kid wakes, it's like a tornado whipping through my home, and my concentration is broken.

I open my door and walk into the living room to a flurry of activity, my usual calm and orderly morning disappearing overnight.

"Morning," Isabella says as Fox whizzes past me.

She tries and fails to catch Fox, who is deciding he doesn't want to get his hair brushed but would rather run laps around my living room, giggling.

"Good morning," I say as I take in the chaos.

Isabella finally corners him, and he squeals like a caged animal as she runs a brush through his unruly hair.

"Fox, please!" she pleads, but he only squeals louder.

Fuck me. Does she really go through this every morning before work?

Five minutes later, she's out the door, dropping the kid to daycare, and I couldn't be happier.

"How do people keep sane with kids?" I mutter to Paola, who's in the kitchen.

"He sure is lively," she replies, scrubbing away the breakfast remnants that Fox had managed to splatter everywhere except in his mouth.

～

The hours race by.

Our attention is divided between the scandal, the looming Bynstrom investment, and day-to-day operations. The scandal involving the senator's fiancée and I had threatened to derail the Bynstrom three-hundred-million investment and IPO strategy we'd been working on for over a year and now is still up in the air.

Many times last night, I wanted to delve deeper into Isabella's life, and ask about the bruise on her cheek and her unruly kid, but I held back. It's not my place to interfere with her personal life.

All my life, I've adhered to a strict code of noninvolvement.

It's simpler that way.

Isabella's like a fragile wallflower—strong on the outside but broken within. Not that she lets it show.

That's something we have in common—we both wear our professional masks well.

Her lips so eager against mine.

Her gentle touch and vulnerable eyes.

We'd promised never to cross that line again. Isabella values her job, and I can't afford another scandal. I need to regain my composure, refocus. This marriage of convenience is the perfect solution. I just have to remember it's only for a year. Then I'll reclaim my life. As a professional, I can manage that.

A gentle knock on my door interrupts my thoughts. The sweet, familiar scent of raspberry ice cream tells me it's Isabella before she even speaks. "Mr. Slater, don't forget your six o'clock appointment this evening."

"Right, thanks for the reminder, Isabella," I reply.

In the midst of the day's chaos, I'd totally forgotten about that meeting.

"That's okay," she says, hovering in the doorway, looking somewhat hesitant.

She's lost weight recently. Another detail I shouldn't be focusing on.

"What's on your mind, Isabella?"

"Doesn't this arrangement seem... strange to you?" she asks, her gaze fixed on me.

I motion for her to come in, and she does, closing the door behind her.

"This is the strangest thing I've ever done, Isabella," I confess, and she slumps into the chair opposite me, letting out a sigh of relief.

"Thank God," she murmurs, a small smile playing on her lips. My eyes are automatically drawn to her lips and the light blush on her cheeks.

"What will people think when they find out?" she asks.

"We have the best PR team in Manhattan. I'm not worried about public opinion. I leave that to them."

"But you are worried about something?" she presses, and I tilt my head in question. She rarely pries.

"You know me well, Isabella," I concede, noticing her swallow hard.

"I'm concerned about your little tornado leaving my house in ruins," I joke, though that's not my primary worry.

I value my privacy immensely, and the idea of sharing my space with someone else, particularly someone as fragile and enchanting as Isabella, is somewhat unsettling. "I'm also concerned about our working relationship," I add. "I don't want this arrangement to affect the professional rapport we've built over the past four years."

"I understand," she acknowledges. "I can't afford to lose this job, Mr. Slater. I'll do my best to keep Fox in check, but we still have to live in your house. We still have to eat, sleep, and live."

"Of course," I agree. "And it's not my intention to make you uncomfortable while you're in my home." I catch myself. "Our home," I correct myself.

"Our home," she repeats, a hint of incredulity in her voice. "Sounds so strange."

"Because it is," I concur. "Jennifer, our head of PR, will email us the strategy and the agreement by tomorrow. Ensure you're familiar with it, and let me know if you want to change anything."

"What will it say?" she asks.

"It'll explain that we were engaged when I had an affair with the senator's fiancée, and I only strayed because I thought you might reconcile with your ex," I reveal, and her gaze drops at the mention of her ex. "What is it?" I prompt.

"I'm not sure if that'll work," she confesses. "What I mean is, things are complicated with my ex. I don't know how to explain this to him without him getting..."

"Angry?" I complete her sentence, a flare of unexpected protectiveness igniting within me at the fear in her eyes.

"Yes," she whispers, taken aback by my intrusion into her personal life. "But it's okay. I'll figure it out," she assures me. "I should let you get back to work," she says, rising abruptly from the chair.

"Wait," I call out, and she turns.

"I shouldn't get you involved," she blurts out hurriedly.

I ponder her words for a moment. I shouldn't be involved, but I need to understand her life if she is to be my wife.

"I am your husband, Isabella," I remind her, the words sounding strange and spilling from my mouth.

"Not yet," she retorts, a smile tugging at the corners of her lips.

"This time next week, I will be," I inform her, noticing her confusion. "You'll receive all the details via email. We'll have a small ceremony at the registry office, just you, me, my brother, Vincent, and his girlfriend, Rosie. If you want to invite anyone as a witness, you can."

"My friend, Harley. I'd like her to be there," she responds without hesitation.

"Fine. Let's get back to it, we have an endless day of meetings, and these conversations are of a personal nature that should be discussed at the house. We need to maintain our professionalism here, Isabella."

"Of course, Mr. Slater." She nods in understanding.

"I'll see you tonight. Go get your little tornado," I say, eliciting a soft laugh from her that resonates in the pit of my stomach, but I quickly brush it aside.

I'm not getting personally involved. I just need to know a bit about her ex-husband to be prepared for potential media questions. That's all.

It's not about the image of her in pajamas with her hair down that's been imprinted in my mind.

"Yes, sir," she affirms before leaving my office, leaving behind a trace of raspberry ice cream and a pang of something I can't quite name.

6

ISABELLA

F ox, my mini whirlwind, is soundly asleep, and Julius made it home an hour ago, disappearing into his office. It's late, and I've already savored the scrumptious dinner his housekeeper, Paola, prepared—a chicken dish rich in tomato sauce with the added sweetness of black olives.

I'm happily satiated and love the idea of having a live-in chef. A part of me starts to relax with this new reality.

Paola, I found out, moved here from Sicily, which explains her extraordinary cooking skills. She doesn't inquire why my son and I are here, and I don't volunteer any details. I sense that his staff matches Julius's professionalism, and he expects them to do so.

I'm sitting in the living room, going through emails on the opposite side of a giant screen, when I hear Julius's bedroom door open, followed by footsteps on the wooden floor.

I peeked around his penthouse before he got home, curious about the man who's been my boss for four years. His place isn't at all like I imagined. Colorful pieces of artwork decorate the living room and hallways, while the large open spaces are filled with plush comfortable furniture. I expected it to be cold, stark, and minimal, much like his personality projected. But maybe, there's more to Julius than the professional exterior he presents at work.

He enters the room, freshly showered, and I can smell the scent of fresh laundry all the way from here. I inadvertently drag my bottom lip, grazing it with my teeth.

"Good evening, Isabella," he greets in his smooth dark voice.

"Julius," I reply, acknowledging the informal setting where I can't really address him as Mr. Slater.

He fetches himself a whiskey from the bar behind the sofa. "Would you like one?" he asks, and I agree, needing a bit of liquid courage for the unfinished conversation from his office that I sense is coming.

The sloshing sound of alcohol, followed by the clang as he replaces the crystal knob, only adds to my nerves as he hands me the drink, his thumb grazing my finger. I try to ignore the electric warmth shooting up my arm. "Thank you," I say, managing to find the words.

"You're welcome," he says, settling down opposite me. "What are you working on?" he asks, eyeing the laptop.

"Just catching up on work emails in preparation for tomorrow," I explain.

He lowers the laptop screen, leaning in closer. "You always work in the evenings? I occasionally get emails from you, but is this a regular occurrence?" he asks.

"Afraid so," I confess, and he closes the laptop.

"You still need a life, Isabella. Tell me what you do for fun."

I let out a hearty laugh. "Maybe wash my hair?" I suggest, and the perplexed look on his face makes me take a large gulp of my whiskey. I swallow the hearty liquid, and it burns the back of my throat. "As a single parent, I don't really get to have fun. There is simply no time," I explain.

"I see," he replies, removing his hand from my screen and settling back into the sofa. "Well, what did you use to do for fun before?" he inquires, prompting me to recall the time before Fox, before my ex-husband. A time when life was simpler.

"I liked to sing," I confess, and take another large sip of my whiskey, clumsily spilling some on my white shirt.

"Dammit," I exclaim, quickly setting down the tumbler and wiping my mouth with the back of my hand.

I catch his eyes falling on my top, which is now sticking to the curve of my breasts. As I raise my eyes, he leisurely trails his intense gaze to mine. His dark eyes cloud with a smoky allure, causing my breath to hitch.

"You're so clumsy, Isabella," he comments, swiftly getting up and retrieving a checkered tea towel from the kitchen for me. "So, a singer then?" he muses out loud as his finger lightly grazes the corner of my mouth.

His touch sends my heart into overdrive, and I quickly grab the tea towel from his grasp. He takes his finger to his lips, sucking the stray whiskey off it in a move that has my thighs aching with a need I didn't know existed.

"Can't let it go to waste now, can we?" he murmurs, his ocean eyes smoldering.

There's a loaded silence between us. Julius's gaze flicks back to my eyes, and a spark of something passes over them before retreating to his seat. I exhale a shuddered breath, not realizing I was holding it in.

"It wasn't serious," I say, bringing us back to the topic at hand and flopping onto the sofa as I resume my efforts to dry my shirt. "Just fun is all."

"That's how Victoria started," he responds. "And now she's top of the charts in Asia, or wherever K-pop or J-pop is."

I let out a giggle. "I didn't realize you knew what that is."

"I'm thirty years old. Not dead," he retorts, and I can't help but smirk. "How old are you, Isabella? I probably should know this, but I don't."

"I'm twenty-six," I reply.

I watch him do the math. "You were a mother at twenty-two. Isn't that young to be a mother?"

Unwanted memories surge forward, threatening to consume me. They're of Travis, his oppressive weight pressing me into the bed, forcing himself on me. Those horrific moments led to Fox's birth nine long months later. But I staunchly push those painful recollections back down into the depths. They're not something I'm prepared to share with Julius.

"Young, perhaps. But Fox is my everything. I don't expect you to understand that," I say, a flicker of frustration in my voice.

His eyebrows furrow, but he doesn't respond. "And your ex-husband? What do I need to know about him?"

"His name is Travis Sneddon. We were married when I fell pregnant with Fox. His family owns Whites Printers."

Recognition flickers across his face, and why wouldn't it? Whites Printers is a large and successful family business with Travis at their helm, although not in the same league as Slater Corp. "And when did you divorce?"

"About a year ago. I walked away, and I've been paying for it ever since," I admit.

"How so?" he asks, and I wish he'd stop with the twenty questions.

Travis threatens me regularly, I want to say but stop myself. "Travis didn't want us to end. He wants us back together and can't seem to understand it's over," I finally say.

"I see," he murmurs.

I put the tea towel down and meet his gaze. I can tell he wants to ask more but doesn't. "I have my son for one week, and his father has him for the other. You can have your peace when Fox is at his dad's," I state, getting up.

"That's not what I meant, Isabella," he replies, standing with me.

I stare up at him and exhale. "Yes, it is. And that's okay. You're not a parent. I don't expect you to see Fox as your son in this arrangement. But I do expect you to be kind to him. He has had enough misery in his life to last a lifetime."

"Is that what you think? That I'm not going to be nice to your son?" He steps forward, closing the gap between us. His body radiates heat, making me feel more heated and uneasy.

"Well, the first impressions weren't exactly stellar. He's taken to calling you the monster now."

"Monster, eh?" He seems amused, but there's also a flicker of interest in his eyes. "That little whirlwind came tearing through here, cursing and ruining a perfectly good silk rug."

"He's just a kid," I respond softly, our eyes meeting.

He shrugs, a casual dismissal of my concern. "It will be fine. I couldn't care less about the rug," he admits, and relief floods me.

Silence passes beneath us, an undercurrent of something else replacing it.

"Think I'm going to head to bed," I suddenly declare, a

rush of nervous energy punctuating my words, amplified by the scotch heating my bloodstream.

"Well, goodnight, Isabella," he says, looking down at me.

I've never noticed the significant height difference between us until now. Without my heels, he looms over me. His blue eyes scrutinize me, just like they did that night in his office. His gaze falls to my damp shirt, which still clings to the curve of my breasts, then travels back up to my face.

"Goodnight, Julius," I respond, turning to walk away, all the while feeling the weight of his gaze on my back.

7

JULIUS

Her fair skin seems to radiate against the pristine white of her dress, and I find it hard to look away.

I'm standing at City Hall when I catch sight of her. She's clad in a pristine white dress that grazes her knees, and I'm decked out in my most formal suit. I find myself momentarily stunned by her radiant beauty.

Her little boy, Fox, is wearing suspenders and long shorts covered in dirt from when he found some and started to play in it. Honestly, this kid. He doesn't even realize what's happening, which is probably good. I can hardly believe what I'm doing myself.

He runs up and down around the small room, bashing and knocking anything in his way. How this kid has so much energy just blows my mind.

I turn and see my brother standing at my side, a grin peeling on his face. He leans in and whispers, "Got your hands full there."

"No shit."

Vincent is equally as well-dressed with Rosie by his side. I've never seen Vincent as happy as he has been these last few months with Rosie living with him. He's in love, it's plain as day, and he's calmer and definitely happier.

My father, who has been dragged here by my mother, sits sheepishly in a seat beside her, and I wish he weren't here. I certainly didn't invite him and haven't spoken to him in three months since we found out he withheld vital information about my brother, Edgar's death.

It's obvious Vincent is just as uncomfortable having him here as I am. But as this is all for show, not having family here would raise more questions than it's worth.

No doubt it was my sister Victoria's doing. She would have ensured my parents attended because she is off performing in Asia.

As the officiant recites his script, I find myself some-what detached, merely going through the motions of this ceremonial wedding. Taking her hand in mine, we exchange the rings Vincent chose for us. Her hand is cold and slick with nervous sweat, and I try to reassure her with a gentle squeeze.

She looks up at me as I slide the ring onto her finger and echo the vows back to her. The words "I do" escape her lips, followed by the sensation of a heavy gold band being slipped onto my finger.

"You may kiss the bride," the officiant announces, and I'm momentarily taken aback. She seems just as surprised, but I find myself leaning in, pressing a kiss to her soft lips, slowly savoring the taste of my new wife.

I'm ready to pull back, but the kiss deepens unexpect-edly, catching me off guard. The memory of her hands wrapped around my neck and her tongue exploring my mouth replays in my mind as if it happened just yesterday, not a few months back.

She pulls back first, and I see a reflection of my surprise mirrored in her eyes. *Fuck, what the hell was that, and why do I need more?*

The applause from our assembled guests snaps us back to reality. Harley, her friend, immediately wraps her in a joyous congratulatory hug. Vincent approaches me, slapping me on the back in a brotherly gesture.

"I know this isn't exactly what you had planned, but it's just for a year, brother," he reminds me with a firm, reassuring squeeze.

As I pull away, I raise my eyebrows in a noncommittal gesture.

"You never know. You might find you enjoy being married after all," he counters with a mischievous wink.

"Congratulations, Julius," Rosie adds, enveloping me in a warm hug. "She's such a radiant bride," she remarks.

She indeed is, I silently concede to myself.

Then, my mother approaches, planting kisses on both my cheeks, followed by my father, who offers a firm handshake. I loathe his touch, but for appearances, don't cause a scene. Despite the arrangement being an open secret, they all congratulate me as if I have just married my soulmate.

Suddenly, a crashing sound echoes through the room, abruptly pulling us away from each other. We both turn toward the source of the noise. Startled and crying, Fox stands amidst the shattered remains of a vase he's knocked over. My gaze shifts to my father, his face contorted in disbelief and annoyance. Then, my eyes return to Isabella, who is now comforting her sobbing child.

In the midst of this chaos, I allow myself to embrace the

moment, a genuine smile breaking across my face despite the whirlwind of activity around us.

My dining room has been transformed. The table is draped in luxurious linens of soft ivory that fall gracefully down its sides, their subtle sheen creating an ambiance of elegance. The texture is soft and inviting, the fabric impeccably ironed to perfection, with no crease or crumple in sight.

Artfully placed upon the linen, an array of floral arrangements take center stage, their beauty hard to ignore. Bursting with color, they are an enchanting medley of peonies, roses, and hydrangeas, their hues ranging from pastel pinks and purples to pristine whites punctuated by their leaves of deep, velvety greens. Each blossom seems to be at the peak of its bloom, radiating an intoxicating fragrance that lightly perfumes the air.

Finishing the last decadent spoonful of my chocolate dessert, I mentally tally the extra gym time I'll need tonight to counterbalance the indulgence.

Fox is engrossed in his own world, banging toy cars together in a corner with a loud and grating intensity. Isabella is too deeply engrossed in conversation with Rosie and Harley to seem to notice. Vincent and Rosie, wrapped up in their own sweet discourse, are equally oblivious. My parents, the least appealing option for conversation, are out of the question. Thus, I decide it is the perfect time to intervene and gently extricate the noisy toy from Fox's firm grip. But before I can, my mother grabs my arm.

"You know it's so lovely being here, Julius. You must come to the house again soon," she says, smiling sweetly.

The truth is I do miss my mother, but I'm just not ready to come back to the family dinners we once had.

"It's too soon," I tell her loud enough for him to hear.

"Not too soon to get married, though, is it?" my father pipes up, and the mere affliction in his tone sends my blood boiling.

"Edward!" Tatianna chides her husband, shooting him a look filled with venom.

"IIow dare you." I seethe.

"Okay, okay. Not now. Not here." My mother attempts to pacify me, applying a gentle, reassuring squeeze to my arm.

"Perhaps it's best I take my leave, Mother," I declare, sliding out of her hold and heading toward Fox.

With a zealous "whoosh," Fox crashes two toy trucks together, oblivious to the tension swirling around him.

"Hey, Nado, let's give it a break," I suggest, using the nickname I've adopted for the energetic child. I gently try to pry one of the cars from his tight grasp.

"No, Monster!" Fox protests, clutching his toy tighter.

I grind my teeth together. "Buddy, the truck needs a rest, just like you do. It's been a long day." I'm not quite sure how to deal with a child this age, but I give it my best shot.

Isabella approaches, her familiar scent wafting toward me before I even see her.

"Mommy, he wants to take my toy," Fox complains.

"Sweetheart, I think Mr. Tonka could use a nap, and so could you. It's been a long day. How about we head to our room?" she suggests in a soothing voice.

Fox's blue eyes, so much like Isabella's, look up at me. "No, Mommy, I want to stay here. I'm not tired."

"Do you ever get tired, Nado?" I ask.

"Nado?" Isabella looks at me, her long lashes fluttering slightly.

"The kid's a tornado. Nado for short."

Her laughter rings out, short and sweet, and it surprises me how much it affects me. She never laughs at work. Not with me, anyway.

"Are you my new Daddy?" Fox asks. The question startles me, and I glance at Isabella, seeing the shock mirrored on her face.

"No, Nado," I reassure him, "You already have a dad."

I see Isabella's momentary struggle before she composes herself. "Foxy, remember what I told you. Travis is your daddy, and Julius is the new man Mommy has married."

"Do you love him more than Daddy?" Fox asks, causing Isabella to blush.

"You're full of questions today, aren't you? Quite the little Einstein," she deflects nervously.

"Is he going to hit you like Daddy did?" Fox asks, and Isabella quickly scoops him up, placing him over her shoulder.

I swallow hard, a lump forming in my throat. *Every mark, bruise, and imperfection on her perfect face was from him? And in front of her son too?*

Sure, I had an inkling, but my rigid boundaries stopped me from prying into her personal life and asking her myself. My body begins to heat as anger and guilt sweep in like a tidal wave.

"Okay, that's enough for today, Einstein," she says hastily. Her eyes dart to me as she stands, and I can't help but feel deep sympathy for her for what she's had to endure and what she's escaped. I don't even know the full extent of the abuse, but the thought of it makes me want to rip Travis's throat out.

8

ISABELLA

So far, in our marriage, nothing has significantly shifted, but then again, I didn't anticipate any grand alterations. Julius and I maintain professional boundaries during work hours, our roles clearly defined.

His workdays stretch late into the night, and often when he returns home, I'm either lost in my own work or fast asleep.

However, one thing relentlessly distracts me, pulling me away from the piles of work that demand my attention —the wedding and that unforgettable kiss. It felt as if the room spun around us, Julius the steady anchor amidst the chaos. His firm lips pressed against mine set my skin aflame, a firework of sensations exploding from my spine to the crown of my head.

Now, on a Saturday night, with Julius out and Fox fast asleep, my mind drifts back to that moment. Tomorrow, Fox goes to his father's, a confrontation I've been avoiding since our marriage announcement.

Travis hasn't taken the news lightly, inundating me with a torrent of texts filled with vile accusations.

As anticipated, the Slater Corp. Public Relations team effectively handled our nuptials, spinning a narrative that the media lapped up. The result? Julius's image is slowly being repaired, and the stock market has rebounded impressively, especially with the announcement of the tech takeover that's been brewing for over a year.

When I step out of my bathroom, a thought strikes me. With Julius out, this would be the perfect opportunity to explore his bedroom, a space I've been curious about but have never ventured into. Wrapping a towel around myself, I push open the heavy doors to his sanctuary.

The room is expansive, luxurious in its simplicity, and far from ostentatious. The king-sized bed adorned with navy satin sheets dominates the space, invitingly plush. My hand instinctively reaches out to caress the silky fabric. An oversized chandelier glimmers above, its mirror counterpart large and directly opposite the bed.

Oh. Hell. He likes to watch. The thought heats my thighs.

I quickly push it away and walk toward his impressive walk-in closet. My fingers trace along the crisp lines of his neatly hung shirts, an array of ties, and a meticulous collection of expensive watches. The air in the room is heavy with his scent, a potent blend of masculine spices and a hint of cologne embodying his formidable aura.

As I step into his en suite, my breath is stolen by the sheer grandeur of the space. He's nowhere in sight, but his intoxicating scent lingers, enveloping me in a comforting blanket of familiarity. Dominating the room is a bathtub that's so large it could easily be mistaken for a mini plunge pool.

Glancing at the time, I note it's only half-past nine. *I*

could indulge myself with a bath in his tub and be out before he's home. The idea is too tempting to resist. I twist the handle, and water jets to life, filling the basin with a comforting rush of warmth.

Discarding my towel, I ease myself into the shallow water. It barely covers my ankles, but I can envision him luxuriating here. *Does he bathe with women in this tub?* The thought sends a rush of heat to my core. My reflection in the fogging mirror is a hazy silhouette, the steam enhancing the softness of my curves. The heat of the water starts to unknot tense muscles I hadn't even realized were tight.

Suddenly, an idea strikes me. Snatching up my towel, I wrap it around myself and return to my room. Opening the drawer of my bedside table, I retrieve my secret weapon for nights when sleep evades me—my trusty Womanizer vibrator. Between the whirlwind wedding, moving into a new home, setting up Fox's daycare, and the looming encounter with my ex, I could definitely use a little stress relief.

Returning to his bathroom, I find the bath nearly filled. I turn off the water and step in again, sinking onto the built-in seat. It's the perfect temperature, and a sigh of relief slips from my lips as I submerge myself deeper. The heat causes my nipples to tighten, and I let down my hair, allowing it to fan out on the water's surface.

Shutting my eyes, I let my mind wander back to the stolen kiss. As the memory surfaces, I position the water-proof device between my thighs. I spread my legs a little wider, hitting the power button, and the motor's hum mingles with the sloshing water.

Oh God, yes. This is exactly what I needed.

The sensation of the vibrator is heaven, and I moan in

pleasure as I press it deeper inside me. Suddenly, I hear a noise and turn to look, but no one is there. I freak out for a moment, but then I remember he's not home. He had a dinner meeting with colleagues tonight, according to his diary.

Returning to the moment, I focus on the pleasure coursing through my body. With each passing second, the tickler does its magic, pushing me closer to the edge of ecstasy. My moans become louder as I approach the point of no return, and I'm so close, the release building inside me.

My hand rises to my breast as I edge closer, and again, I think I hear something in the distance, but I push the thought aside. The pleasure overwhelms me, and I come loudly and quickly, lost in the blissful release of pent-up tension.

9

JULIUS

After a grueling day, I return home to the sanctuary of my penthouse, the city's cacophony fading away as the elevator doors close behind me. I expect the place to be quiet, with Nado already asleep and Isabella retired to her room. But as I step inside the living room, a faint sound draws me toward my room.

A gentle splash echoes through the hallway, mingling with the low hum of running water. I approach my bedroom and the adjoining bathroom, my footsteps falling on the oak flooring in near silence.

Someone's in my fucking room.

I step up to the open door that's never open.

What greets me stops me dead in my tracks.

Isabella is in my bathtub.

Naked.

My heart lurches as I take in the scene. Her hair, loose and wet, clings to her bare shoulders. The curve of her breasts peeks out from the frothy surface of the water. Her eyes are closed, her lips slightly parted, and she's engrossed, a vibrator in her hand.

Oh my fucking God.

My hands ball to my sides. I'm immediately frustrated and aroused all at once.

Desire floods me, a primal urge to join her in the bathtub to replace her stupid toy with me. I clench my fists, fighting the urge to make that fantasy a reality. This isn't supposed to happen. I'm not supposed to see this, to feel this. Our marriage is a business arrangement, nothing more.

Yet, here I am, unmoving by the sight of her, the sound of her soft moans echoing in the vast bathroom. I watch as she arches her back, the water rippling around her, the soft glow of the bathroom lights casting an ethereal glow on her skin. I've never imagined her this way.

I choke back a groan, the frustration building. I need to leave to escape this temptation. With a last, lingering glance at her, I force myself to turn around, making my way to the living room as quickly as I can to leave her behind.

Frustration surges through me, and I rip off my tie, tossing it onto the armchair. I've just arrived, but fuck, I need to leave. I cannot be here. I can't be here knowing what I can do to her in that bathtub.

Descending the elevator, I try to rid myself of the image of her plaguing my mind. The action does nothing to quell the heat coursing through me. The image of her in my bathtub is seared into my mind. I'll need a cold shower and a good amount of self-restraint to keep myself from returning to her.

Dammit, Isabella. What the fuck have you done?

When I return three hours later, the penthouse is quiet, the city lights twinkling through the floor-to-ceiling windows. The stillness, however, does nothing to douse the memory of Isabella in my bathtub. It's etched into my mind, a hauntingly beautiful reel of sexual arousal I can't escape. I look down at the tie discarded on the armchair, the knot still intact.

I rip it open, the sound echoing in the silence. Listening for any sounds or movement down the hallway where the bedrooms are, there are none. The coast is clear.

I walk to my bedroom, my body drawn like a moth to a flame, to the spot where I last saw her. The bathroom is empty now, the water long drained, but her scent lingers, intertwining with the steamy residue in the air. I can almost hear the echo of her soft sighs against the splashes of water.

Hot and insistent desire claws at me. My fingers fumble with the buttons of my shirt as I rip it off and down my shoulders and drop it to the floor. I unbutton my pants, unzip the fly, and let them fall beside the bed. My strained erection falls out heavy like gunmetal, and goddammit, I shouldn't be doing this, but I can't fight the urge any longer.

My hand wanders down, taking hold of my engorged cock. The image of her and the sounds she made fuel my fantasies as I stroke myself. Each touch and stroke are filled with the desire I feel for her. If I were man enough to break my strict code of conduct, I imagine finishing the job for her.

Instead, I play out my own fantasy where I join her.

I walk behind her, grabbing her hair and tilting her head, exposing the column of her throat.

"Join me," she whispers breathlessly as I stroke myself harder from base to tip.

I take the vibrator from her hands and sink it further inside her. She moans and arches her head back in ecstasy. I make her come with ease, then toss the device to the side. I push her thighs open and take a deep breath before dipping my head underwater. When I take her clit in my mouth, she writhes under my touch. I resurface, take a quick breath and this time dive deep between her legs, taking her cunt in my mouth until I hear her moans from underwater.

My climax hits me hard, the waves of pleasure washing over me and leaving me breathless. Her name escapes my lips in a throaty whisper, a plea in the silence, "Isabella..."

As my heart rate slows down, I open my eyes, catching my reflection in the mirror. A slight figure diverts my attention near the door.

Our eyes lock.

Fuck.

Isabella watches me. Standing by the slightly ajar door, the darkness does little to hide her wide eyes and flushed cheeks.

She turns quickly and clumsily, and I quickly pull up my pants.

What the fuck?

"Wait!" I say as I follow her out the door, running after her.

The hallway is dark, and she's in her god-awful tartan pajamas.

Thankfully, I catch up just before she reaches her bedroom door.

"I'm sorry, " she says hurriedly. "I woke thirsty and went to get a drink when I heard er... something."

I stare down at her, her breath rising and falling in her chest like she's just run a triathlon.

Shit, did she hear me come with her name on my lips? How the fuck do I explain that one? No. No way she could have heard my whisper.

65

But instead of fixing this, I blurt out, "And did you like what you saw?"

She looks up at me, her gaze locking with mine, and as she nervously takes her lower lip between her teeth and bites down on it, a surge of anticipation courses through me.

We have to work together in a few hours, but I can't wait for her response. "Isabella," I push, my voice filled with a hint of urgency. "I asked you a question."

"I shouldn't, but yes," she quickly responds, and her eyes fall down my chest.

I want to touch her to make her mine, to finish that late-night kiss in the office months ago. Fuck her hard and lose myself inside her, but this would only complicate things, and I've fucked up things enough lately to consider fucking a single mom.

"Well, a taste never hurt anyone," I say, and she leans back, hesitant.

That's all we both get.

"A taste?" she asks meekly.

I tower over her, and she looks up, that column of her neck exposed like I imagined when I took my cock in my hands moments ago. I brush my fingers over her bottom lip, imagining my mouth claiming hers. "Yes, Isabella, a taste…"

Goddamn, she's a temptation I cannot let myself be embroiled in. "Go to bed, Isabella," I say, but it comes out as a command, bossy and authoritative.

Her eyes are wide, her chest rising and falling as my fingers linger on the warmth of her skin. "Then you should let me go," she whispers.

I suck in a breath and remove my finger, unaware it still lingered on her mouth.

"We will not speak of this again," I say.

"Absolutely," she agrees with a curt nod before turning and retreating to her room.

She closes the door behind me, our eyes glued on one another until the barrier severs the connection.

IO

ISABELLA

Sleep evades me, and I show up to work like an apocalyptic zombie.

All I can see is his long, hard dick and him taking himself so strong, his biceps pop and curl with each stroke, each muscle in his chest contracting and moving with his motion. I don't think I've ever been so aroused in my entire life. Then I think, but can't be sure, he whispered my name, *my* name pulling from his lips when he comes hard.

I'm overwhelmed by a mixture of emotions, but there's no denying the intense arousal that sweeps over me at the sight of him. I'm instantly wet, my body reacting to his presence in the most primal way.

Yet, here we are, entangled in this strange dance of attraction, all while knowing our marriage is nothing more than a convenient arrangement—a business transaction disguised as love and commitment. We've set the clock for twelve months, after which we'll dissolve it as swiftly as we entered. It should be simple and straightforward. And yet, as I stand on the precipice of this unknown, it feels like I'm stepping into a world of unpredictable possibilities.

The reality is I have too much going on in my life to entertain thoughts of a relationship, especially with a man like Julius. He's from another world and class. I couldn't trust him to want more than a fleeting pleasure from me. We come from two different worlds, and let's face it, he doesn't exactly adore Fox. So, the thought of us being anything more than temporary spouses or fuck buddies is ludicrous.

My mind should be focused on work and the never-ending tasks that lay before me. But I find myself scattered, my concentration ripped to shreds by the undeniable attraction that lingers between us.

Julius, for his part, seems to be avoiding me, not that I can blame him. After all, I was the one lurking at his door, completely invading his privacy. Thank hell, he didn't know I was in his bathtub earlier. The truth is, I'm not entirely sure how I'd feel if he'd caught me in there.

As the day wears on, my duties as a mother call. I pick up Fox from daycare, then we have to say our goodbyes. This is the worst part—not seeing my son for a week. It tears me apart.

Every.

Single.

Time.

The sun sets as I pull up in front of my ex-husband's house—our old house. A pang of nostalgia hits me, but it's quickly replaced by an undercurrent of tension. Fox's little hand holds mine firmly, and I can tell he doesn't like spending time here, but with the courts not budging on the shared custody arrangement, I can't do a damn thing but love my little boy as much as I can when I have him.

To his credit, Travis is freshly shaven and in his suit, appearing mostly sober. He sends Fox to his room to unpack his things, leaving us in an oppressive silence.

He's angry. That much is clear.

His ex-wife just married a man he hadn't known existed. Of course, I can't tell him about the arrangement with Julius, bound as I am by a confidentiality agreement. The secretiveness of the situation adds another layer to the uncomfortable atmosphere, and I steel myself for the conversation to come.

"You fucking whore," he says, and I immediately turn around to leave. He grabs me by the wrist, his grip burning tight as he squeezes me.

"I don't have to listen to this," I say calmly.

"You will listen to what I have to say. You think you can sleep your way to the top? Were you fucking him when my dick was inside you?"

"Of course not!" I defend. "And how dare you."

"I don't know who you are, Isabella, or what you're playing at by marrying a Slater."

"I'm not playing at anything. We're happy, that's it," I say, trying to leave it alone, but his grip only pulls around me tighter.

"Let me go," I plead.

"Once a whore, always a whore."

"How fucking dare you," I snap, trying to wriggle out of his grasp. At least we are out front, and people are around should I need to scream, but he only persists.

Reluctantly, I stop fighting with him. He is too strong, and I know I can't win.

He grins at my submission. "You think he'll make you happy?" he asks. "Has he got a bigger cock than me? Is that it?"

"Stop it, Travis. Fox is inside."

"I don't give a fuck."

"Now I know why you left me. Your fucking legs were open for him late at night. You were spread out at your office like the two-bit whore you are." He pulls me aggressively close to him, the tobacco on his breath and the revolting scent of rum overwhelming.

I know if I just wait, let him say his peace and maybe hit me once or twice, I can be gone. So I don't argue, and for that, I feel more ashamed than for what I'm about to endure.

The last thing I yearn to do is dress up and attend a dinner, but it's part of my agreement with Julius. As his wife, I have a role to fulfill. It's what's expected of me.

It's been a month since I've been married for the second time. As promised, we have kept things strictly professional between us, and there has been no mention of me watching my boss stroke himself in the most delicious ways, even though the image floods my dreams.

I dare not mention it, nor do I want to do anything that would jeopardize my job or our marriage of convenience. Doing so would put the funds needed to battle my ex for full custody at risk. Without that, there isn't another way to take Travis on and the endless resources at his disposal through his family's wealth.

All I know is it's a dinner party at a business associate's house. Not that it matters. In truth, we haven't made a social appearance as a couple since we tied the knot. We keep to our individual routines, as dull as mine might be.

After I get dressed, I hardly recognize the person gazing

back at me in the mirror. I'm cloaked in a dress far beyond my usual spending habits. My hair is elegantly pinned up, with loose tendrils framing my face, which is highlighted by intense eyes and understated lips. I flick out the length of the dress, slit high. It shimmers, reflecting the light.

This isn't the only addition. Since our wedding, my wardrobe has expanded with numerous outfits for such events. I would be a fool to think this is something I could get used to. Just another means to an end.

I emerge, looking around for Julius, but he's nowhere to be found. I glance at the time, ensuring my punctuality, as I know he appreciates running ahead of schedule and maintaining control. Even with all my searching, I still can't find him.

The house feels weirdly quiet without him or Fox around. And I can't help but wonder how he is and if Travis is treating him okay. I quickly push my worries aside the best I can, knowing it doesn't do me any good.

I decide to head into the library and step inside the door that's slightly ajar, where I find Julius engrossed in a book. He's dashing in his tux, his hair slicked neatly to the side.

When he lifts his eyes to meet mine, he's caught off guard, and for a moment, he's speechless. As his blue eyes rise to meet mine, a look of surprise washes over him, rendering him momentarily speechless. His gaze travels down my dress, and the intensity of his stare sends tingles up my spine.

"It's the dress," I blurt out, smoothing down the pale pink dress and feeling nervous at his genuine adulation.

"Yes, it is the dress," he agrees and stands, crossing the library toward me. "It is a very beautiful dress," he murmurs in that seductive tone of his, and I can't ignore the fire behind his dark eyes.

"I, um..." I drag my gaze to the floor.

His fingers lightly touch my chin, tilting my face upward until I have no choice but to meet his gaze. My heart feels like it's soaring in my chest, and butterflies do their frenzied dance in my stomach.

"You look down too often," he murmurs. "I like your eyes on me." His words flow like silk, making my thighs tighten involuntarily.

"Sorry," I reply, maintaining my gaze up at him.

His gaze momentarily dips to my lips, sparking a ripple of that electric tension that often passes between us. His jaw tenses, then he takes a step back. "Stop apologizing. You apologize too damn much," he says, his voice slightly irritated. "You are my wife, Isabella, my equal."

I gasp, taken aback at his use of 'wife.' I'm about to apologize yet again when I catch myself. I notice his nostrils flare slightly. *What's gotten into him?*

"Let's go. The car is waiting," he declares, striding out and leaving me to wonder what on earth just happened.

During the car ride, he's mostly silent. When we arrive, he introduces me to his colleagues and their wives, and apart from a courteous hello, I'm left standing awkwardly, fully aware I'm in a world so far from my own.

He leaves me to the company of other guests, and I engage in small talk when I can. But for the most part, I find myself marveling at the vast interior of his associate, Tyler Wagner's swanky Chelsea townhouse. With its gleaming marble floors, cream walls adorned with contemporary art, and floor-to-ceiling windows offering a view of the Hudson River, there's more than enough to keep me occupied when Julius isn't around.

The dining area flaunts a finely set table for a luxurious dinner party, with crystal stemware, silverware, and monogrammed napkins atop delicate china, while a string quartet sets a gentle musical backdrop. However, despite this magnificence, Julius continues to neglect me during dinner, too immersed in business talk with Tyler, leaving me frustrated and ignored.

After we finish eating, I catch some fresh air on the balcony. Julius probably won't even notice I'm gone. Leaning on the cool metal railing, I look out into the pitch-black Hudson. The summer night feels good, but its peacefulness is fleeting as a muffled, haughty laugh causes me to pivot quickly. Something about it feels familiar, and my breath releases in a rushed whooshed to find it's not Travis but someone else. As I turn back, I'm on edge. A surge of memories of Travis forcing himself on me bubble up, causing my stomach to twist in discomfort. I hug myself, trying to ease the feeling. Making things worse, those women buzzing around Julius earlier have turned their focus to snickering behind their fancy-manicured hands.

The smirks and scornful looks they're throwing my way cut deeper than the diamond necklaces they're wearing. Sure, I'm the woman who managed to snag the billionaire playboy. It's a surreal reality, and I'm likely the punchline for these high-society ladies.

I feel out of place, ticked off, and ready to bolt.

Glancing over, I see Julius engrossed in conversation with a group of men, utterly unaware of my discomfort. It's like I've been thrown back into a snooty high school scene with these high society WAGs.

Looking down, I gather myself, but when I raise my gaze again, they've inched closer like bees to honey. "We're just trying to figure out how you did it," one says.

She's tall, slender, and flawlessly beautiful, just like the gemstones she's flaunting. She looks down at me, trying to intimidate me.

"How I did what?" I ask, my smile firmly in place. I won't let them rattle me, choosing to take the high road.

"How you managed to marry Manhattan's most eligible bachelor." The group breaks into laughter and cackles.

I raise my drink to my lips, curving them around the glass rim, and take a generous sip. I look back inside for Julius, but he is nowhere in sight.

I need more...

...a lot more.

II

JULIUS

Truthfully, it's quite a task to remain absorbed in conversation when my mind is brimming with thoughts of Isabella in *that* dress. She's an absolute vision in the soft, pink outfit that cinches perfectly at her waist and hugs her curves just right. The thin straps showcase her elegant clavicle, adding to her allure. Her understated beauty, accentuated so magnificently, definitely stirs something within me it shouldn't.

On the balcony, society's most glamorous women are conversing with her, many I'm ashamed to admit I've slept with in the past. Yet it's Isabella I'm drawn to. She appears taller than usual, her back rigid as if on the defensive.

I've kept my distance from her tonight, fearing getting too close and breaking my strict professional code.

Darius follows my line of sight. "Your new bride seems to be fitting in well," he says, admiring her from afar. "She's a beauty, Slater. How is it with her son living with you?" he asks, raising a skeptical eyebrow.

I sigh, thinking of Fox and the countless destruction he's caused at my house—the stained rug, broken ornaments, and numerous meltdowns I've overheard. "Fortunately, he's at his father's every other week," I admit.

The men grunt and nod in understanding.

The truth is, the boy is a handful. His behavior is beyond the usual mischief. I'm no father, but I can tell something's off. However, his words from our wedding day still echo in my mind, *"Are you my new dad?"* and even more disconcerting, *"Are you going to hit mommy too?"*

The mere idea of anyone laying a hand on Isabella causes my blood to boil.

Masking my emotions with a strained smile, I disengage from my group and head toward the balcony where Isabella stands. Bethany and Veronica, two of Manhattan's stunning ex-models, are conversing with her.

As I approach, their smiles broaden. Both women, with whom I've shared past encounters, don't seem bothered by their present marital status or mine. Earlier, as I was making my way out of the restroom, Bethany latched onto my arm with a playful twinkle in her eye, hinting that we sneak off to one of the empty bedrooms.

"Julius, it's about time you join your bride. She's been alone most of the night, haven't you, sweetie?" Veronica, ever so bold, straightens my lapels right in front of Isabella.

I subtly step back and loop my arm around Isabella's waist. A flash of annoyance flickers in Veronica's eyes, and her smile stiffens, barely masking her displeasure.

"Business is always the focus at these events. As a businessman's wife, you'd understand that, Veronica," I respond with an accusatory smile.

Isabella moves slightly away from my grasp. It's a minute shift, but I notice, and I do not like it one bit.

"Surely, one must take some time to relax, let loose," Bethany teases.

Isabella makes a noise beside me. "I'll meet you in the car, Julius," she announces abruptly, then turns, freeing herself from my grasp, and strides away.

I return a glance at Veronica and Bethany, who act innocently. "What? Was it something I said?" Veronica quips.

"Goodnight, ladies," I reply sharply, swiftly bidding the hosts and his wife adieu. Then, I make my way to the car, where Isabella is already waiting.

The ride home is steeped in silence. I can sense her anger toward me, and it's unbearable, gnawing at me until I can no longer ignore it. I turn to her, "That was rude. How you left."

She whips her head toward me, her face tight with anger. "Rude? Shall we talk about rude, Julius?" She turns fully in her seat, visibly bristling. "You left me all night with people I didn't know. I can handle myself. I've been through a lot. But you intentionally left me with those women, knowing how they are. How dare you," she retorts, clearly frustrated.

"They're harmless socialites," I argue.

"Maybe to you. I saw how they behaved around you. You're supposed to be a married man, yet you didn't reject their advances."

"They were just being friendly," I explain, my voice taut. "Stop overreacting, Isabella."

Is she jealous? The possibility of that stirs a strange sense of satisfaction in me.

She lets out a deep sigh, burying her face in her hands. "I've gotta get out of here," she almost shouts. Clearly upset, she lowers her hands, her bracelet clinking loudly against the door handle.

I stare at her in confusion, her face contorted with

anger. I've never seen her this way in the years we've worked together. I hadn't realized what I'd done could upset her this much.

"Let me out, Julius, or so help me God…" Her voice is low and harsh, and although I'm struggling to understand her, I know I need to let her leave.

"Stop, Carrick," I command, and my driver smoothly guides the car to the side of Washington Street.

"Where are you going?" I ask, not wanting her to leave.

She pushes open the car door and strides out to the dark street. "Just leave me alone. I thought I could trust you. I thought, of all people, I could trust you, Julius, to have my back. How could I let myself think…" Her voice trails off as I slide over and rush out to try and catch up to her.

"Isabella, stop," I beg of her.

"Please, just leave me be," she pleads, but I can't. I can't just leave her alone now. Something is profoundly wrong, and I need to understand. I need to help, even if she doesn't want me to.

I grab her by the wrist, the force jerking her back and into my body. Her face is in my chest, so I tuck two fingers under her chin, lifting to see her eyes. I feel something, something that I push away.

The clang of her bracelet falling to the ground snaps me out of whatever that was, and she steps back, physically retreating from me.

I bend down to pick up the fallen bangle and hand it to her. She snatches it hastily, but not before I spot the blue-gray bruise it was hiding. Something inside me snaps. A wave of fury washes over me as I lean in closer. "What is that?" I demand, pointing at the concealed mark.

She swiftly retrieves the bangle from my grip, covering

up the bruise. "It's nothing," she dismisses, looking past me and toward the distant car.

"It isn't nothing," I say with a strained jaw. Every muscle in my body is tense, bound like a million elastic bands tensioned within their limits.

She averts her gaze. "I don't want to talk about it."

"Bullshit," I retort, moving closer to her. The lapel of my jacket brushes against her bare skin, and I glance down to see the gentle rise of her chest above the soft fabric of her dress.

Her chest heaves rhythmically—a clear sign of her anger. But right now, I couldn't care less.

Over the last few years, I have noticed a steady increase in marks adorning her body. I was too focused on maintaining a strictly professional and personal life to ask questions. But now, she is my wife, and I can no longer avoid asking. I can no longer pretend not to see the marks on her skin. I am done pretending not to care.

"Julius," she says softly. "Don't."

"You can trust me, Isabella, but I need to know. Tell me everything." She drags her eyes up to me and chews on her lip. "I will not ask again."

She rests her hand on a nearby tree and steadies her breath as if preparing to confess something to me. "Travis can't seem to let me go." She looks up at me, and I give her the go-ahead to continue. "We've been separated for a year now, and he blames me for the breakup. He has a temper, you know. And a drinking problem. Our marriage started out rocky, but when we had Fox, I thought I could make it work. I wanted to make it work for Fox's sake. But things just got harder and harder."

"Did he hurt you?" I ask.

Her gaze hits the ground. "Yes. Many times during our marriage."

A sound escapes my lips. "And now? Is that because of him?" I say, picking up her wrist, my thumb automatically rubbing up and down the exposed part of her skin. She inhales sharply at the connection, and our eyes meet.

She blinks, and it's over.

"Yes. He was furious when he found out about our wedding. I'd been ignoring his calls and messages, but when I dropped Fox off at his place..." Her voice trails off.

"Tell me," I persist, needing to know what she's dealing with and who this man is who could possibly hurt this fragile woman, the mother of his child.

"He called me a whore. He thinks we were sleeping together, and that's why I ended our marriage. That's when he grabbed me hard by the wrist and threatened to take Fox away from me for good."

She wipes away a tear quickly and blinks, almost embarrassed to show emotion in front of me. *Am I that much of a bastard that she has to hide this from me?*

My fists clench at my sides as rage engulfs my bloodstream like a raging inferno. "I took an oath to protect you, and I swear to you, from this day forward, I will do that." With that solemn promise hanging in the air, we head back to the car.

The tension between us is palpable as we ride home, a silent journey marked by thoughts louder than words. I'm fucking furious with myself for not asking these questions sooner, for not protecting Isabella when she has always been so loyal to me.

Once home, I pour myself a stiff drink of whiskey, trying to make sense of this emotional whirlwind. I hear Isabella's footsteps fading toward her bedroom, and I don't make any move to stop her. But then there's just silence.

To my surprise, she's back in the living room. "Whiskey?" I offer her as she rounds the corner and looks down at me.

"I think I need one," she says and walks over to the armchair.

A slight smile forms on my lips as I grab another glass, and the liquid sloshes around. I hand it to her, ignoring the warmth of her skin as it trails up my arm when our fingers touch.

I am locked in a battle of emotions, furious with myself for not having the courage to speak up and help her when I knew deep down that the bruises she would haphazardly appear with at work were not caused by clumsiness. At the same time, I am fiercely attracted to her when I know I shouldn't be.

"I'm still angry at you, you know," she says over the rim of her crystal tumbler.

"Are you now?" I reply, hearing the slight smirk in her tone.

"How can you call those people friends? Especially those women?" She takes a huge drink and swallows it, the movement drawing me to her throat.

"They're just about bearable," I confess, savoring the smooth burn of my whiskey.

"Huh," she sounds out in thought. "You're like prime rib to those women."

I crack a smile at her words. "Are you jealous, *wife?*"

"No!" she shoots back immediately, her eyes flashing defiantly. She hides her blushing cheeks behind her drink, taking a quick sip before straightening.

"Since we're on the subject of honesty, we should talk

about that contract we both signed. It's pretty clear we need to remain faithful to one another during this contract, which is absolutely no problem for me because... well..." her voice trails off. "Anyway, I feel this could be a problem for you, considering you've got a different woman for every meal," she teases.

I chuckle, the sound muffled by my drink. "And see where that's gotten me? My company was practically on the brink."

"So the senator's fiancée wasn't your only scandal?"

"I'd rather not go there."

"Well, I kind of want to," she fires back, a spark in her eyes I haven't seen before.

I find it intriguing, even dangerously so.

"I fucked Giletta, yeah, but it wasn't anything serious. She told me she wasn't engaged anymore. If I'd known she was, we wouldn't have... wouldn't have ended up in this media circus with my company's stock taking a nosedive and everything I ever worked for in jeopardy."

She takes a thoughtful sip of her drink, her gaze never leaving mine. "And now you're playing the celibacy card to fix your image and save your company?"

"Something like that," I admit.

She drains her glass and uncrosses her legs, the slit of her skirt revealing just enough to stir my imagination—her, in the throes of passion, in my bathtub.

"So I've spilled some of my secrets. Anything you haven't told me that I should know about you, *husband?*"

I inhale deeply, relishing the way she says 'husband.' My eyes lock onto hers once more before I knock back the remainder of my whiskey, steeling myself.

I've decided I need to tell her I saw her in my bathtub. "I saw you," I confess.

She blinks, not sure what I mean. Leaning closer, my eyes trail down her figure to her bare thigh. I place my tumbler back on the table, and as our eyes meet, I notice the rise and fall of her chest as she comprehends my words.

"You did," she admits, realization settling in, her cheeks turning a vivid shade of pink while she nervously runs her fingers along the rim of her tumbler.

I nod in confirmation, sinking back into my chair with a sigh. "Are you annoyed with me?" I ask, a trace of apprehension creeping into my voice. The thought that she might consider me a voyeur for witnessing her climax in my bathtub, a blatant invasion of privacy, gnaws at me.

Mirroring my posture, she leans back into her chair, her gaze never wavering from mine. "I'm not sure."

Now that we're both reclined, silence envelops us, and the air is charged with a palpable, almost suffocating tension.

"I enjoyed watching you," I confess, my voice low and steady. "Very much, Isabella. The sound of your soft moans echoing through the room aroused me more than I care to admit. So much so that I had to attend to my own needs later that evening, which you witnessed."

She bites her lower lip gently. "I suppose that makes us even then," she replies, hot and breathy.

"I suppose it does."

Another pause.

"What if I were to say I wouldn't mind watching you some more?"

She blinks, caught off guard by my words. "Wouldn't that complicate things?" she queries, her voice unsteady.

"Only if I touched you, which I promise I will not," I assure her, my tone as earnest as I can manage. "I will never cross that line."

12

ISABELLA

The words coming out of Julius's mouth have me stunned. And the crazy part? It sounds like exactly what I want. What I fucking need.

The fact that he watched me in the throes of ecstasy in his bathtub should freak me out and have me running for the hills. But it's doing the exact opposite. I'm feeling hot, lightheaded, and craving more, knowing he was there, watching me give myself over to pleasure.

It's the same as I felt when watching him, filled with need and desire.

"Okay," I reply, smirking and my face aglow in the light of his blue eyes.

I'm floored when he begins to unbutton his shirt. My eyes can't help but be drawn to the golden skin and dark hair on his chest. His strong jawline and those deep blue eyes are aflame with a desire that makes me want to be his. I know I shouldn't be feeling this way, we both shouldn't, but we're adults with needs.

We're in a marriage of convenience, and this steamy proposition is just an added perk. Two adults with a mutual need for release and the fact that we can watch each other, it's just too hot to pass up.

He continues to unbutton his shirt, freeing it from the confines of his pants and unveiling the enticing V-line of his waist. "Touch yourself, Isabella. I can't stand seeing you in that dress without you touching yourself."

"Wh-what? Right n-now?" I stammer, my gaze fixated on the tantalizing dips and curves of his muscular chest.

"Spread those long legs of yours. I want to see that delicious cunt," Julius commands, his voice dropping to a husky whisper.

Well, damn. A dirty talker. The anticipation has me clenching involuntarily, but then I realize I can't get there without a little mechanical help.

"I need to get my... my, you know... vibrator," I splutter out.

His eyes widen, and he presses his lips together, a hint of frustration crossing his features before he gives a curt nod.

Adrenaline rushing through my veins, I dart toward my bedroom, already nervous about the impending scenario. I retrieve my vibrator from the side drawer and make a beeline back to my seat, the city lights casting an ethereal glow around us.

"How do we..." I start, my nerves making it hard to articulate my thoughts.

"Open your legs," he instructs, and I obey despite the butterflies fluttering wildly in my stomach. His gaze travels up my thigh, finally resting on my lace thong.

"That's a good girl. Now slide your panties off and give them to me."

Oh God.

With my free hand, I push down the fabric of my underwear, letting it gather around my ankles before passing them to his outstretched hand. He seizes my lace thong, drawing it up to his nose and inhaling sharply as his eyelids shutter closed momentarily. When they reopen, they blaze with an undeniable desire.

That look has me completely under his control. I spread my legs wider for him, and a low growl of approval escapes his lips. *Thank fuck, I took care of grooming this morning.*

His hand slides down, and he wraps my panties around his cock.

Jesus Christ. The sight alone has me growing wetter.

"Touch yourself, Bella," he urges, and I do. I can't wait anymore.

My hand ventures underneath my dress, and the moment I switch on the vibrator, the hum fills the room. I watch him watch me, sending a new desire rushing between my legs.

He frees his arousal, and it's smooth, long, and hard—a sight that sends a jolt of need through me. The vibrator needs to be inside me now. And as I slide it in, a moan escapes my lips.

"Imagine that's my hard cock sliding in and out of that wet cunt of yours," he urges, his directive sending a tantalizing thrill down my spine that only adds to the dampness between my thighs.

I'm on the edge, so close to the brink already. I force my eyes to stay open, riveted on Julius grunting and groaning, imagining his cock and what it would feel like inside me. Claiming every inch of me.

"That's it, wife. That sweet pussy belongs to me," he grits out, his release imminent.

His commanding words push me past the edge. "Yours," I manage to whimper out, my voice a barely audible, breathless gasp as a tidal wave of release sweeps over me.

Seeing my climax pushes him over the edge, his groan filling the room as he comes on my panties.

Jesus Christ!

We're left panting, riding out the aftershocks of the most intense orgasms we've ever experienced.

I carefully remove the toy, a sudden wave of self-consciousness washing over me as I watch him clean up. I rise, ready to retreat to the safety of my room, when his voice stops me.

"That's the last time I want to see you come with a vibrator," he asserts.

I turn abruptly. "Well, then that's the last time you'll see me climax," I retort.

His expression morphs into one of confusion. "What do you mean?"

"I can't orgasm without it," I confess, meeting his gaze head-on.

His surprise quickly gives way to anger. "You can and you will. I will teach you," he declares with a resolve that leaves no room for argument, yet I can't stop myself.

"You won't be able to," I counter, remembering how neither my past partners nor I have achieved the same result without my trusty battery-operated friend.

"Watch me," he replies, a determined glint in his eyes as he strides away.

After the intense orgasm, I passed out feeling absolutely satisfied, but now, a week later, it's like our hot-and-heavy weekend show was a dream. Thoughts about how he would teach me have plagued me, but there has been nothing of the sort, and I'm beyond frustrated.

Julius is all professional and swamped with work lately, especially since the Bynstrom deal has gone ahead, and they are busy restructuring the company. And I'm running around like crazy, trying to keep up with his hectic schedule.

Slater Corp. is also in the process of buying up a bunch of companies, so it feels like Julius is needed every second of the day. His calendar is nuts. He's even double-booking dinners just to squeeze everything in.

He's busy. I get it, but it's also left me feeling restless.

Julius is out at yet another business dinner, and Fox isn't due back until tomorrow from his dad's, and I can't wait. This week-on, week-off thing is rough. It's too much change for Fox and not enough time for me. But with my ex playing hardball over custody while also trying to worm his way back into my life, it's all a bit of a mess.

Deciding to treat myself, I pour a glass from Julius's fancy whiskey bar and open my laptop. My inbox is crammed with a bunch of emails that I'll need to get to, but one from Julius catches my eye. It's fresh, only about ten minutes old, which is weird because he's supposed to be at dinner right now.

With my curiosity piqued, I click on it. I'm hoping it's not something that needs immediate attention, as it's way too late for any more work crises.

From: Julius Slater
To: Isabella Moore

Dear Isabella,

You are not allowed to touch yourself without me there to watch you.
Your husband.

Julius Slater
CEO
Slater Corp.

A startled gasp escapes me, and a giggle follows, but it quickly becomes a flash of irritation. All I wanted was to climax and unwind from the day, with the image of him pleasuring himself lingering in my thoughts. I hurriedly tap the reply button and begin to compose my response.

From: Isabella Moore
To: Julius Slater

That's unfair. You're never here, husband.
Your wife,
Isabella

I swallow the whiskey, and it heats my bones as I nervously wait for a reply. I'm having fun for the first time in a long time. A reply sounds as it quickly comes back in.

From: Julius Slater
To: Isabella Moore

Dear Isabella,

Don't you dare... and why is your surname not mine?
Your husband.

Julius
CEO
Slater Corp.

Why would I take his surname when this is only temporary? Just seems like more unnecessary paperwork when things have to go back to normal. I quickly type out a reply.

From: Isabella Moore
To: Julius Slater

Because this is only temporary.
I can do as I wish, husband, so if I feel like releasing, I think I might just go now and do just that.

Your wife,
Isabella

I bite my lower lip, a smile spreading across my face as I eagerly await his response. I almost think he isn't going to respond as it takes a bit of time to come through, but then I hear the soft ding and smile when I see his name flash up in my inbox.

From: Julius Slater
To: Isabella Slater

Dear Isabella,
I'm leaving now.
Your husband.

Julius
CEO
Slater Corp.

Ps: Your name is now correct, wife.

"What the…" I blink at the screen in surprise. Sure enough, my name now reads Isabella Slater, and it's a strange sight.

Ignoring the feeling it gives me, I quickly double-check his calendar to confirm where he's supposed to be. He should be just starting at his second dinner meeting at this hour.

My mind whirls with confusion.

Is he skipping the meeting to attend to me?

In my current state of heightened anticipation, I don't really care about the why. I quickly drain the remainder of my whiskey and switch out my practical cotton underwear for a sexy lace thong hidden beneath a silk robe.

In less than ten minutes, the soft chime of the elevator doors rings out, followed by his footsteps echoing through the apartment and the sound of him loosening his tie. Then there's a knock on my bedroom door. In our short time together, he's never entered my private space.

"You're here," I observe, sitting on the edge of my bed. Julius's gaze meets mine, his eyes burning with an intensity that mirrors my own. He licks his lips and takes a step forward, only to hesitate, taking a step back.

Eventually, he settles into a chair a few feet away from

the bed. "I am. Now, let's see you open that robe and slide a finger into that pretty pussy of yours, Bella," he says, his words surprisingly forward. It's crude but also tantalizingly dirty.

As he unzips his pants and frees himself, I can't help but stare. He's already hard, the sight of which sparks a trail of desire in me. I wonder how it would feel to be claimed by him.

"I'm not a patient man, Bella," he says. "I need to see your fingers sink inside you."

Despite my initial hesitation, I do as he asks and slide my hand lower, slowly pushing one finger inside myself. It feels different but not unpleasant, and his attentive gaze only adds to the arousal.

"Good. Now two fingers, deeper, slower, until you hit your back wall," he instructs in a low, husky voice laced with need.

I do as he says, trusting him implicitly, his watchful eyes analyzing every move I make, every reaction of my body. "Drag those sweet juices up to your clit and move your fingers hard and fast," he orders, and I follow his instruction, my fingers moving to the rhythm he dictates.

"Fuck your hand, Bella. Harder," he commands, and his hand moves faster, matching the pace he's set for me.

I moan at the sensation of my fingers inside me, the fullness that envelopes me as I throw my head back in ecstasy and unravel in ways I've never experienced before.

I would overthink this moment if I weren't reeling in the aftershocks of such a shattering release.

"Jesus fuck," he groans out at his release, and I open my eyes to find him spilling out onto himself. I involuntarily lick my lips at the sight.

"You don't know how much I want to suck your fingers

right now," he says. "The same fingers dripping with your cum from my dirty words."

I watch as he wipes himself up with a nearby towel, a sly grin appearing on his face and a knowing look. If I had to describe it with one word, it would be cocky, and I don't even care if it means I can have orgasms like that.

"You can," I offer breathlessly, then my breath halts at the silence that follows.

His eyes flare with something, and it's like he's wrestling on the spot, torn between coming to me or leaving.

"Goodnight, Isabella," he says and walks out the door, leaving me wanting more, even though I know I shouldn't.

13

JULIUS

There isn't a sweeter sight of my wife pleasuring herself and me fisting my hard cock to her.

Our marriage hasn't been all that bad. I'm surprised I've opened myself up beyond my usual boundaries. I thought it would be harder, seeing how clear my boundaries have been in the past and how determined I was to keep my personal and professional lives separate to build an empire.

Perhaps it's because I've been so busy with work, but the thought of her pleasuring herself without me had me coming home and leaving my dinner meeting to be with her this week.

Looking and not touching is something I've never done before, and damn, it's so fucking hot. Maybe voyeurism is a kink worth exploring. But strangely, there isn't anyone else I'd rather watch unraveling before my hungry eyes.

But the fact that last night was her first orgasm without a device or man? *What the actual fuck?* Isabella is a beautiful twenty-six-year-old woman with needs. *Imagine what I could do with my cock inside her.* Quickly, I push away the thought. We made a deal, and that's it. We touch ourselves and not each other. That barrier can *never* be crossed.

As I finish for the day, I feel relieved knowing I don't have any meetings tonight.

Through the glass, I spot Isabella packing up as well. She usually leaves a bit earlier on the days she has to pick up her son.

Honestly, I find myself wanting to go with her. I don't want her to face her ex-husband alone, especially considering what he has done to her in the past. I can't deny that a part of me yearns to go there right now and deliver a satisfying punch to his face for all the trauma and abuse she's endured. However, I understand that crossing that line would only cause more harm. It's a line that doesn't need to be broken.

My phone rings, and I glance down to see it's my sister calling.

"Victoria," I say, answering the call.

"Julius, well, hello! You never call me," Victoria says, all huffy.

"I'm sorry. You know what it has been like around here," I reply.

"And I just performed in front of fifty thousand people last night, but that's no excuse."

Okay, she has a point.

"Jesus, sis, that's insane. Where was that?"

"Japan, still here a while, before finishing up in Australia. How is your new wife? I can't wait to meet her when I eventually get back to the States. Rosie said she's perfect for you."

"She's tolerable," I reply, and a wicked smile spreads onto my lips as the memory of her fingers sinking inside her folds and her head spilling back in the throes of a moan.

"Is that a smile I hear in your voice?" she teases.

"Perhaps. Tell me about the tour," I say, trying to change the subject.

"Some crazy fan is stalking me, but apart from that, it's fine."

"What do you mean?" I ask, needing clarification.

"It's nothing to worry about. My security is handling it."

"They better be."

"Oh, you worry too much. I'm flying out to Kyoto today for another concert, and..."

I half-listen as I see Dougall Fritz approach Isabella. He's a mid-level management player, and lately, I've noticed him talking to Isabella more frequently. I don't like it. He knows we're together. In fact, the whole world knows we're together. He leans on her desk, sitting on the corner, and I see him smiling as they share a laugh.

My grip on the phone tightens into a stranglehold.

"Julius, are you there?" Victoria asks, pulling me out of my haze.

"Yes, sorry. I have to go. Can I call you later?" I say, not liking what I'm witnessing at all.

"You better."

I hang up the phone and hastily open the door to my office. Both Isabella and Dougall turn their heads at the sudden movement. He's playing with her bracelet, and my ears feel like they're emitting steam. I try to assess the dynamic. *Is she flirting with him?* I know he's flirting with her, but does she want him? Am I preventing her from her own happiness by keeping her chained in this marriage of convenience?

"Julius."

"Dougall," I say curtly. "Is there a reason you're

distracting my secretary, or is there something you actually want?"

A slight glint in his eyes ignites rage within me. That fucker wants *her*. I knew it. He knows exactly what this is and isn't afraid to challenge me.

Isabella senses my mood and quickly resumes her secretarial duties. I step forward, causing Dougall to stand.

"Leave my wife alone," I say, my rage under control but palpable.

"I don't know what you're talking about," he says, looking slightly taken aback. But it's all an act. Dougall has a reputation worse than mine. He knows exactly what he's doing, and I won't stand for it. "I see it's best I leave," he says, glancing between Isabella and me.

I quickly notice Isabella looking up at me, uncertainty in her eyes.

"Don't come back unless you want a demotion to janitor," I retort sharply.

He turns, wide-eyed and gasping in shock, then quickly walks out.

Fucker.

Still staring at him, I hear Isabella's voice. "That was a little rude, don't you think?"

I widen my eyes at her. "There is no flirting here. You are my wife."

"I wasn't flirting," she insists.

"Yes, you were. And so was he. If you want to keep your job, I suggest you act professionally at all times." My words are coarse and harsh, but I won't tolerate it.

The shock on her beautiful face transforms into a scowl. We engage in a stare-off as the energy charges around us like a swarm of bees.

"Yes, of course," she finally says, and I exhale sharply, heading for the elevator to leave for the day.

With each determined stride, my anger and frustration build as I step away from her. I feel her gaze on my back, and as I enter the elevator, I turn around to find her staring at me.

The elevator doors close, and I catch a glimpse of disappointment across her face, and I push away my disappointment in myself.

No attachments, Slater.

Work comes first—always.

It's late when Isabella comes home with Fox. I feel like she has been avoiding me all evening, choosing to eat out with her son instead of being at home.

Fox rushes in, screaming as he always does, and I find myself retreating to my library, checking the last of my emails while sipping on a smooth 1976 whiskey. It's past eight o'clock, and even though I'm not a parent, I can tell that a four-year-old's bedtime is long overdue.

Fox comes bounding around the corner, his little footsteps disrupting the quiet of my sanctuary, sounding like a thousand elephant steps. "Jules Monster!" he says.

He has taken to calling me that, and I don't particularly like it.

"Nado," I say as he approaches and tumbles to a standstill, his little legs carrying him clumsily. He looks up, taking in the towering piles of books that reach the ceiling.

"What you doin'?" he asks, coming over and standing beside me like an annoying little fly.

"Work," I say tersely.

The boy is a mess, with a dirty shirt, hair that looks like he's been electrocuted, and smells as if he hasn't showered for days. I can't help but feel sorry for him, imagining the kind of care he's been receiving from his dad over the past week.

Isabella is rustling outside, and I find myself compelled to ask, "How was your week with your dad?"

He picks up my pen and shakes it violently. "Otay."

"Just okay?" I ask, wanting this four-year-old to try and expand his vocabulary a bit.

"Daddy lets me watch whatever I like and gives me treats... sooo many treats. I tink that's why Mommy doesn't like him."

I swallow the distaste in my throat. No, son, your mommy doesn't like him because he abuses her. I want to say that, but I fear this child has seen enough trauma in his life for me to relive it for him.

"And how was Dad? Was he mad?"

He motions my ballpoint pen like an airplane, saying, "Whoosh, whoosh, whoosh. Higher," he says, climbing onto my lap. I hold out my arms as the boy 'sign-writes' in the air with my pen-turned-airplane.

"There you are," Isabella's familiar voice floats in. She stops in her tracks and sees Fox on my lap.

She blinks.

"I'm sorry. He shouldn't be..." Her voice trails off. "Fox, darling, let Julius work, please."

The pen in his hand goes into supersonic mode as he loses his balance. I quickly grab him before he falls to the floor.

"Wow, that was fun!" he says, and I smirk. This kid is a wild child.

"Fox, come on," Isabella says over the commotion.

"Again, again!"

"Fox!" Isabella yells, and her reaction sounds strange. "Now!"

I put Fox down, and he hangs his head. "Next time, Nado," I find myself saying, attempting to pick him up as he sulks toward the door.

Isabella doesn't even look at me. Instead, she grabs his arm, ushering him out the door. The next thing I hear is him throwing a tantrum in the bath at something she said, followed by the soft lull of her voice echoing down the hallway as she reads him a bedtime story.

∼

I can't sleep.

It's becoming a regular occurrence these last few months of marriage.

A muffled noise catches my attention, a low whimper I can't quite place. I sit up, pull on a shirt, and slip out of bed. I've been staring at the ceiling for half an hour anyway, unable to quell the gnawing frustration.

After putting Fox to bed, Isabella avoided me. Despite her insistence that it was innocent, I'm angry at her for her playful banter. I'm angry at myself too because this arrangement is binding us together in a way I hadn't anticipated.

I pad down the hall, the floorboards cool beneath my bare feet. As I approach her room, the sound of the shower turning off greets me, followed by the faint noise again. *Is she...* We had an agreement to only find pleasure together. But if she's that upset with me, is she?

I quicken my pace, reaching the locked door to her room. I rap loudly, my voice firm. "Open the door, Isabella."

"Julius?" Her voice is shaky and uncertain.

"Open this door, Bella. Now," I demand, my patience wearing thin.

The sound of the lock clicking open reaches me, and she cracks the door open slightly. I push the door open the rest of the way and step into a room filled with steam and the sweet scent of roses from her conditioner. Her hair is damp, and she's clutching a towel to her body.

"What are you doing in here?" she asks, her voice strained.

"We made a deal," I remind her, my eyes scanning the room. "We can only come with each other."

"I wasn't," she protests, her cheeks flushing.

"I heard you." My gaze falls back to her, and that's when I see it—bruises and marks marring her shoulder and snaking down her arm. I stare in shock, then my anger morphs into a primal protectiveness.

"What the fuck did he do to you?" I demand, my voice barely a whisper.

"Nothing!" she retorts, turning her back to me. More bruises reveal themselves, a trail leading down her spine.

Ignoring her protest, my hands wrap around her stomach, and I feel her relax against my touch as she curves her back into my chest. "I'm so sorry, Bella," I whisper, feeling her stiff posture tense further in protest.

I don't know how long I hold her before she melts against me, giving in to my support. She sobs softly, and I can't bear her facing away from me. I gently guide her, turning her to face me before pulling her against me once more. She continues crying into my shoulder, and I tighten my hold, offering what comfort I can.

We remain entwined for a time, her muffled cries gradually subsiding. When she finally looks up at me, her eyes are swollen and red. "Let's take care of those bruises," I say, leading her out of the bathroom and into the kitchen, where I keep my medical supplies.

I sit her on the chair and fetch her a calming tea. Then I finally find my medical supplies and remove the cream for bruising. I unscrew the lid as I sit on the stool next to her. The towel is still knotted around her, and I find myself momentarily distracted by her natural beauty—her full lips, natural blush atop her high cheekbones, and porcelain skin.

I push away the unfathomable attraction I have that is seemingly growing by the day and squeeze the cream from the tube. I'm hell-bent on making her whole again. I know these are only the physical marks on her skin, but I hate to think about what's going on inside her.

I gently rub her bruises, one after another, as she sits quietly. The weight of her stare presses upon me, the silence eating between us.

"Fox was getting his things when he decided to take out his drunken rage on me. This time he was wearing his ring. His family crest. When I tried to turn, he grabbed me, kicking me to the floor."

I shake my head, her words making me nauseous. "Where was Fox?" I ask, hoping he didn't witness the violence.

"Luckily, he was getting his bag in the other room. He has seen way too much for his four years. No one should ever have to see their mother like that." She inhales sharply.

"I can't bear to see you going through this. I want to take you to the police and report this," I say, looking up at her with determination.

"No," she says, her voice trembling. "We can't do that.

I've done it before, and he's only gotten angrier. It's my word against his."

I pause, my heart sinking at her words. "Look at your body. This is evidence right here. We have to go to the police. We can't let him get away with this."

She starts to hyperventilate, her eyes wide with fear. "Please, no," she pleads, her voice filled with terror.

Anger rises within me, a boiling fury at the injustice of it all. I can't stand the thought of her suffering in silence, protecting her abuser. I want to scream, to break something, to make it all stop. But I know that won't help her in this moment.

Taking a deep breath, I pull her close, my grip tight but gentle. "Okay, okay," I say through clenched teeth, my voice filled with frustration. "We'll find another way. We'll figure this out together."

"From now on, either my driver will go fetch Fox, or I will," I assert, my voice firm. She squirms out of my grasp and looks at me, her eyes filled with apprehension.

"The driver will do," she insists. "We don't need to rile him up more, and with you... I'm not sure." She shakes her head, her expression filled with uncertainty. "You have to remember, Julius, after our sham marriage wraps up in nine months, I'm on my own."

The thought of her being alone once our arrangement ends tugs at my heart. I gently tilt her chin up, meeting her gaze with a determined look.

"No police, then. But I want to take some photos, just for our records," I declare, my voice resolute.

She gives me a reluctant nod, and I draw her closer.

It's about time I pay a visit to the man who's been hurting my wife.

14

ISABELLA

I t's Wednesday afternoon, and I'm drowning in emails and work commitments. The weight of it all pushes me to leave and find a sugary pick-me-up to help me get through the rest of the day.

As I enter the coffee shop, Sojo's, I spot Rosie, and she calls me over. Navigating through the busy café, I see Vincent with her, his arm wrapped around her in a warm embrace. They are so adorable together, and it stirs something dark and yearning within me. But deep down, I know it's something I can never attain.

Over the past few months, with Rosie frequently visiting our floor, we've gotten to know each other. The love between her and Vincent feels like something from a *Bridgerton* novel. I've witnessed their connection firsthand and even overheard their passionate moments, which were so incredibly arousing that I had to step out for some fresh air.

"Hey, Bella, come join us," Rosie says, beckoning me over, and Vincent pulls out a seat for me.

"Is my brother annoying you so much that you had to leave?" Vincent asks with a playful smirk.

"No, not at all. I'm just desperate for a coffee and a treat," I reply, trying to conceal the thoughts swirling in my mind.

"Let me get it for you," Vincent offers and promptly leaves. By now, he knows exactly what I like. It's no secret I always order a macaroon and a flat white from Sojo's.

"Thank you," I say as he walks away, his hand brushing against Rosie's shoulder. I can't help but be drawn to the connection they share. There's something about it that feels oddly familiar.

"So, how's it going? It's been about three months now that you've been living together on Park Avenue with him," Rosie asks, her smile filled with curiosity.

I blush involuntarily, unable to control the flush that spreads across my cheeks when I think about him pleasuring himself and me touching myself at the same time. "Well... it mustn't be all bad," she says with a sly grin.

I push away the blush on my cheeks. "It's not that bad. He is at work mostly, and we keep to ourselves."

She raises a skeptical eyebrow before adding, "And your gorgeous son, Fox. How is he coping with the new environment?"

I look at Rosie, amazed by how put together and composed she is, so wise beyond her years. I envy her ability to seamlessly fit into Vincent's world, something I haven't quite mastered.

"He's been quite a whirlwind for Julius to get used to. But Fox is a handful, even at the best of times. He hasn't fared well with the separation and the back and forth with my ex. It's like he's become a commodity in all of this," I explain, frustration evident in my voice as I swipe away a strand of hair from my face.

I find myself growing frustrated with the endless legal battles and the constant drain on my finances. The slow pace at which lawyers operate feels unbearable at times.

"Julius is very set in his ways," Rosie says, contemplating her thoughts.

"You're telling me," I reply with a sigh.

"Just give it time, and you'll see a side of him that I'm only just starting to see." I nod, still somewhat doubtful. "He will let his guard down. Just give it time," Rosie reassures me. "I remember starting as an intern and being handed that thick code of conduct booklet," she says, a laugh escaping her lips. "And look how that ended up for me," she adds, laughter filling the air.

We share a genuine laugh just as Vincent places my flat white and raspberry macaroon before me. "Thank you."

Vincent sinks back into his seat. "So, where were we?" he asks, glancing at us.

"I was just curious about how Bella and Fox are settling in with the ever-professional Julius," Rosie pipes up.

Vincent bursts into a hearty chuckle. "Julius and kids, something I never thought I'd witness."

Intrigued, I can't help but ask, even as I take a sip of my flat white, "And why's that?"

"Bella, Julius is a complex guy," Vincent replies.

"Seems to be a Slater trait," Rosie chips in, and Vincent pulls her close into a bear hug.

"I'm going to let that slide," he retorts, kissing Rosie's forehead. "Julius might not have shared this with you, but our childhood was pretty turbulent. He was shipped off to boarding school at a really young age, way earlier than me. He spent most of his holidays at boarding school alone while I came back home. And when he did come home, our father was either absent or just... busy and not present."

I'm confused and saddened by his admission, imagining a young Julius left to fend for himself at such a young age without the guidance and love of a family. "That's really sad," I reply, my voice filled with sympathy.

"It's just how it was," Vincent confirms, his tone holding a touch of resignation.

"While we're on the topic of parents, I noticed yours were absent at the wedding," Vincent remarks.

I'm taken aback by the sudden change in topic, "Yes," I reply, unsure of where he's going with this. He widens his eyes, seemingly expecting more, and I can sense his dissatisfaction with my response. "They live in Detroit," I add quickly, yet my tone has a finality.

Rosie senses my discomfort and quickly intervenes. "Hey, why don't we invite you over for dinner at our place sometime?" she suggests, stepping in to ease the tension.

"Oh, um..." I hesitate, unsure about spending more time with them outside of work.

"Come on, it will be fun. You can bring Fox if it's the week you have him," Rosie continues, her enthusiasm evident.

Vincent looks at Rosie, his expression unsure about the request. He knows his brother all too well.

"I'm not sure if Julius has the time to..." I begin to say, my voice trailing off.

"Nonsense. If I ask, he won't say no," Rosie insists confidently.

Vincent lets out another bark of laughter.

"I'll ask him when we get back," Rosie declares determinedly.

"Okay," I reply, feeling a mixture of surprise and curiosity.

I pick up my macaroon and take a large bite, trying to process the situation. Is it just me, or does this feel like a date arranged by none other than Rosie herself?

I return to my office with Rosie a hot step behind me. Vincent has retreated to his office, and true to her form, Rosie is tailing it beside me to invite Julius.

"I can make my famous strawberry pie," Rosie says excitedly.

"He hasn't even committed to dinner yet. I think you may be getting ahead of yourself."

"Puh-lease!!" she says, knocking on his door loudly and confidently. I can't help but hover behind her.

She opens the door and steps inside. I'm behind her and stand at the side as she is too tall for me to see over her.

He takes us both in.

"What can I do for you, Rosie?"

I wander over and bring him a coffee, placing it on his desk. His hand brushes against mine, and we have a moment where there is this built-up sexual chemistry, one which haunts me in my dreams. It's becoming a touch I need, crave, and feel in my dreams, but it's more than that.

"Thank you, Isabella," he says, then clears his throat.

"Vincent and I would like to invite you and Bella to dinner."

"When?" Julius asks.

"Saturday night?" she questions, her eyes trained on Julius.

"How is my schedule for Saturday night, Isabella?"

His gaze comes up to meet mine. "It's clear, Mr. Slater."

Rosie turns to me, looking shocked. "Wait, you call him Mr. Slater still?"

"Rosie, we do what works," Julius adds, his voice firm.

Rosie looks at me, and I feel a mix of nerves and anticipation. My eyes dart to the floor, unable to hold her gaze.

"Count us in," Julius tells Rosie, and I can't help but look up, my eyes meeting his. I'm taken aback by the surprise in his expression as he stares at me.

Something flickers in his eyes, and I can't quite decipher what it means.

15

JULIUS

My team has pinpointed a window through meticulous monitoring where Travis Sneddon is finally alone at his house. Catching him alone has been nearly impossible between his recent travel and hotel sexcapades in the city. And as soon as they tell me he is alone, I cancel my afternoon appointments feigning a migraine and steer my car toward the address synced to my dashboard.

Situated in Short Hills, New Jersey, the thought of Isabella having to rely on public transportation for her daily commute makes me cringe. I do not want her to endure unpredictable schedules, crowded trains or buses, and the potential for delays and discomfort.

That's why I made the easy decision to provide her with a personal driver. Knowing that she no longer has to rely on public transportation brings me a sense of relief. It's a small but significant way to ensure she can commute comfortably, safely, and without the stress of dealing with public transportation challenges.

But more importantly, my driver, Carrick, serves a

purpose beyond transportation. I purposely kept this information hidden from Isabella, not out of deceit but out of a desire to keep her safe. Carrick gives me peace of mind, knowing that Isabella has someone capable she can rely on for help if she needs it.

I kill the engine of my Aston Martin and glare out the window. The house is contemporary, appealing even. Clearly, money isn't an issue for him.

From delving into his family affairs, the Sneddon family has their fingers in a profitable pie of IT franchises. I won't lie. I've thought about buying them out and running them into the ground just for kicks. But I urge myself not to get involved, no matter how hard it is.

I berate myself for maintaining such a distance all these years she's been in my employ. I had built an impenetrable wall between us, all because of my stubborn determination to succeed on my own and not let anyone in.

Approaching the door, I knock, and the muffled sounds of movement inside reach my ears, followed by a loud crash. "Fuck," a disgruntled voice rings out.

My second knock resonates louder, laced with impatience.

"I'm coming," the voice bellows back.

As the door swings open, a potent smell of alcohol escapes the house, carried on the breath of the man standing before me.

"Juliusss Slater. What the hell do you want?" he rounds out on a slur. "You've got a nerve showing up here."

"I want you to leave my wife alone," I say. "And Fox too. If I hear you've hurt him in any way, I will come after you with every resource at my disposal."

He stumbles back slightly, surprised by my resolve. There's a flicker of something in his eyes, a hint of fear maybe, quickly replaced by stubborn defiance. "You can... t-tell mmme what to dooo..." he slurs, his speech sloppy from the alcohol. "... 'specially not 'bout my own kid."

"I can, and I will when it comes to protecting my wife and her son," I retort, my gaze unblinking. "You hurt her again, and you'll answer to me."

His laugh this time is short, a nervous sound, his façade starting to crack. "You're not their savior, Slater," he says, attempting to sound menacing. "Just the rich fool who married a single mom to clean up his image."

"You know nothing about me. About us." I growl, my temper flaring at how insignificant he is making our marriage. "And if you lay a finger on either of them again, you'll find out just how far I'm willing to go to protect my family."

The silence that follows is charged, my warning hanging heavily in the air. I turn on my heel and walk away, leaving him to stew in his drunken haze. He's been warned.

As I turn to leave, Travis hollers after me, "Go to your whore, Slater! She's no different than the rest of 'em."

A volcanic rage surges within me. Swirling on my heel, I charge back toward him, fists balled and eyes blazing. "Watch your filthy mouth, Sneddon." I snarl, my voice low and deadly.

His drunken smirk falters, yet there's a stubborn glint in his bloodshot eyes. Despite his obvious inebriation, he seems to understand that I'm not just another businessman to shrug off. I'm a man whose woman he's insulted. He senses the peril he's just invited but stands his ground.

Travis Sneddon may be many things, but a coward isn't one of them.

My clenched fist hovers, threatening and poised. "One more word about Isabella, and I'll ensure you won't have the luxury of uttering another syllable ever again," I growl out, my eyes burning with unspoken threats. Travis remains silent, his stubborn defiance strong even in the face of danger.

I keep my eyes fixed on him, letting the silence stretch until it's almost unbearable. Then, without another word, I turn on my heel and stride away. The gravel crunches under the weight of each heavy step of my polished shoes as I head back to my car.

I don't give him the satisfaction of a second glance. The message has been delivered. Travis Sneddon is now acutely aware of the storm he's invited. As I pull out of the driveway, I can still see him in my rearview mirror, standing in the doorway, watching me leave. I know I've left an indelible mark on his arrogance.

It's done. The line has been drawn. Now that he knows who he's dealing with, he won't dare hurt Isabella again, or he'll have to deal with me.

It's Saturday night, and Isabella and Fox are with me en route to my brother's penthouse.

When we arrive, I stand to the side to let Isabella go ahead of me and inside the elevator. "What are you doing, Jules?" Nado tugs at my pants.

"I'm letting your mother through first."

"Why?" It strikes me that her ex never did this, so this is new for Fox to witness.

I get down on my knees so I'm at his level. "Because good manners and a kind gesture is a sign of respect and courtesy."

Nado nods, then takes off into the elevator like a wild animal unleashed.

I get up and step inside, Isabella's gaze meeting mine as she smiles. "Thank you," she whispers, her voice soft yet firm. "Not for letting me on the elevator... well, for that..." She clears her throat, a shy blush seeping into her cheeks. "But for teaching my son the kind of values that a father figure hasn't been able to do before."

Midway through our exchange, Nado darts between us, nudging his mother off balance, and she stumbles into my open arms.

"Fox!" she blurts out, surprise etched on her face as I instinctively steady her. Her fragrance wafts up to me, and she smells divine, like a tantalizing mix of wildflowers and vanilla.

I look down at her, our eyes locking in mutual surprise. Her dark brown hair cascades around her shoulders in loose waves, swaying gently with each movement. She looks ethereal tonight, but I bite my tongue before the compliment escapes my lips.

The reality is, ever since she sauntered out of her room in the floral halter-neck dress, I've been captivated. The thought of how simple it would be to unclip her dress's clasp and trace my lips along her neck is dangerously tempting.

I'm distantly aware of Nado running around his mother and me, playfully chasing invisible monsters within the confines of the elevator. But it's all a blur. She's within reach, and the temptation to lean in and kiss her is overwhelming.

The abrupt screeching of the elevator, followed by a jerk to a halt, snaps me back to reality, and I quickly step back.

"Oh shit, Mommy!" Fox declares, standing guiltily next to the now infamous emergency button.

Isabella's horrified expression, paired with our sudden entrapment in the elevator, ignites a fit of laughter in me. Honestly, this kid brings a whole new level of craziness I never knew existed.

"This isn't funny, Julius!" she chides, yet her eyes are sparkling with suppressed laughter.

"Sorry, Mommy!" Nado giggles, joining in with me.

"No, it's not just funny. It's downright hysterical," I concede, stifling my chuckles as she finally gives in to the bubbling, contagious laughter.

16

ISABELLA

Eventually, the elevator doors open, and we tumble out unscathed. Although as far as being trapped in elevators, this, by far, was the best fun I've ever had. My claustrophobia seemed to disappear with Julius's animated storytelling keeping Fox and me in raptures.

"You're alive!" Rosie approaches with a beaming smile. She's donned a stunning outfit. A pair of tailored jeans hug her body, while a lilac cashmere sweater adds an extra touch of elegance.

She wraps me into a warm embrace, expressing her delight, "I'm so glad you're here. Tonight is going to be a blast!" she says loudly before pulling me closer. "Let's just loosen Julius up a bit. You'll see how fun he can be."

"Shh," I reply, hoping he didn't hear her. But the prospect of seeing Julius let his guard down has me intrigued.

As I rest my head on her shoulder, I feel a sense of relief, able to be myself, especially around Rosie. She has been my confidant since my marriage of convenience.

"Isabella, it's great to have you here," Vincent says,

kissing my cheek gently. "We should have invited you over sooner. Work has just been a whirlwind."

"It's nice to be here," I add. "Vincent, you remember my son, Fox?" I say, trying to get Fox's attention as he starts to spin on the spot, fast to be as dizzy as possible.

Stop, for the love of God.

Fox untwirls and slows to a wonky stop. Vincent engages him, and my attention diverts to Julius, who is laughing at something Rosie said as they break apart from an embrace. A twinge of jealousy seizes me, watching him unwind in her company and wishing he'd be more open with me. However, the moment is cut short when Julius greets Vincent with a firm handshake before Vincent embraces him.

"So what's all this about?" Julius questions as he glances between Vincent and Rosie.

"What do you mean? It's just dinner. Can't we share a meal? Besides, I'd love to catch up on Fox's latest exploits," Rosie says.

Bending down to meet Fox at his level, Rosie pulls him in for a tight hug. "Hello, Fox. Nice to see you again, little man!" she coos, and he promptly melts into her embrace, instantly recognizing her welcoming warmth.

"I'm hungry," he blurts out, and we all laugh.

"No need to fret, Fox. Rumor has it that you're quite the hot dog fan," she teases, referencing the tidbit of information she'd obtained from me earlier in the week about Fox's favorite meal.

Fox's wide eyes dart up to meet mine, brimming with excitement. He turns to Rosie and asks, "Do you have ketchup?"

I catch Julius's eye, and we can't help but crack up, sharing a moment of easy laughter.

~

After a tour of Vincent's fancy penthouse, we sit at the dining table. But I can't help noticing their homes are like night and day. Vincent's place is like something out of a designer magazine, all dark marble and sleek lines, but Julius's is cozy, full of color, and very down-to-earth. It's a bit weird, to be honest.

Rosie's voice brings me back to the conversation. "Tonight, we're having an all-American feast for Fox's love of hot dogs... smokey barbecue ribs, pulled pork, brisket, and all the fixings."

The smell alone has me drooling then the platters of delicious food are laid out before our very eyes. "Wow, this is not what I expected," I exclaim.

"This is mouthwatering," Julius comments as the waiter sets down three mini hotdogs before Fox. His eyes sparkle like a fireworks display, and his joy kindles warmth in me.

"Fancy food isn't the same as comfort food. And I love comfort food," Rosie shares, taking a big scoop of pulled pork from the platter nearest her.

"We're definitely on the same page there," I say, nodding in agreement and helping myself to the smokey brisket.

"Those posh dinners are so dull," Rosie adds, her hand resting on Vincent's arm. It's a quiet reference to all those stuffy charity dinners they go to. "But with you, my love, they are tolerable."

"As they are with you, little one," he says, and they share a moment.

Julius catches my eye. It's like he's zeroed in on me, and I can feel myself blushing.

"Bet you've had to suffer through one of those boring events now that you're Mrs. Slater?" Rosie asks, breaking the moment.

I turn away from Julius, stating, "Actually, it was pretty rough. The women there were like vultures."

"They have no shame," Rosie remarks dryly.

"It's because they're jealous of you, Isabella," Julius chimes in.

As agreement echoes around the table, I swivel toward him in surprise. My napkin tumbles from my lap as I jerk toward him, "You could've mentioned that then instead of defending them."

Julius picks up my napkin, and his fingers brush mine as he hands it back, sending a little shiver up my spine.

"I don't think I ever defended them," he admits, holding my gaze.

Our eyes lock, and I see a spark of something. It's different from his usual look. This one is softer, warmer, and a hotter kind of predatory.

As the night unfolds, I can see Julius letting his guard down. Each glass of wine seems to chip away at his cool façade like sunlight slowly melting a chunk of ice.

Julius has excused himself, and Vincent is checking on dessert, leaving Rosie and me watching over Fox, who decides to run up and down their hallway.

"It's fine, honestly, you worry too much," Rosie says as I stare at my son, worried he'll break something of value in here.

"Have you made any more headway with custody?" Rosie asks, pulling my attention from Fox.

"Not exactly. The lawyers are so slow. Everything is a process. But as you know, I will have more means by the conclusion of this arrangement to really pull the trigger."

"I understand."

"Fox needs more stability. I need to give him that. It's not with his father. He's a..." I let my voice trail off, thinking of the unspeakable horror that man has caused in our lives. When I look back up, I see Rosie's caring expression.

She extends her arm, letting it rest upon mine. "I don't know what you've been through, Isabella, but I have faith you'll win custody. You're strong as nails and an amazing mom to Fox."

"Thank you." I smile at my good friend, my heart swelling with emotion.

"Fox!" The deep voice of Julius booms down the hallway.

"What's he up to now?" Quickly, I scoot my chair back and race to find the source of the commotion.

When Julius comes back in, Fox is hot on his heels, sprinting past him and racing toward me.

"I saw his sausage!" he blurts out so unexpectedly that I can't hold back my laughter. "I saw his sausage!" Fox says again, giggling as he watches Julius's face turn a shade of red.

"He caught me in the bathroom," Julius admits, his face flaming.

I'm laughing so hard I can barely breathe, and Rosie's cracking up too.

"His sausage is much bigger than Daddy's." Vincent walks in just in time to hear Fox's comparison, and he starts howling with laughter.

Rosie leans in and whispers, "That's a Slater trait, my friend." Then falls back into her chair, laughing uncontrollably.

"Looks like Fox has taken quite a liking to you," Vincent manages to get out between laughs.

Julius stands, trying to look stern. "I see you're all getting a kick out of this."

Vincent gives his shoulder a comforting pat. "Ease up, brother. He's just a kid."

Blushing, I catch Julius's eye. "I'm sorry," I mouth over the laughter. His eyes are soft when they meet mine.

"If it's all the same to you..." he starts, turning to Fox, "... I'd like to finish up my business *alone.*"

Fox rolls his eyes, repeating "sausage, sausage, sausage," as he runs off, causing a fresh wave of laughter to fill the room.

When dessert hits the table, Fox has decided to curl up and nod off to a movie in the theater room. Now I've returned to a table full of more dessert. I'm so full, but I can't pass up the delicious strawberries covered in chocolate. I watch as Vincent feeds Rosie a strawberry. She takes it, and he delicately wipes the chocolate off the edge.

"Look at you two. Seriously, who thought my brother would end up staying here in the States and being the happiest he has ever been?"

"Things can change in the blink of an eye, brother. When you least expect it, a tornado can twist into your life, uproot everything you ever thought you wanted, and change it forever."

Rosie looks at Vincent adoringly as he takes her hand and turns to her. He lowers onto one knee, and I instinctively grab Julius's leg as I understand what's going on in front of us.

Rosie gasps loudly, then covers her mouth with her hand to silence her shock.

"I was going to wait for the right time, but anytime with you, my love, is the perfect time. Rosie, my sweet Rosie. You have made me the man I'm meant to be. You are everything I never knew I needed, I can't live without you, and I love you to the ends of the earth. Will you do me the honor of making me your husband?"

My eyes are glued to the man on the bended knee in front of Rosie and me.

Immediately Rosie replies with, "Yes. Yes!" screaming out in pure love.

Vincent pulls out a small box, opening it to the ring. Another gasp pulls from Rosie's lips as he glides the ring down her finger.

She's crying tears of joy, and he lifts her into his arms, crying with happiness. They kiss, and I'm filled with joy and jubilation that they have found their match.

I turn away and give them this moment as I see Julius staring blankly. He can't believe it. But it looks more than that as he's deep in thought.

"Isn't this wonderful?" I touch his arm, and he turns abruptly, shaking out of his stare.

"Yes. Yes, of course. It's unbelievable," he says.

"Congratulations, guys," he says and stands to move over to where they are, looking into each other's eyes with blissful love.

I join Julius in congratulating Vincent and Rosie, their joy enveloping the room like a warm blanket. After a hearty round of well-wishes, we decide to excuse ourselves, giving the lovebirds some much-deserved alone time.

As we carefully navigate our way to the car, Fox snoozes peacefully in my arms, worn out from the excitement of the evening. The drive home is bathed in the soft glow of streetlights, providing the perfect backdrop for a heart-to-heart.

Julius seems lost in thought as we stop at a set of traffic lights, his gaze unfocused. "I didn't see this coming," he says suddenly, his eyes flicking toward me before returning to the road, "Vincent, settling down. It's not what we grew up expecting, especially with our father's track record." I can only offer him a puzzled look. Julius has never talked about his family, let alone his father's supposed infidelity. "I guess we never really talked about it," Julius admits, a wry smile pulling at his lips, "Our father... he wasn't the most faithful husband. He had affairs, and it wasn't a secret. I even witnessed one when I was at boarding school."

The confession hits me like a punch to the gut as the lights turn green, and Julius continues to drive, his grip tight on the wheel. The idea of a young Julius encountering such adult betrayal leaves a sour taste in my mouth. "Julius, that's... I'm sorry. That must have been tough," I manage to say, squeezing his hand to offer some comfort.

He shrugs, a touch of vulnerability peeking through his typically confident demeanor. "It made me question a lot of things. Monogamy, marriage... I wonder if they're really for me."

"Well, that makes sense, Julius," I offer.

He pulls into the garage and kills the engine. "How did you know you wanted to marry Travis?" he asks, and I suddenly can't breathe.

My heart takes flight, and panic sets in at the memory.

I feel a heaviness pressing against me, a weight that awakens me to find Travis on top of me. He's rough, and before I can fully comprehend, he's inside me.

"Travis." My scream rips from my throat as I writhe beneath him, attempting to escape his crushing weight.

"Get off me, Travis!" I demand, my voice cracking as he

continues to forcefully invade me, violating my trust with each thrust.

"You know you want it, baby," he grunts out into my ear, his breath heavy with the stench of alcohol.

"No, I don't!" I protest, but he only holds me tighter the more I struggle.

Eventually, I stop fighting, laying there motionless as he finishes. It's as if my mind has disconnected from my body, making me a detached observer, helplessly watching as my body is violated.

His grunting fills the room, his weight overbearing. I feel a wave of sickness creeping in, bile threatening to rise, but then it's replaced by numbness.

His pace quickens, and his final act is rushed and aggressive. Once he's done, he rolls off me, leaving me more broken than before, my legs spread, a result of the violation that happened in my sleep.

He doesn't utter a word. He just rolls over and succumbs to sleep.

Shaking uncontrollably, I manage to slide out from beneath the covers and head toward the bathroom. As I sink to the cold floor tiles, Travis's snores echo in the distance. A single tear escapes my eye, signifying the knowledge that I will never be the same again.

A month later, I discovered I was pregnant.

"I... I don't know. Let's get Fox inside." I push open the door before he can do it for me, panic gripping me like a glove.

17

JULIUS

My brother is getting married.

What the fuck is happening?

The whole notion is playing on my mind so much that I can't fucking sleep. I never thought in a million years he would marry, be happy, and push past the vengeance in his heart and the trauma of losing our older brother.

But then I reflect on tonight. Isabella was, well, more than a secretary, more than a marriage of convenience. Apart from being stuck in the elevator for half an hour and the shock of finding Fox in the washroom, I actually had a great night. The subtle looks and glances were not lost on me. I know we have something. It could be more if I lean into it. If I let my guard down and put aside everything I've ever known, maybe we could be more.

A noise interrupts my thoughts from down the hallway, seemingly from one of the bedrooms. I glance at the clock, and its glowing digits stare back mockingly. It's three fifteen.

The noise subsides momentarily, followed by silence, but I hear it again.

"Stop!" This time louder and more alarming, I instantly recognize it as Isabella's screams. I launch out of bed, tear open my door, and run down the hallway.

As I burst open the door, her screams continue to resonate. I hurry to her side, the faint glimmer of light casting a shadow on her. Her eyes are closed tightly, trapped in a nightmare.

"Bella," I say, attempting to wake her from her torment. Despite my touch and attempts to rouse her, she remains within the nightmare's clutches, so I shake her more firmly this time, speaking louder.

"Bella, wake up!" I implore, cradling her face in my hands. Her eyes flutter open, her skin slick with sweat. She appears startled to see me as she comes to terms with being shaken from her nightmare.

"Julius?" she asks, propping herself upright, appearing dazed.

"You had a nightmare," I say, holding her face.

"Oh," she murmurs, a flicker of fear or regret flashing in her eyes. I brush away a strand of hair across her cheek. Then, I notice her oversized T-shirt bunching around her thighs, barely covering her. I swallow down the sudden surge of desire for her.

"I'm sorry," she apologizes, scooting further up the headboard.

"There's nothing to be sorry about."

Her eyes glance down at my bare chest, and when they meet mine again, there's that look she gives me.

"You can't look at me like that, Bella, and expect me not to want you."

"Look at you like what?" She breathes out hot and heady

My gaze drops, my hand trailing to rest on her exposed thigh. I shouldn't want to touch her, but I do.

"Help me forget, Julius," she pleads, tugging at the hem of her shirt. She lifts it over her head, and I inhale sharply at the sight of a naked Isabella before me. Her breasts spill out, full and tempting.

"Dammit, Isabella, I want nothing more than to claim you as my wife... but..." I trail off, my arousal straining against my pants.

"I know we can't," she finishes my sentence.

"Then you can't look at me like you want me to fuck you," I say, biting my lip.

"I know, it's complicated," she admits. I find myself leaning in, and she does the same as I lower my gaze to her lips.

"I want you to spread those pretty legs and touch yourself, Isabella." My tone darkens, becoming commanding, filled with need. I'm so close to her I could easily finger fuck her, but instead, I guide her hand down the curve of her stomach, past the dip of her belly button, until her hand rests between her legs.

"I want you to please that greedy cunt of yours."

"Yes," she gasps as I watch her fingers circling her sensitive bud, and I struggle to remove my hand from hers.

"And you..." she begins, touching herself, letting out a choked moan.

"No, I want to watch you, Bella."

I caress her leg, watching her squirm under my touch.

"Do you like watching me?" she questions. My arousal strains against my gray sweats, painfully prominent at her words.

"You are a painful addiction," I confess.

As her back arches off the bed and her fingers delve deeper, I can't just stand by and watch. My hand starts tracing a path up to the delicate curve of her breast, and I gently tweak the hardened peak of her nipple, drawing out a pleasurable moan from her lips. The rhythm of her movements quickens, prompting me to apply more pressure. Her gasp feeds the desire raging within me.

On their own accord, my lips find their way to her hardened peaks, my tongue dancing over her pebbled nipple. I shouldn't be touching, tasting, sucking, but I can't seem to stop.

Her free hand finds its way into my hair, her fingertips pulling at the roots and cutting through the barriers I've erected. Years of professionalism and a fortress around my heart crumble under her touch.

"I can think of a thousand ways to make you shudder," I whisper into the heated space between us. My words seem to ignite something within her as she loses herself in an intense climax.

A primal urge takes over, and I bring her slick fingers to my lips. I take one in, tasting her sweetness, savoring every drop from knuckle to tip. A low groan vibrates through her body at the intimate contact. "God," I murmur, my taste buds tantalized by her juices.

Our fingers remain intertwined, but the realization hits me with a force of a freight train—I need to leave. I want her in ways that blur the line of propriety, but I can't allow myself that indulgence. I will end up hurting her after this endd, and she has endured enough hurt.

She deserves more than that.

More than I can give her.

I start to pull away, but she holds on. "Don't go," she pleads, her hand falling limply to her side.

"I must, Bella," I insist, my voice strained.

"Do you really?" Her question hangs in the air, a tantalizing promise. The look in her eyes and the warmth that radiates from her threaten to shatter my resolve. Just as I'm teetering on the edge of surrender, she speaks again. "You should go," she murmurs, pulling the blanket over her exposed body.

Her words are like a splash of cold water, grounding me. With a deep, shuddering breath, I manage to rein in my conflicting emotions. Giving her one last lingering look, I rise and head toward the door, each step heavy with regret.

Upon shutting the door behind me, a profound quiet engulfs the corridor. Each footfall on the plush carpet reverberates in the silence, echoing the turmoil churning within me. As I reach the sanctuary of my bedroom, the cool, crisp air does little to quell the lingering warmth of Isabella's touch and the raging thickness in my pants.

I stand by the window, staring out into the quiet street, the normalcy of the world outside in blazing contrast to the storm raging within me. My mind is ablaze with memories of her—her delicate curves under my touch, her eyes glinting with desire, the taste of her on my lips.

Marriage—this arrangement we agreed to—was never meant to invoke such raw and potent feelings. It was a means to an end. Convenient. Logical. But with every shared glance and innocent touch that sparked a wild flame, the lines began to blur.

My reflection in the window is a stranger, a man in conflict with his desires and duties. The ache in my body is almost tangible, a gnawing reminder of what I'm denying myself, denying us.

The king-sized bed looms large and empty, a stark reminder of the physical distance I've imposed between us. I sink into the sheets, the smell of my cologne a poor substitute for the sweet scent of Isabella.

Sleep proves elusive as I toss and turn, wrestling with the growing turmoil.

How can I maintain this façade *of marriage and not claim her as my own? How long can I resist before the hunger consumes me?*

I need to figure out a way through this maddening maze of emotions. With that grim determination, I eventually drift into a restless sleep, haunted by dreams of forbidden desires and a woman I can't seem to let go of.

18

ISABELLA

For the most part, the honeymoon period of our marriage has been surprisingly peaceful and blissful. My ex-husband has chosen to be civil, perhaps due to the presence of the driver that Julius insisted accompanies me whenever I drop off or pick up Fox from his house in New Jersey. It also seems to have had a positive impact on Fox, as he appears more settled and even happier. He now calls Julius Jules instead of Jules Monster, which is a clear sign of improvement.

I try not to think about the inevitable return to our cramped apartment and the end of our marriage arrangement. With Julius around, I feel safe and protected.

However, I can't help but feel unsure about how things will go back to normal, especially after our voyeuristic escapades of watching each other. It's the hottest thing I've ever done, and a few times a week, we continue with our intimate sessions of observing without touching.

Until that night, but it was probably a one-off. We set a boundary. We've established it to separate work from home.

He is Mr. Julius Slater at work, and at home, he becomes the seductive, dirty talker who knows how to fulfill my desires. And now I want more.

But I try not to dwell on that too much. I know how it always ends for me with men. They are not to be trusted, even someone as handsome and caring as Julius.

Julius's aloofness is like a wall—cold, hard, and unyielding. It's a vivid contrast to the man who sometimes decides to let me in, in the desire in his eyes. The man who, two months ago, touched me like no other man ever has after he roused me from a nightmare. The nightmare, all too familiar, where I wake to find Travis invading me, yet again after loading me with alcohol and having me pass out.

The man who showed vulnerability when his brother announced his engagement, the surprise in his eyes, the hesitation in his smile.

I try to understand Julius and penetrate the fortress he's constructed around himself. But his stoic demeanor is as impenetrable as steel, his professional façade never cracking. It's almost as if he's afraid. Afraid of what breaking those walls might reveal. Afraid of the chaos that might ensue. I am too.

There's no happy ever after for people like him and me. This fake marriage is just in name only. *Isn't it?* And all it will ever be with the rules clear from the outset. I don't know why I let myself think of the possibilities. Maybe it's because I think I see something in his eyes when he looks at me, maybe because it's a look no other man has given me.

His need for control is almost palpable, a stringent boundary between work and pleasure that he's meticulously drawn and never dares to cross. It's almost maddening how rigid he is. It's as if he's suppressing something, some emotion or desire that he's afraid might tumble out.

But why? Why is he so determined to maintain these boundaries? Why does he resist intimacy when it's crystal clear we share a connection? Is it because I'm not from the same circles he typically mingles with? Or because I'm a single mother? Is he afraid of becoming his philandering father? These questions continually swirl in my mind, their answers as elusive as Julius himself.

His reaction to Vincent's engagement was telling. I saw a flicker in his eyes—surprise, sure, but also fear? Regret? As if his brother's happiness stirred something within him, a longing or a realization that he quickly stifled.

This hot-and-cold dance we're stuck in is becoming infuriating. One moment, he's the attentive husband, the next, he's the detached boss. The sudden switch leaves me confused, yearning for more than the honesty in his eyes, for the warmth in his touch.

Yet tonight, as I push through the busy restaurant, I try and rid Julius from my mind. Moving through the bustling patrons, I do my best to shake off the nagging worry about Julius and his sudden *Tokyo trip.*

Rosie's waiting. Maybe she can help me get my mind off things.

Rosie and Harley are deep in conversation when I spot them by the window. I have to grin seeing my two closest friends chatting away like old pals, even though they only met a few months back at City Hall for my wedding.

"Hey, look who finally made it!" Rosie cheers, standing to plant kisses on both my cheeks. "Sorry I'm late," I apologize, squeezing in next to Harley.

With Julius out of town, it feels like my workload has doubled.

"Swear to God, your boss is going to work you into the ground," Harley quips, pulling me into a hug.

I surprise myself by defending him. "It's not his fault there's so much to do."

Harley blinks at me, surprised. "Wow, is this the first time you've defended him?"

I pause, remembering all the times I've vented about my crazy schedule to Harley—all the late daycare pickups and trying to balance work with single-mom duties. But I never shared any of this with Julius. From the get-go, it was clear that personal lives weren't up for discussion at work. That much was obvious when I was handed a thick code of conduct booklet to sign on my first day.

It was driven home that first week when I asked Julius about his family during his mother's visit. I'll never forget the ice in his eyes or his blunt reply. *"We do not discuss our personal lives at work,"* he'd said, making it crystal clear how he wanted our professional relationship to be.

"We went ahead and ordered. You were so late," Harley announces, already nibbling at the bruschetta in front of her.

"Great, I'm starving!" I respond. "Have you heard anything?" I ask Rosie, unable to keep the worry from my voice.

"All we know is that she's been taken. They're doing everything they can to get her back. Vincent's got his contacts and some ex-CIA guys trying to find her in Tokyo."

I cover my mouth, stunned. "What?"

Rosie looks equally shocked. "You didn't know about Victoria's abduction? I thought Julius would've told you. It's bound to be all over the news shortly."

How could he not tell me? He left abruptly, saying his sister needed him. *But this?* This is what happens when I let my guard down and let someone in. I should know better. I shake my head, trying to push away the disappointment of my husband not confiding in me. "He just mentioned his sister was in trouble, that's all."

Harley gasps. "Victoria's been kidnapped? Who would hurt her?"

"I can't believe it." My mind reels. "Shouldn't we be doing something?"

Rosie shrugs helplessly. "Vincent, Julius, and their parents are already in Tokyo. There's not much we can do from here."

Harley nods in agreement. "What else do you know?"

"The last update I got was a tip about her possible location. They were getting a team together to extract her."

"Holy shit. I hope she's okay." I can't help but worry.

"Who would do such a thing?" Harley wonders aloud. But we all know there are evil people out there. I've met them. Felt their cruelty firsthand.

"What do they want with her?" I press on, trying to push past the fact that Julius kept this from me.

"Money, most likely. Isn't that what kidnappers usually want?" Harley says matter-of-factly.

The image of Victoria in danger sends a chill down my spine. The waiter sets our pizza and beers on the table, but I've lost all my appetite. I feel a strange mix of anger and concern. I should've known about this. But the only thing that really matters is Julius. He shouldn't be facing this alone. I quickly send him a text as Rosie and Harley grab a slice of pizza.

Me: *Rosie just told me about Victoria. If you need anything, I'm here.*

"Have you picked a date yet, Rosie?" Harley asks, trying to lighten the mood.

"Well, no... not with everything that's going on." Rosie shakes her head, "I'd love something small and cozy. But Vincent's mom, she's envisioning a big showy affair. You know, society expectations and all."

"And what about Vincent?" I pitch in, my curiosity piqued.

"He just wants to marry me. As soon as possible," she confesses, a giggle escaping her lips.

"Just try to keep some activities out of Vincent's office, will you?" I joke. Rosie's eyes widen in surprise, then embarrassment.

"Oh God!" She covers her face, laughing.

"That's right," I confirm, my laughter matching hers.

"He's insatiable!" Rosie shrugs, grinning broadly. "Then again, so am I. Sorry, not sorry." She giggles even more, and soon we're all laughing so hard our sides ache.

We're onto dessert when Rosie's phone rings, and my phone beeps, abruptly grounding us back to the reality of what's happening a world away. We look at each other, dreading the worst but hoping for the best.

I check my phone message while I hear her round out Vincent's name.

Julius: *Thank you, We have her. I'll make sure she's okay, then come home to you.*

I hear Rosie breathe a sigh of relief, her hand coming to her mouth as a tear rolls down her cheek. "Oh, thank God." I watch as she listens to Vincent, her eyes large and in shock. Whatever it is, it can't be good.

Harley takes my hand as we wait for her to finish the conversation and hang up.

She wipes away her tear. "She safe now. That's all that matters," she says as she brings a tissue to her tears.

My eyes are drawn to the door the moment it opens. I

watch Julius walk in with a heaviness I've never seen before. His usual confident and in-control demeanor is replaced with a quiet vulnerability that takes my breath away.

I'm at his side in an instant.

"Julius," I whisper, touching his arm lightly. He turns toward me, the weight of his worry clear in his eyes. "How is she?"

"She's... okay, considering. They roughed her up, but she's strong. She's... okay." His voice cracks slightly, the words heavy with unsaid fear. His sister's safety clearly shook him more than he is letting on.

"Tell me everything," I say.

I guide him toward the couch, sitting him down gently before making my way to the bar. I know his drink—a whiskey neat. The golden liquid fills the glass, and I bring it over, offering it to him. He thanks me with a nod, then takes a long sip, the amber liquid casting shadows on his worried features.

As I sit next to him, I can't help but glance at him. The usual barriers he's so hell-bent on maintaining seem to be crumbling tonight. It's almost as if the whirlwind events of the past forty-eight hours have brought him back down to earth and made him more human.

There's a long pause. The hesitation in his eyes is apparent, the internal struggle between his natural inclination to keep things to himself and the raw desire to confide in someone.

Finally, he takes a deep breath and leans back, his eyes closing momentarily as if trying to gather his thoughts. "When I got the call..." he starts, his voice barely above a whisper, "... I thought it was a mistake. Some cruel prank.

But it wasn't. My sister... my little sister... she was taken, Isabella."

His voice trembles at that, and my heart clenches. I can see the depth of his worry and guilt. I reach out, laying my hand gently over his. He gives a slight start but doesn't pull away. Instead, he turns his hand over, and our fingers intertwine.

"I've never felt so helpless," he continues, his eyes opening to meet mine. "I was half a world away while she was in danger. When we got there, they had already... they had already hurt her."

Tears well in his eyes, but he blinks them away stubbornly. The strength it's taking for him to share this, the vulnerability he's showing, is breathtaking. My grip on his hand tightens.

"But we got her back," he says, determination setting in his features. "We got her back, and those bastards will pay for what they've done."

I can see in his eyes the burning need for vengeance and the resolve to protect his family. But under all that, there's something else—a raw, undisguised emotion that's both terrifying and exhilarating to see in him.

Desire.

He's looking at me like he's never looked at me before. It's not the formal, businesslike gaze I'm accustomed to. It's a hungry, yearning look. One that's mirrored in my eyes as I look back at him.

"Julius..." I start, my voice trembling as much as his did.

He cuts me off, his fingers squeezing mine as he pulls me onto his lap. "Isabella," he whispers, his voice hoarse. "I... I need you. I've been trying to deny it, to keep us... professional. But I can't. Not anymore."

His confession hangs in the air between us, a fragile

thing that has the power to change everything. I can't find my voice, but I don't need to. My hand in his, my eyes locked with his, say all that needs to be said.

His hand releases mine, only to circle my neck and pull me closer. Our lips crash together in an overwhelming, raw, and passionate kiss. There's an intensity in him I've never seen before, a fervor that engulfs us. His touch is insistent yet gentle as if he's trying to convey everything he's been holding back through this one connection.

I respond with my fingers digging into his shirt's fabric, my body leaning into his. This isn't the composed, aloof Julius I'm used to. This man is bared, raw, vulnerable, yet strong and relentless. And it's this man I want. This man I've craved, even when I didn't know it.

The taste and feel of him is intoxicating. His lips move over mine, parting, seeking, exploring. His hand tightens around my neck, pulling me impossibly closer. Our bodies mold together as if they were always meant to fit this way, and we were always meant to be this close.

The world around us fades into insignificance. There's only Julius and me, the heat between us, the undeniable connection that's been simmering under the surface for far too long. A connection that we've finally given in to.

When we finally pull away for air, our breaths mingle, our foreheads resting against each other. His eyes search mine, and I see it—a quiet resolve, a silent promise.

Julius isn't going anywhere.

He's here.

With me, and he's not letting go.

19

JULIUS

Her sharp and soft gasp echoes in the quiet room as I effortlessly lift her petite body into my arms. There's an odd sense of rightness with the weight of her against my chest. I've been dreaming of this moment, of her in my bed, ever since she came to live with me. It's a thought that's invaded my mind more times than I care to admit, and now that it's happening, I can hardly believe it.

A realization dawns on me as I carry her toward the bedroom. I've been denying the truth, refusing to acknowledge the depth of my feelings. The desire, the longing, the connection that has been quietly building between us since the day she stepped into my life was always there. Yet, I hid it beneath the mask of professionalism, behind the carefully constructed wall of aloofness.

Carrying her through the door into my bedroom feels like crossing an unspoken boundary. A boundary I had placed, built on fear and uncertainty. But as I lay her on my bed, all I see is her. All I feel is her. And right now, I know there's no room for fear or uncertainty.

Her hair fans out across the pillow, the moonlight casting a soft glow on her face. She's beautiful, incredibly so, and the sight of her stirs something deep within me. As I look down at her, our eyes locking, I see a mirror of my emotions reflecting back at me—the desire, the anticipation, the uncertainty, and most importantly, the trust.

Now, I understand the truth of my feelings for her. I want Isabella. Not because we're chained to one another for convenience but because she's become a vital part of my life —a part I'm unwilling to let go of. My hand reaches out, gently tucking a loose strand of hair behind her ear as I lean down to claim her lips once again.

This is no longer about denying or hiding. It's about embracing what we have, what we could be. It's about breaking down the walls between us. And as our lips meet, the world outside ceases to exist. It's just Isabella and me right here, right now.

And for the first time, I allow myself to truly feel, to truly want, and to truly love.

Her soft moan echoes in the room as our bodies connect, a raw sound that sends shivers of desire down my spine. I can feel her heat beneath me as I slowly peel off her T-shirt, my hands sliding down to unbutton her pants. She lies beneath me in her underwear and bra, her body a canvas of soft curves and flushed skin I can't wait to explore.

Standing, I start to undress, my eyes never leaving hers. Isabella's gaze is locked on me, her eyes darkened with desire, reflecting a fiery passion that sends a thrill through me. I'm naked before her in moments, my body taut with anticipation, my arousal evident.

"This time, Bella," I whisper, my voice husky with

desire. "I get to be inside you, every inch of you. This time, I get to make you mine."

She gasps out a breathy "Yes." Her agreement is a sweet surrender that spurs me on.

Laying back down beside her, my eyes drink in the sight of her, beautiful and so incredibly sexy. My fingers slip under the waistband of her panties, sliding them down her legs until she's bare before me.

"I've been wanting to taste your cunt since the moment I licked you off your fingers," I confess, my voice barely above a whisper.

"Yes," she breathes out with desire, her teeth sinking into her lower lip.

I lean down, my tongue tracing a path over her, making her gasp and shiver beneath me. My hand settles on her stomach, holding her steady as I explore her, teasing her with slow, deliberate strokes.

Her body is responsive, arching and writhing beneath my touch, and it's intoxicating. Every sigh, every moan she lets out makes me want her more.

"Oh Christ, Julius." She gasps, her hand finding the crown of my head. She tugs at my roots, riding out her release. I leave my fingers inside her, bringing another one close behind.

"I... I can't," she stammers, her eyes wide with surprise as another orgasm washes over her. I can't help the smug satisfaction that swells in me. This is how it should always have been for her. The feel of her pussy sucking me in is too much. I need to have her.

I snatch a condom from my bedside drawer, swiftly rolling it onto my throbbing length. "Do you have any idea how long I've been resisting you?" I murmur, my voice a low growl as I position myself above her, the tip of my arousal teasing her entrance.

"Show me," she breathes out, her voice laced with anticipation. With that, I drive deep into her, drawing out a deep, guttural growl from myself and a sensual moan from her.

Feels. Like. Heaven.

"Bella..." I murmur, my fingers tracing the contours of her face, her name falling from my lips like a prayer.

I move inside her again, a little deeper this time, and she lets out a shaky breath, her body adjusting to me.

"Julius," she responds, the sound of my name on her lips rolling a shiver down my spine. There's a trust in her voice, a willingness I've never heard before.

Feeling her relax around me, I take it as a sign to move. I slide deeper into her, completely sheathing myself inside her warmth. We both gasp, the sensation of being fully connected overwhelming.

She's never been more beautiful or desirable, and the realization hits me like a punch to the gut. This woman is no longer just a convenient arrangement for me.

We establish a rhythm, each thrust harmonizing into a symphony of sounds. Her soft whimpers intertwine with my harsh grunts, and the salacious sounds of our bodies colliding echo in the room. Our eyes remain locked, every wave of pleasure mirrored, every electrifying sensation magnified.

Feeling the tension coil within me, I know I'm on the edge. But this moment isn't about me. It's about her. I want her to find her release, to lose herself in the pleasure I'm offering her.

"Cream on my cock, Bella," I say, my voice a gruff whisper in her ear.

I pick up the pace, the room filling with the sounds of our bodies moving in unison, the tension building to a crescendo.

When she tenses below me, her eyes fluttering closed, I know she's close. Holding her tightly against me, I give one last, deep thrust, and we both shatter, our cries mingling in the quiet room.

As our breaths slow and our heart rates come back down, I wrap my arms around her, pulling her close. There is a change in the room, a shift in our relationship.

"This isn't just a marriage of convenience," I confess, kissing her forehead.

She looks up at me, her eyes shining with an emotion I don't quite recognize. After a few moments, I pull out of her gently and lay beside her. We're both breathless, spent, our bodies sated.

She lays on my chest, her hand toying with my chest hairs. "You're a new man, Julius, one I don't recognize," she says as she glances up at me from her long lashes.

"Bella, these last forty-eight hours have shown me that life can be taken away from you in an instant. You and me, I tried to deny it, but we have something," I confess, stroking her hair that's spread out over her bare back. "I don't see the point in denying it any longer."

"I know," she whispers, her voice low and packed with an understanding that she has been trying to fend off the same undeniable truth.

"Life's too short to deny it," I add, feeling her swallow against my ribs. The fear is palpable. It's in both of us, but I'm willing to take a leap to see where this can lead us. I draw her closer, and she places a tender kiss on my ribs.

"This is your room now too," I tell her, and at that moment, I realize this is just the start for us.

I've had a taste of what life could be like with Bella, and there's no going back now.

20

ISABELLA

The morning light slips through the crack in the curtains, dust particles flickering in the sun's beams. It's a quiet, peaceful scene, so different from the chaos of the world below. And the truth is I have never slept better.

I didn't wake to the sound of my screams or in a frightful sweat. Instead, I feel the warmth radiating from Julius behind me, his body spooning mine in the soft confines of the bed.

His steady breathing tickles the nape of my neck, a comforting rhythm that sends a wave of contentment washing over me. I am not dreaming. This is real. And it's a reality that scares me beyond anything else because of what I feel for this man lying beside me.

"Morning, beautiful," he says, his breath warm on my ear.

A sigh escapes my lips as his fingers continue their tantalizing journey up my thighs, then, oh God.

He sinks a finger inside me, and my heart races and my

breaths grow shallow. His hardness rests against my back, and I press into it, wanting so much more.

He chuckles low in his throat, the sound vibrating against my back. "Such a good girl, the way your pussy is so wet for me," he praises.

His other arm tightens around my waist, anchoring me to him as his hand continues to explore, each touch sending jolts of pleasure through me.

Unable to keep quiet, I let out a soft moan, pressing closer to him. "Julius," I whisper, my voice shaky with the intensity of my feelings. I reach behind me to grip his thigh, seeking some form of stability as my world narrows down to his touch. His scent. His presence.

His lips brush against the shell of my ear, sending shivers down my spine. "Yes, Bella?" he prompts, his voice holding a note of satisfaction as if my response is exactly what he wants.

"More," I breathe out, my mind spinning as his fingers delve deeper, coaxing another moan from me. He hums in approval, obliging to my plea as his movements become more purposeful.

"Always more for you, Bella," he promises huskily, his words further stoking the fire within me. I can hardly believe this is happening.

For now, I don't want to think about tomorrow or after the year when this reality comes crashing down.

I want to live in this feeling.

The commute to work this morning has a different vibe. There are times when I accept his offer for a lift, typically when I don't have to drop off or pick up Fox that week.

Those rides usually involve a quick rundown of his daily agenda and meetings. But today, it's different. There's a new energy between us. A shared secret that leaves us both quiet, our minds spinning around the recent developments.

I notice the quick sidelong glances he throws my way, and each one sends a flutter through my stomach. No matter how much I try to fight this feeling, it's a lost cause with every glance he sends my way.

I'm so deep into work it barely registers that it's almost lunchtime. Wanting to complete another task, I try to push on, but a voice breaks my focus.

"You look absolutely radiant today, Bella. There's an undeniable glow about you."

Lifting my eyes, I spot George, a middle-management colleague, standing by my desk. He's trying to start a casual conversation, his intentions transparent in his lingering gaze.

George isn't one to back down. He asked me out after he found out I was divorced. He is a handsome divorced man with an eight-year-old, so what started as familiar kid-related chats morphed into him asking me out a few months after my divorce was finalized. I refused, vowing to steer clear of men after my damaging experience with Travis. It seems like love had quit on me after my divorce.

"Thank you," I add. "What can I do for you?" I ask, trying to keep it professional.

He blinks. "Oh, right. Just wondering if we know if the meeting has been pushed back today with the strategy team."

I look at him. He could have easily emailed rather than coming up to the fortieth floor.

. . .

I'm in the middle of formulating a polite but curt reply to George when my phone rings. It's a shrill interruption, almost like it knows the urgency of its timing. I hoist the receiver to my ear even as I maintain eye contact with George.

"Isabella." Julius's voice is crisp and authoritative on the other end. "My office. Now."

The order is unambiguous, and I don't miss the underlying warning in his tone.

As I lower the phone, my eyes shift to Julius's office, finding him watching our interaction. His gaze, intense and warning, is directed at George.

George stiffens, seeming to sense the change in atmosphere. "I suppose I should get back to work," he murmurs, retreating just as I stand to head for Julius's office.

"It's the same time," I reply.

As I enter, Julius crosses the room, closing the gap between us, shutting and locking the door behind us. His stare is intense, almost possessive. This should frighten me. It's a side of Julius I haven't seen before, but it doesn't. Instead, it stirs something within me. His possessiveness doesn't feel like a trap but rather a confirmation he wants me as much as I want him.

Without a word, his hands find their way to my waist,

pulling me close until I can feel his breath on my skin. His eyes bore into mine, a silent question hanging between us.

"Julius," I whisper, my hands coming up to rest against his broad chest. My heart is pounding, matching the fast rhythm of his. I can feel his desire for me, just as intense as mine for him, and it's incredibly heady.

His fingers dig into my hips, drawing me even closer. The proximity and intimacy is overwhelming, and yet, I crave more. I tilt my head up, my eyes meeting his. They're dark with desire, his usual cool demeanor replaced with raw passion.

"I don't like to share," he growls out, his voice thick with need. His fingers trail up my sides, pulling me flush against him. I gasp, not expecting such a bold move in his office.

"I'm yours, Julius," I say, my voice equally husky, wanting him to take me here in his office.

"Mine," he repeats, staring down with a need in his eyes that matches mine.

Our shared admission hangs in the air, the tension between us palpable. But the ticking of the clock on his office wall brings us back to reality.

He has a meeting in five minutes.

"Tonight," he says, his voice rough. "Tonight, I'm going to fuck that delicious pussy of yours until you scream only my name."

He drags his lips to mine in a heated kiss, then we part on a promise, a vow I eagerly look forward to.

We separate with a final heated glance, immersing ourselves in the workday that still stretches ahead. But his words, the promise in his voice, linger in the back of my mind, providing a tantalizing distraction throughout the rest of the day.

Later that afternoon, I find myself pushing open the worn-out door of the daycare, the loud creak echoing in the otherwise quiet hall. The familiar smell of cheap disinfectant, mingling with the faint scent of mashed peas, greets me. The woman at the front desk, Miss Fran, looks up from her stack of paperwork, the edges of her pinched lips downturned into a frown.

"You're early, Isabella," she notes, a hint of disapproval lacing her tone.

Yes, for once, Fox isn't one of the last kids left to be picked up.

I'm not in the habit of arriving early, and the unexpected change doesn't seem to sit well with her. Her steely gaze roves over me, an unspoken accusation that I'm disrupting the carefully managed routine. But I ignore her, letting her judgment roll off me like water off a duck's back.

"Yes, I am," I respond simply, getting fed up by the unsaid insinuations they continue to make.

Shuffling down the familiar corridor lined with children's chaotic artwork, I arrive at Fox's classroom. The moment I step through the door, Fox spots me. His face lights up, a bright smile eclipsing everything else in the room. He rushes toward me, nearly knocking me over with his enthusiasm.

. . .

"Mommy!" he shrieks in delight, wrapping his little arms around my neck. His happy squeals fill the air, and his giggles ring in my ears, replacing any trace of Miss Fran's disapproval.

When we get home, I decide to make dinner for the three of us. Julius mentioned he'd only be an hour or two behind me, which gives me ample time to prepare some steak and roasted vegetables.

I'm not a culinary expert by any means, but there's something incredibly satisfying about cooking a meal for my family.

Julius arrives just as I'm pulling the veggies out of the oven and setting the steak aside to rest. Fox is playing at my feet, his toy cars zooming across the kitchen floor.

I turn to see Julius watching us, a gentle smile gracing his lips.

Upon hearing the familiar footsteps, Fox yells excitedly, "Jules!"

"Good evening, Nado!" he greets warmly, stopping at the kitchen bar and casting an appreciative look over the stove.

"I'm cooking dinner," I tell him, and he responds with a beaming smile.

"It smells delicious," he replies, his voice taking on a darker tone that hits me somewhere deep in my chest.

. . .

Fox interrupts the moment, crashing his toy car against Julius's feet. "Vroom, vroom."

I can't help but stifle a grin. Julius kneels, watching as Fox methodically traces a toy car up and down his polished shoes.

"Going off-road, are we, Nado?" Julius plays along, his eyes sparkling with amusement.

Then Fox leaves a visible scuff mark on Julius's shoe with the toy car's wheel. Fear strikes his delicate little features. "I'm sorry, I'm sorry!" he cries out when he sees the mark on Julius' shoe.

Immediately he panics and starts to cry, leaving Julius confused at his reaction. But it's nothing new to me. I quickly move around the kitchen island to collect Fox in my arms, comforting him.

"It's okay, darling," I say, getting down to his level and wrapping him in my arms. The abrupt change reminds me of his fearful reaction he'd have around his father when everything was fine one minute and Travis would harm me the next.

"Nado, I don't mind," Julius tries to placate him. He bends down to wrap his arms around my son so we both are holding him. The sight makes my heart swell.

I return to the kitchen after he is settled and playing with his toys. As I move around, I feel the electrifying presence of

Julius behind me. A glance confirms Fox's attention absorbed in his toys, away from us.

"Who knew cooking in my kitchen could be such a turn-on?" Julius murmurs, his warm breath caressing my neck. He pulls me into him, the solid heat of his body pressing against my back. I gasp, flushing as his words ignite a wave of desire in me.

"Is that so?" I manage to say, trying to steady my racing pulse.

"If Nado weren't here, I'd sit you on the kitchen counter, lift your legs above your head and sink into your tight heat until you're full of my cock."

Jesus, yes.

His words create a visceral image in my mind, leaving me momentarily breathless. The sizzling in the pan fades into the background, drowned out by his voice echoing in my head. But the fantasy shatters when Julius's phone rings, pulling me back to reality. He groans as I watch as he slides his phone out of his pocket, his gaze flicking to the caller ID.

Gavin. VP of Acquisitions. *Why is he calling at this hour?*

"I need to take this," Julius says, detangling himself from me quicker than I'd prefer. As he strides away, I'm left staring at his retreating back.

"Is everything okay with the Bynstrom acquisition?" I call after him, concern knitting my brows together.

· · ·

"Yes," he replies, then his office door closes behind him, leaving me alone in the kitchen.

Later, as we sit for dinner, I find myself observing Julius's interactions with Fox. The atmosphere feels less strained and more natural. It's heartening.

"Mom sure knows how to cook," Julius comments appreciatively, cutting into his steak with a grin directed at me.

"Yes, Mommy's the best!" Fox chimes in, gripping his corn cob enthusiastically. In his excitement, the cob shoots out of his hand and lands in Julius's lap, butter-soaked and rogue.

An awkward pause descends upon us, and then Julius looks down at his stained trousers, muttering a surprised, "Well, fuck."

Unable to hold it in, I burst into laughter, a startled Fox joining me. "Fuck, fuck, fuck!" he parrots, triggering more horrified laughter from Julius and me.

Warmth permeates the room, a tangible sign of the bond slowly forming between them. It's a sight that fills me with hope and an unexpected sense of peace.

But, as always, I find myself wondering, *how long will it last?*

21

JULIUS

After Isabella prepared an incredible meal, I catch myself standing in the doorway, watching her read a bedtime story to Fox, somehow strangely mesmerizing and beautiful. I only wish it was a memory I could have had as a child rather than a room of boys in boarding school.

As everything falls into place, there's one lingering thought I can't shake.

Earlier, Fox's inadvertent destruction of my shoes and pants provoked an unexpected guilt within me. I realized how unaccustomed Fox must be to the immaculate condition of my penthouse. He should feel free in his own home, not walking on eggshells. My four-thousand-dollar shoes or my expensive Brioni pants mean nothing compared to his comfort and happiness.

"Jules, can you read me a story?"

Isabella looks up, taken aback. She's about to decline on my behalf when a pang of longing stops me. Childhood memories of story times I never experienced, parental affection I never received, it's something I would've given anything for.

"Sure," I respond, detaching myself from the doorframe and moving toward the bed.

"You don't have to," she whispers, meant only for my ears.

"I want to," I assure her, sharing a warm smile that fuels a comforting sense of camaraderie between us.

I replace Isabella on the bed, settling next to Fox, who starts rummaging through his box filled with toys, books, and a few Legos. The sight transports me back to my boarding school days when all my personal belongings were restricted to a single box. It represented my identity and held my only connections to home, which included a yearly Christmas card from my mother.

One day, overwhelmed by frustration and desperation, I remember forcing the school to contact my mother. I pleaded to come home but was brutally rebuffed. The pain in her voice as she said, *"Dad doesn't want to see you,"* is an echo that has never left me.

Years of solitude and detachment followed. When I finally returned home after graduation, I had to rebuild relationships with my siblings and parents while my father continued to keep his distance. It was then that I began to comprehend his emotional withdrawal, rooted in the loss of my brother. The grief had splintered our family, causing my father to retreat further from us all.

"This one, Jules!" Fox's excited voice interrupts my dark musings. He thrusts a book in my direction. Accepting it, I observe him cuddling his much-loved teddy bear, the scene yanking me back to the present.

"Do you just have one box of things?" I ask, hearing Isabella's retreating footsteps in the distance.

"Yes!" he says, his face radiating pride. "It's easier that way when I go to Daddy's house."

"Do you like going to Daddy's house?" I can't stop myself from asking, but I know I shouldn't.

He shrugs. "Sometimes."

He stares up at me, and I see a little fear in his eyes.

"Why sometimes, kiddo?" I question further.

He twists his lips. "Sometimes he's a bit crazy and mean."

My fists ball at my sides. "Does he hurt you?"

"No, just Mommy," he says sadly.

My nostrils flare with rage and guilt.

"I promise you, Fox, he will never hurt your mother again," I say with a force so strong.

"Okay, can we read now?" he asks, oblivious to the strength of my promise and the blood flowing in my core.

As I close the book's final page, I glance up and notice Nado's eyes are closed. His little chest rises and falls rhythmically in the throes of sleep. His hand clutches his trusty stuffed bear to his chest.

In silence, I rise from the bedside and lay the book down gently. I find myself gazing at him, this innocent boy sleeping peacefully, and in that quiet moment, I make a silent promise. I resolve to fill Fox's world with more toys, books, and, most importantly, love and attention. This child deserves the richness of joy, and I'm fully committed to ensuring he experiences it.

Exiting Nado's room, I go to the master bedroom, anticipation threading through me. Since last week, Isabella's been sharing my bed. But always, she sets the alarm for the crack of dawn, a determined effort to avoid causing any confusion for Fox, especially given our marriage's impending expiration date.

There she is.

In front of the mirror, she methodically brushes her long brown hair, seemingly unaware of my presence. Her beauty is striking. It never fails to draw me in.

The sight of her in her long black rock band T-shirt that lightly skims her curves, her hair falling in glossy waves with each brush stroke, the gentle sway of her hips. It's a far cry from the refined lingerie I'm accustomed to seeing women wear. Yet, her unguarded, genuine self truly sparks my interest and desire.

"Are you going to keep staring, or are you going to come over here?" Her voice breaks through my thoughts, her eyes meeting mine in the mirror's reflection.

"Keep staring," I reply, a smirk tugging at my lips as I begin to unbutton my shirt, gradually closing the distance between us.

An amused yet provocative glint flits across her eyes. "Is that so," she retorts, setting her brush down and threading her fingers through her hair in a sultry challenge.

Seizing her hair, I gather it in my hands, looping it around twice. Her head leans toward me, her breath hitching as I brush my lips against hers. My tongue teases her lower lip, my teeth nipping at it gently.

She lets out a soft groan.

"Do you want me to fuck you, Bella? Give you exactly what I promised?" My voice is husky, laced with the heat flowing throughout my body.

Her eyes smolder as she gazes up at me. "Yes," she responds, her voice barely above a whisper.

With a swift motion, I tilt her head back, trailing my lips along her neck, her head tilting up to expose more of her skin. She releases a quiet sigh as my tongue traces the column of her neck.

"Do you want my dirty mouth fucking your delicious cunt?" I ask, my voice low as I nibble her earlobe.

Her soft sighs echo around the room as I trail my lips down her neck, my hands roaming over her body. Each touch is like a spark, setting off a fire within us. The world outside is forgotten.

She nods, and it takes me no time to shred my clothing. Slowly, she pulls her T-shirt over her head, naked underneath.

Just for me.

It's like a punch to the gut. She's so damn beautiful it's almost unreal. My gaze traces over her, drinking in every curve, every detail. I can feel my control slipping, replaced by a raw, primal need to possess her fully.

I lean in, brushing my lips over her collarbone, moving lower down her chest, over her hip, and along her thigh. Each touch has her gasping, her body arching into my touch, craving more. She tugs me down with her onto the bed, and I'm on my knees, ready to give her everything her body needs.

Everything I want.

I swipe across her sex once, then again. Her skin is intoxicating, the salty sweetness driving me wild. She's responsive, every touch and kiss setting off a delicious shiver that shoots straight to my core. I can't get enough of her. I don't want to. I map out her body as if committing each and every inch to memory for fear of losing her. The way she pushes against my mouth, with me, is driving me wild. And when she finally shatters, her cries filling the room, it's like a dam breaking.

Quickly, I get off my knees, and she opens her legs, sensing my desperation. I wrap my hard cock then as I slide into her, I feel her pussy suck me in. All thoughts evaporate, replaced by our bodies' raw, carnal connection. She fits snugly around me, warmth enveloping me in a tantalizing grip.

Her body yields to mine, and with every stroke, I sink deeper. Faster. Together, we lock into a rhythm, a potent pulse driven by unchained lust. It's raw, untamed, leaving no room for soft whispers or tender sighs. The room thrums with the rhythm of our fervent movements, underscored by our panting breaths and stifled moans.

In the dim, hazy light, we clash and grasp onto each other, our bodies arched in the pursuit of heightened pleasure. The air thickens, heavy with the intoxicating blend of sweat and desire.

With each powerful thrust of my hips, she rocks with me, meeting me head-on, igniting the wildfire between us. There's no trace of gentleness, no space for slow, languid movements. This is raw and unfiltered, a blatant exhibition of our insatiable craving.

As we barrel toward our climax, the world narrows to just us, a tangled mass of bodies in the relentless chase of ecstasy. Every thrust, guttural grunt, and sharp gasp accelerate our journey to the sweet precipice. We're claiming, taking, and demanding. This is a fierce exchange of passion, a dance of dominance and surrender, and an undeniable testament to carnal desire.

It feels right, more right than anything I've ever known.

I hold her, the silence of the room filled with our synchronized breathing. There's something inherently intimate about this moment and shared vulnerability.

"I could get used to this," I admit softly, my voice barely above a whisper, the words hanging in the room.

Despite the looming complications and impending end, right now, everything feels just as it should be.

22

ISABELLA

The past couple of weeks have had me riding on such a high I'm practically bracing for the ground to shatter beneath me. Every night, I find myself tangled up in Julius's sheets, lost in the intoxicating labyrinth of his arms. Despite the convenient label we've stuck on this marriage, I can't ignore the niggling feeling that I might be kidding myself. I've been erecting these sturdy walls around my heart, making it a fortress against trust and intimacy. But Julius Slater is like a sledgehammer, effortlessly chipping away at my defenses.

Logically, he doesn't belong in my world, right? And I definitely don't fit into his. Neither does Fox. I'm certain the moment some high-born princess crosses his path, she'll captivate him, whisking him away into the world he's accustomed to. The world that got us into this pretend marriage in the first place.

But the sight of him with Fox, reading him a bedtime story with such raw tenderness when he thought I wasn't looking, that image is stubbornly etched in my mind. I yearn for my son to have a semblance of normalcy, a father figure that adores him as his own.

He deserves that, doesn't he?

My train of thought is derailed by a soft squeeze on my thigh. I swivel my gaze to Julius, who kills the car engine and announces, "We're here."

One of Julius's business associates invited us to a birthday party. He mentioned it to me last night, seeming a tad uncertain. Well, we're here now.

"Yay!" Fox squeals, peering through the windshield. "Wow, Mommy, look at all the balloons!" His delight is infectious.

An elaborate balloon archway welcomes us, each balloon proudly proclaiming 'Samuel' in baby blue letters. It's extravagant enough to make me mentally calculate its worth, a figure that could comfortably cover a month's pay easily.

"Let's go take a closer look, kiddo," Julius suggests, unclipping his seat belt.

He winks at me, and I can't help but return his smile. Ever since he came back from Tokyo, there's been a drastic shift in his demeanor. He's softened around the edges, his actions and emotions transparent.

For now, at least, he's completely invested in the present, and I can't help but find it endearing.

The extravaganza spread before us is less of a children's party and more like I'm looking down the barrel of a diamond-encrusted kaleidoscope. Despite the undeniably opulent setting, the space brims with the giddy laughter of kids high on life and plenty of sugar.

Julius's reassuring grip on my hand anchors me as we weave through the crowd. Fox's tiny fingers clutch my other hand, his enthusiasm practically pulling us along.

The glittering throng of the upper crust of society looms into sight, their attire straight off fashion runways.

Their gaze flits between us, murmurings rippling through the crowd. The anticipation sharpens my senses, readying me for the imminent encounters.

"Julius! What a surprise!" The perfectly modulated voice of Marianne, a renowned socialite and a long-time admirer of Julius, slices through the hum of conversations. I remember the cool reception she gave me after being introduced to her at the first party we attended as newlyweds.

Julius's smile is cordial. "Marianne. Lovely to see you." His grip on my hand doesn't waver, a silent reassurance.

Marianne's eyes flicker toward me, her smile polite, albeit a tad cold. "Isabella," she acknowledges, then turns her attention back to Julius. "How have you been?"

"Doing great, thank you." Julius's voice is calm and assured. Then he subtly steers the conversation to safer ground. "You remember Fox, right?"

Marianne's gaze softens as she crouches down to engage with Fox. His unbridled joy and innocence seem to strike a chord, even with her. For his part, Fox is more interested in a clown performing a few yards away.

The rest of the afternoon unfolds in much the same way with us presenting a united front to every curious eye or veiled insinuation.

Julius never strays from my side, his presence a silent but potent declaration of support. But he's just keeping up appearances, right? Ours is an unconventional unit. Pretend. Yet it feels real, perhaps more so than the façades around us.

"You seem deep in thought." Julius draws me in, looping his arms around me.

"Me? No, just trying to locate Fox in all of this. He could

be anywhere." I say, jesting about our extravagant surroundings.

A smile graces his face, and it instantly warms my heart. "Do you reckon he has enough to keep him busy? Juggling, karate, a karaoke corner, and a ball pit. He could truly be anywhere." A soft laugh escapes my lips, and he pulls me even closer, stealing a kiss.

His public show of affection is overwhelmingly tender. Yet, a small, broken part of me still questions if it's all for show.

Suddenly, a sharp, piercing cry shatters our bubble of happiness. The animated chatter halts as an abrupt silence sweeps across the crowd. Julius tightens his grip on my hand as we, along with everyone else, fix our gaze on the source of the commotion.

"Stop it, stop it now!" A woman's voice, frantic and shrill, rises above the sudden quiet, tension spiraling in its wake.

Turning toward the sound, I spot Fox in the center of it all. My heart leaps into my throat as I see him involved in a tussle with a boy who seems to be the same age. Fox, my normally sweet and good-natured boy, is wildly kicking at the other child with a fierce scowl.

In a flash, Julius releases my hand, a look of alarm crossing his face. With a speed that surprises me, he outpaces me, darting toward the boys. His long legs eat up the distance between us and the squabbling boys, his usually calm demeanor replaced with concern.

As I rush to catch up, my mind whirls, scrambling to process what's happening. Fox, who's been nothing but excited all day, suddenly engaged in a fight? I don't understand it.

The chatter around us resumes, hushed whispers and

curious gazes fixed on us as Julius reaches Fox. I can almost feel the weight of their scrutiny, their judgments forming even as the drama continues to unfold. But right now, I only care about getting to Fox, understanding what has gone wrong, and comforting him.

Julius swiftly intervenes, separating Fox from the other boy. On quick inspection, neither seem badly hurt, a relief washing over me.

"Your son assaulted mine," accuses the woman, yanking her child away from us as if we carry some contagious disease.

"Fox wouldn't... he's not aggressive," I defend, aghast, my hand instinctively moving to Fox's shoulder. "He's not the type to start fights."

"Are you implying that I'm lying?" she retorts, her glare piercing.

Choosing to disregard her hostility, I focus on Fox. "Honey, can you tell me what happened?"

He remains silent, the incident clearly upsetting him.

"Fox," Julius begins with a stern yet caring voice, "We should never resort to violence. Can you tell me what happened?" he says, lowering to his level.

However, the woman isn't done. "I don't know who's raising this child, but he doesn't belong in a place like this," she spews out with palpable disdain.

A surge of anger pulses through me, but Julius rises to his feet before I can respond. "That's enough," he states firmly. "Boys can have disagreements. They're children. They're learning boundaries and limitations. Fox is now my son, and I know he would never hurt someone without being provoked. Fox belongs wherever I am."

The confidence and pride in his voice stuns me. Fox looks up at Julius, his eyes wide with surprise and a flicker of admiration. The only father figure he's had in his life is an abusive one, and the awe in his face renders me momentarily speechless.

People around us gasp in surprise, but I'm too busy focusing on my son to look around.

"Let's go," Julius proposes, pivoting and offering his hand to my son and me.

Fox's small hand reaches for his, and I watch as Julius visibly softens at the contact. His eyes meet mine, and I place my hand in his. He shoots the woman a scathing glance before leading us down the path toward the exit.

As unconventional as our relationship might be, I find myself happy. Something I thought I could never be again.

As we drive back home, the experience leaves me contemplating the sturdy walls I've built around myself. The day's events seem to have chipped away at them, leaving me a little more open, a little more willing to trust.

After all, it's not every day you find a man who not only holds your hand in a crowd but stands by you against the world.

23

JULIUS

F ox kicking another boy at a birthday party was certainly not in today's itinerary, nor was the shock from the crowd. It left me grappling with unexpected feelings, a hint of what Isabella must endure navigating through socialites at these events.

After Fox's outburst, I retreat to my room, allowing Isabella and him some private space. As I pace around, lost in thought, Isabella calls my name. Immediately, I dart out of my room, heading toward Isabella in Fox's room.

As I step in, she looks up, uncertainty clouding her eyes. "Fox wants to tell me what happened, but only if you're here too," she says.

"Absolutely, Nado," I respond, moving to sit beside Isabella on Fox's bed.

"*Now,* will you tell us what happened, Foxy?" Isabella gently prompts, her hand finding Fox's, offering a comforting touch.

Fox's face scrunches up as he tries to piece together his thoughts. "Momma, I hit him because he needed to learn a lesson."

Her surprise is clear as she asks, "Oh, sweetie, why on earth would you think that?"

His answer throws us both for a loop. " 'Cause he called you a gold-digging slut."

I feel the anger surge, heat rushing to my face. "He said what?" I blurt out, glancing at Isabella.

She places a hand on my thigh, but she isn't mirroring my anger. Instead, she appears saddened. Her quiet sigh as she asks Fox, "And do you know what those words mean?" shows she's more hurt than enraged.

"No, Mommy. But I've heard Daddy call you a slut before, then he hits you. I didn't want him to hurt you."

Fuck me.

She lets out a gasp. "Oh, sweetheart," she says as she pulls him into her chest. He starts crying, and I can tell by the movement in her shoulders she is crying too. And my rock-hard exterior starts to melt. Melt hard for these two people who have been through struggles I can't bear to imagine.

The moment hangs heavy in the air, almost as if time has decided to pause and bear witness to this heart-wrenching revelation. I can't tear my eyes away from the sight before me, a brave little boy holding onto his mother, their tears intermingling in the dimly lit room. The pain they've endured is written across their faces, and I can't help but think how cruel not only Travis but the people in my circles have been to them both.

"He shouldn't call you that, Mommy." Fox's small voice trembles, his words muffled against Isabella's shoulder.

"You're right, sweetie," she murmurs, her hand gently stroking his back in soothing circles. "It wasn't a nice thing to say. It wasn't right."

"Then I'm glad I punched him," Fox declares, pulling

away from Isabella to look her in the eyes. It's not the words he speaks but the resolve in his eyes that stuns me. The courage of this little boy defending his mother is extraordinary, and for a moment, I find myself in awe of him.

Isabella's face softens, and she smiles through her tears at Fox. "I appreciate that you wanted to stand up for me, Fox, but violence is never the answer. There are better ways to handle situations like these, okay?"

Fox nods, sniffing back his tears and wiping them away with the back of his hand. I feel a surge of respect for this little fighter and even more for his mother.

Finally, I break my silence. "You're one brave kid, Nado. You stood up for your mom, and that's something to be proud of. But mommy's right. We need to use our words, not our fists, okay?"

Fox nods at me, his lips curving into a small, unsure smile. "Okay, Jules."

"Good boy," I murmur, giving his shoulder a comforting squeeze.

The moon is the only source of light in the room, casting a dreamy haze on everything. Bella's beneath me, her body on full display, and damn, it's a sight that sends my blood pumping. I'm lost in the dips and curves of her body, a roadmap of pure temptation.

"Bella," I murmur, my lips brushing her neck while my fingers lazily skate down her side. Her body quivers under my touch, and I feel that magnetic pull between us growing stronger.

She opens her eyes, looking at me like she's trying to

solve a puzzle. "Thank you for today. For defending my son when you didn't know if he was to blame."

"You, me, and Nado, we're in this together," I say, needing her to know I mean this. I want her to feel safe and loved. Her past doesn't get to define us.

She gives a small nod, her eyes lighting up with a spark of hope. That's all I need. I lean in and kiss her, pouring all my emotions into it. As my arousal grazes her entrance, a shiver of expectation trembles through us.

"I need to feel you, Bella. Fully. No barriers, no condoms." I look up, seeking the consent in her thoughtful eyes.

She nods, giving me the permission I need, and I sink fully inside her. A soft gasp escapes her as she adjusts to the new sensation, and I'm nearly undone.

"Fuck." A harsh, guttural expletive escapes my lips, and my eyes roll back in sheer ecstasy.

Our bodies start finding a natural, rhythmic sync, primal and instinctive. Her fingers knot in my hair, yanking me closer into her gravity.

My hands roam her body, memorizing her. She clenches around my cock, and I'm barely holding it together. We lose ourselves in each other, our bodies swaying together, riding the waves of this intense emotion that's building between us.

We're lost in each other, driven by need and desire. Isabella's fingers are digging into my back, her legs wrapped around me in a hold that's more intimate than anything I've ever experienced. She's swept up in the sensations, her eyes closed.

Isabella's response is instinctive, a magnetic pull I'm helpless against. She wraps her thighs tighter around my waist, her body arching into mine, matching my rhythm with a precision that sends waves of pleasure coursing through me.

"Look at me, Isabella," I choke out.

She opens her eyes, and damn, just like that, we're on the edge, teetering, ready to fall. Her body molds perfectly against mine, her gasps and moans filling the room, intertwining with the low growls escaping my throat.

And then we're over, our bodies spiraling in pleasure. The world narrows down to this moment, to the two of us lost in each other.

When the high subsides, I roll beside her. We're still tangled up in each other, sweaty and spent. Her head rests on my chest, her breaths in sync with the pounding of my heart. I wrap my arm around her, holding her close. And I hope, more than anything, that this memory can help push away the shadows of her past.

The words are out of my mouth before I even fully comprehend them. "He's not going to hurt you or Fox again, Bella," I assure her, my hand instinctively cradling her cheek. The smoothness of her skin beneath my touch is a sweet, grounding reality.

The mention of Travis sends a shadow across her features, a stark reminder of the pain she's had to endure. "Julius—" she begins, but I interrupt her.

"I promise you, Isabella," I state with determination. "Travis will never lay a finger on you two again."

A tear slips from the corner of her eye, and I brush it away with my thumb. This woman, this incredible force of nature who's battled more than her fair share of demons, makes my heart constrict. I watch as she lets her guard down, lets me in, and these moments of vulnerability pull me closer to her.

Even as my fondness for Nado grows, even as I fall for

Bella, the fear that I may tread a path I'm ill-equipped for grips me. The notion of failing them or morphing into the man my father was sends a chill down my spine.

I want to try, for Bella, for Nado, and for this unconventional family I find myself inexplicably drawn to.

"Thank you, Julius," she whispers, her eyes meeting mine. "I believe you." There's a trust there, in her gaze, a trust I haven't earned yet, but I'm determined to.

"You're safe, Bella," I reiterate, my fingers brushing through her hair, wanting her to feel the sincerity behind my words. "You and Nado both."

Her hand finds mine, her fingers tangling with mine. "I've been alone for so long, Julius. Even with Nado, it was just... it was us against the world."

"And now?" I prompt, wanting to hear her say it, needing to hear her say it.

She turns to look at me, a soft smile on her lips. "And now, it feels like we're not alone anymore. Like we have someone in our corner."

Her admission hits me harder than I expect. I've been living a life devoid of meaningful connections for so long, sleeping around. The weight of her words takes my breath away. But in an instant, my throat clogs, and my heart races. Visions of my father's cold indifference, his blatant infidelity, and the resulting abandonment all flood back.

The shared experience of neglect that Nado and I unknowingly share makes me wonder if I'm destined to walk the same path. Am I capable of causing the same damage? Of wounding those who are beginning to mean more to me than I could've ever anticipated?

I don't let that fear show. Instead, I pull her closer, wrapping my arms around her. "We are more than a marriage of convenience, Bella. We are a family. And I promise you, I will do everything in my power to protect this family."

There's still so much I want to say, so much I need to tell her about my fears, insecurities, and the ghosts of my past that still haunt me. But tonight, it's about her, about us. The rest can wait.

For now, this is enough.

This moment, with her in my arms, it's more than enough.

24

ISABELLA

As I arrive at the office, the air is quiet, filled with an almost reverent hush that always marks the start of another day on the executive floor. Julius's office door is closed, indicating he's already immersed in a meeting, despite the early hour.

My desk is tidy, as always, save for one stunning anomaly—a single, pristine red rose. It's a bold dash of color against the otherwise neutral palette of the office and a clear indication of Julius's growing affection—a silent gesture just for me.

As I gently touch the petals, there's a rustle of movement. Looking up, I see Vincent ambling toward me. His eyes are focused on the rose, an enigmatic smile playing on his lips.

"Morning, Isabella," he greets, an eyebrow arched in intrigue.

"Morning, Vincent," I return his greeting with a polite smile, my fingers instinctively curling around the stem of the rose.

He glances between the rose and me, not saying

anything directly, but curiosity is evident in his eyes. He doesn't ask, the silent question hanging between us.

"Ready for the board today?" I deflect, attempting to steer the conversation toward safer ground.

"Oh, absolutely." Vincent chuckles, catching my drift and rolling with it. "Though it seems you've already had quite the pleasant start to your day."

I give him a noncommittal shrug, trying to keep my emotions in check. "Seems so," I reply casually, my heart fluttering a bit.

We both know he's not really talking about the workday. He's alluding to the rose, to the unspoken affection it represents. And yet, he doesn't press the matter, showing respect for the boundary between Julius's personal and professional life.

A soft chime indicates the end of Julius's meeting, and as the office door swings open, I glance up at my husband. He's dashing in his navy suit and chalk-white shirt tailored around his broad shoulders.

My mind drifts to him in his bed last night, cradling, holding, and possessing me, making me feel like the only woman in his life. Possibly making love to me with unspoken feelings and touches.

My heart flutters as our eyes connect, nervous suddenly. He smiles widely, then sees Vincent and stops himself from what I think he was going to do—coming over and kissing me.

He's become more affectionate at work and not just the sex. That is off the charts with my dirty-talking husband. But it's more, the handholding, the gentle kisses, the promises of more.

I know he's committing to this marriage, and I am falling. What the fuck am I saying?

I've done it.

I've completely toppled over the precipice I swore I'd never approach. Heart guarded and wrapped in layers of caution, it was supposed to be off-limits. And yet, here I am, admitting to myself that I've unintentionally let Julius slip past my defenses.

"Good morning, brother," Vincent greets, the corners of his lips curving up in a knowing smirk.

Julius returns his smile, a twinkle in his eye that matches the sunny day outside. "Indeed, it's a great morning," he retorts, sending a quick glance my way, making me feel more special than any rose ever could.

Vincent doesn't miss the look and chuckles. "I see we've all had a fantastic start. My fiancée made sure of that for me, and apparently, you had similar luck with your bride."

Julius shoots his brother a good-natured glare, a silent 'mind your own business,' but I can't help the smirk that creeps onto my lips.

"Okay, smart aleck," Julius says, playing along. "Let's get moving."

Vincent, unperturbed, carries on, his grin stretching wider. "It's refreshing to see you loosening up around the office."

"Keep pushing, and you'll regret it," Julius warns him, though his tone is light.

I can't help but giggle at their banter. The genuine connection between the two brothers and their back-and-forths, however teasing, fills me with a warmth I never knew I craved.

"My lips are sealed, at least in front of your bride," Vincent quips before turning serious. "Speaking of which, I'd like both of you to keep your schedules open next weekend."

Julius raises an eyebrow. "Oh? Why's that?"

"We're all flying out to Sardinia for our engagement celebration."

My heart skips a beat. "Really?" The idea of traveling outside the country, something I've never done, sounds exciting and terrifying all at once. Then another realization hits me.

Fox will be at Travis's next weekend.

The thought of leaving my son there isn't pleasant, but my lawyers reassure me it won't be for much longer. With the might of the Slater legal team behind me, I'm closer to gaining full custody. Travis, for all his faults, will soon be a part of the past we're both trying to escape.

"Yes," Vincent confirms my question, his eyes lighting up at my excitement. "It's going to be an unforgettable trip. So, I'd really love it if you both could make it."

"I'm sure we can arrange that," Julius replies, shooting me an encouraging smile.

"But... Fox," I begin, my voice wavering. "Fox will be at Travis's next weekend."

Vincent looks between Julius and me, his playful demeanor replaced by a more understanding expression. "I'm sure we can figure something out for Fox," he assures me, probably sensing my anxiety. "Can you swap weeks?" Vincent asks, and I've already thought of that knowing the response.

"Afraid not. Travis won't budge on anything like that, nor would he sign off on me taking Fox out of the country."

"I wish we could change the date, but it's when Victoria has a break in her schedule. We really should have thought of your... situation," Vincent offers. "Sorry, Bella."

"No, no, please, it's your engagement party. Don't apologize. I'm sure it will be fine."

Julius takes my hand from behind the desk and squeezes it. "We're in this together, remember? We'll figure out something for Fox. You don't have to worry."

I manage a shaky nod, touched by his reassurances. It's not easy for me to trust, especially when it involves my son. But with Julius, it feels different. It feels safer.

Vincent's gaze flickers between the two of us, his eyes wide with realization. The unmistakable affection displayed by his brother, an aspect of Julius he's not accustomed to seeing, visibly stuns him.

Suddenly, Vincent's secretary calls out, her voice slicing through the momentarily awkward silence.

"Mr. Slater, you left behind the projection summary for your meeting."

Vincent flicks his eyes between us one last time, an unreadable expression on his face before he strides off toward her.

My gaze falls on Julius returning from a grueling board meeting. The stern set of his jaw tells me he isn't pleased with the proceedings. I want to ask him about it, but at the same time he reappears, so does an unexpected figure. Mrs. Slater.

She's the epitome of class, dressed impeccably, her hair sleekly drawn back in a chic bun. Age hasn't dampened her allure. Instead, it has refined her. That's what affluence does, I muse. "Tatianna," I greet her.

A warm smile graces her lips, "Hello dear, lovely to see you."

That's the thing about his mother. She doesn't make me feel like an outsider. And it strikes me odd that we haven't visited her and his father during this arranged marriage. Not that I've mentioned it to Julius, of course. But isn't that what families do?

On the occasions I've seen Tatianna at work, she's always maintained an impressive, tailored image. An occasional lunch with Julius seems to be the extent of their interactions. So, her presence now leaves me pleasantly surprised.

"Mother, what are you doing here?" Julius approaches, positioning himself beside my desk. He greets his mother, leaning in to kiss each of her cheeks.

"I've arranged for the three of us to have lunch together," she announces, catching Julius and me off guard.

"I'm tied up with work today, and Vincent has just left," he replies, his voice serious.

I turn to look at him. He doesn't have a lunch appointment, and didn't his mother mean me, not Vincent? The feeling that he doesn't want me to get to know his mother weighs heavily on me. His words in the bedroom, the sincerity, what does it all mean if he doesn't want me to get to know his family?

"Nonsense, and it's you and Isabella I want to take out," she replies sharply, and suddenly I feel like the rose between two thorns.

He grits his teeth. "Fine, we'll make it a quick one," he says.

She throws us both a triumphant smile, and I'm suddenly nervous.

Nestled amidst the heart of the city, *Le Ciel Bleu* is the epitome of luxury and exclusivity, a place frequented by the

Slater brothers. As we approach, I can't help but marvel at the architectural grandeur. The soaring glass façade reflects the city's skyline, imbuing it with an almost ethereal charm. This is a world where opulence meets culinary excellence.

Stepping inside, the ambience is an impeccable blend of intimacy and grandeur. Soft, ambient light bathes the room, bouncing off the intricately carved mirrors and glistening chandeliers, casting an inviting glow on the mahogany tables draped with immaculate white tablecloths. The furniture exudes elegance, upholstered in plush velvet, and the walls display sophisticated, abstract art.

The centerpiece of the restaurant is an open kitchen, showcasing chefs performing their artistry. The aroma of exotic spices and gourmet dishes fills the air, making my stomach rumble in anticipation. This is a far cry from Sojo's, the café around the corner from work.

Despite the restaurant's extravagance, there's a certain warmth to it. The courteous staff, the subtle melodies playing in the background, and the genial murmur of conversations all contribute to a comforting ambience.

As we're escorted to a private corner booth with a stunning view of the city, I realize that while this may not be my usual setting, it's a world I could certainly grow to appreciate.

"Darling, I have extended numerous invitations to you both over the past six months. I genuinely wish you'd visit us soon," Tatianna says delicately, her eyes drifting toward Julius, gauging his reaction.

I observe the exchange between mother and son and

notice Julius physically straightening, tension evident in his posture.

"I have no desire to see Father. I wish you'd stop insisting on this," he states firmly.

Tatianna persists, "With the upcoming wedding and him being there, can't we put the past behind us? Victoria has forgiven him, so have I. I implore you to consider forgiving him too. He's not getting any younger, you know."

"You're seriously not using his health to guilt-trip me, are you?" Julius retorts, taking a long sip from his coffee cup.

"All I'm saying, Julius, is life is short, and perhaps it's time we learn to forgive."

I sit here, feeling a twinge of nervousness creep in. I have no clue what they're talking about. Then I remember the conversation Vincent had with me at Sojo's—his turbulent upbringing and the fact he was left at a boarding school to basically grow up. I wonder if this has to do with that. I'm tempted to shrink back in my chair, but I focus on my husband instead, hoping to understand him better.

"There isn't just one thing to forgive, Mother, and you know it." His eyes swiftly move to mine, subtly sharing a silent message, something I'm yet to understand, before returning to his mother.

She swallows hard, her jaw clenching as if grappling with an internal battle. With a heavy sigh, her meticulously manicured fingers come together in a steeple on the immaculate tablecloth, a stark contrast to the turmoil within her.

"You're right. I can't make excuses for him. He's wronged you. He's wronged me too." Her voice laces with regret, and I can't help but wonder what she means. "But we are Slaters. We regroup. Family is important."

A bitter chuckle escapes Julius, "Family is important, huh? That would have been nice to hear when I was a kid feeling like my only family was the kids at boarding school. Listen, Mother, I agreed to this lunch, and I'll attend Vincent's engagement in Sardinia, but anything more than that, you're overstepping."

Julius's phone interrupts the tense moment, and he leaves the table, offering his mother and me a quick, apologetic smile. We're left amidst the elegant setting of white linens and gold-rimmed crystal flutes, an uncomfortable edge between us.

Tatianna takes a sip of her drink, placing it down gently before leaning in slightly. "So, dear..." she begins, her gaze soft but piercing. "How are things really between you and Julius?"

I hesitate for a moment, collecting my thoughts before opening up about our initial struggles—the daunting move from our modest apartment to Julius's opulent penthouse and the whirlwind introduction to high society. She listens attentively, a quiet understanding in her eyes.

When I mention the frosty reception I got from some of the women in Julius's social circle, she interrupts me, her tone firm. "Pay no heed to those women. They are mere social climbers, my dear. Julius... he's always been a target for such women, which led us to this predicament."

Caught off guard by her candidness, I remain silent. She, however, softens as she continues. "I believe you're the best thing that's happened to him, Isabella. I see a grounded, real person in you. Perhaps things pan out for a reason. I just hope Julius's unwavering determination won't hinder his chance at real happiness."

But her knowing smile unsettles me, and I sit taller in

my chair. *Are we projecting more than what we're supposed to? Are our feelings becoming too obvious?*

"This is a marriage of convenience, Tatianna. I am fully aware of the expiration that's looming, and so is Julius."

Her gaze meets mine. "I see," she utters, disappointment barely concealed.

~

Julius shows up just as I've finished tucking in Fox for the night, giving me a bit of a surprise. His soft "Night, Nado" echoes in the room as he leans over Fox to gently kiss his forehead.

I can't help but feel a warmth spread through me at this sight, a sight that was never meant to be part of the picture. My heart shouldn't be melting like this. I wasn't supposed to envision Julius as a father figure in Fox's life. Yet, here he is, perfectly slotting into the role, doing all the things a father does, the things Fox never had.

It's as if we're slowly becoming a family. We're sharing meals together and engaging in ordinary family activities. And just yesterday, I watched in astonishment as Julius sat down on the living room floor to play a game of Snakes and Ladders with Fox. The sight of them, engrossed in the game while I busied myself with emails on the couch, made me feel an unanticipated surge of joy.

It's these little moments that are slowly changing the dynamic of our relationship. Moments that are breaking down the walls of our 'marriage of convenience' and allowing glimpses of something far deeper to peek through. For a moment, I let myself imagine what it would be like if this were real, if we were a real family. It's a dangerous thought that threatens to upend everything, but in that fleeting moment, it feels beautifully right.

That night, as we retire to bed, the silence of our bedroom is disrupted only by the soft rustle of sheets. Julius turns to face me, his hand gliding up my side suggestively. But something is weighing on my mind, something left unsaid at lunch earlier this week. Something he hasn't bothered to elaborate on or bring up after the heated discussion with his mother. But, it's gnawing at me, making it impossible to let it go.

"Julius," I say, breaking the moment. He stops, glancing up at me, the fire in his eyes disappearing at the tone of my voice. "There's something I wanted to ask you. At lunch... when your mother mentioned forgiving your father... what was she talking about exactly?"

He takes a deep breath. His features are shadowed in the dim light, but his blue eyes are clear with a hint of sadness.

"I was wondering if you would bring that up," he says quietly, acknowledging the unspoken tension that had marked the conversation.

He pauses, the silence growing heavy between us. I can tell he's debating how much to reveal, wrestling with old wounds that still feel fresh.

As I wait for him to continue, my heart beats a little faster. It's strange how there's still so much we don't know about each other, even after all this time.

25

JULIUS

Ready to spill my past to Isabella, I'm battling with myself about how much to let out. But, having spent half a year with my wife, I've felt a happiness I didn't know I could, and it's all because of her. The way she looks at me like she really cares, it's not something I'm used to, but it's making me want to open up to her.

"You know I went to boarding school like how other wealthy parents send their kids," I begin, my voice calm and steady. "But what you don't know is that, unlike most boys who return home for breaks and holidays, I didn't. My father didn't want to see me. I wasn't the favorite."

"Vincent was?" she interjects when my voice trails off, her brows knitted together in confusion.

"No," I shake my head, offering her a thin smile. "We had another brother, Edgar. He was murdered when I was young." Her face registers surprise, but I barrel onward, not giving myself a moment to hesitate. "I don't really remember him even though, that one time, I was at our country home in Connecticut when it happened."

Isabella's eyes fill with sadness, and she reaches out to rest a hand on my arm. "I had no idea, Julius... I'm so sorry."

"I don't remember him. There was a significant age gap between us," I admit, longing for a brother I barely knew. "He and Vincent were close. He was shot while he carried Vincent on his shoulders."

A tear escapes her eye, and she quickly brushes it away. "I'm so sorry," she apologizes again, her voice barely above a whisper.

"You don't have to apologize. It's... nice to have someone care about me," I confess, watching as she looks at me with empathy and surprise.

"Your mother cares for you, Julius," she reminds me softly.

"Yes, but not enough to want me back with the family during my formative years. Anyhow, without a family there for me, I grew up quickly. I threw myself into building this company with Vincent. We found that we had a shared love for business and creating something from nothing. And that's how Slater Corp. started. As for relationships... I never really let anyone in before you, Isabella. I never wanted to."

She cradles my cheek in her hand, a gentle touch warmed by the truth I've just shared. I let out a sigh, steeling myself for what I'm about to say next. "Then this year, to top things off, I discovered Dad withheld some facts about my brother's murder. That was really the final straw for me with him."

"What? Why would he do that?" She gasps, her eyes widening in shock.

"Vincent made it his life's mission to find out who the killer was. Even though there was a man in jail convicted for my brother's murder, Vincent was convinced it wasn't him. He believed there was someone else involved. He found them, but it turns out my father knew all along that this family was involved."

"Family?" she echoes, her voice quivering slightly.

"Yes, the Gambino Mafia. Father had dealings with them through his brokerage company. They were after him. It should have been him that was murdered that day, not my Edgar. When I found out, I punched him so hard that his lithe body hit the floor. That was nearly eight months ago now."

The weight of my past hangs heavily between us, the silence in the room deafening as I wait for her reaction.

"So, our wedding was the first time you saw him since you punched him?"

I nod. "And next, it will be Sardinia, hence Mother's timely lunch."

"Oh, I see. So that would mean... the same time you found out about your father's involvement was..." She trails off, her eyes filled with realization.

"The same time I slept with the senator's fiancée," I confirm, a bitter chuckle escaping me. "Yes. I was messed up. She assured me her engagement to the senator was off, and she was single."

Isabella looks surprised at my confession. "I promise you I would never knowingly break up a relationship. I know the damage it does to a family."

"Your father?" she ventures tentatively. "Did he cheat on your mother?"

"All the time. She turned a blind eye to it all. After all, image was important. She enjoyed a world of luxury while he took his pleasure elsewhere."

"My father did too," she admits suddenly, and I realize this is the first time I've heard her mention her parents.

"You've never talked about them before," I point out, my interest piqued.

"Like you, we all have secrets," she says, a wistful smile playing on her lips as she echoes my words from earlier.

"I need to know you, every part of you, Isabella," I say with conviction.

"Not much to say. I grew up an only child in Detroit ,then we moved to Jersey for my father's work. We lived simply. Middle class, I guess you could say. My father met the Sneddons through the country club. We met, and Travis was charming at first, and I was, well, so naïve." She gives her head a little shake, seemingly trying to dislodge the memory. There's a brief nibble at her lower lip, a clear sign of her nervousness to reveal something to me.

"You can trust me, Bella," I tell her.

She takes a deep breath before confessing, "I... I got pregnant with Fox after... after he... he raped me."

"Jesus, Bella." I gasp, her revelation shaking me to my core.

"I agreed to marry him because he promised it wouldn't happen again." She breaks down into a soft sob. "I just wanted Fox to have both his parents around, a normal upbringing full of love and memories. Seems naïve, doesn't it?" Her voice trembles with the weight of her emotions.

"It didn't stop, did it," I state, more of a bitter realiza-tion than a question. The thought of what she's had to endure makes me sick.

"No, if anything, it got worse. I was at rock bottom. I knew I had to tell someone. I was so low, so desperate to escape the black hole that had become my life, so one day, I decided to gather the courage and tell my parents the atroc-ities Travis inflicted on me."

"And what was their response?" I find myself asking, although a part of me dreads the answer.

She shakes her head, words seemingly failing her. A lone tear trickles down her cheek, which I gently wipe away.

"You must've told them about his abusive behavior... that he was a monster. They should've stood by you," I say, my anger brewing at the thought.

"The truth is, they didn't believe me," she confesses, her voice barely a whisper, but the words echo loudly in the silence of our room. "Or maybe they did and chose not to acknowledge it. In their minds, they had already married off their daughter to the best family possible, and any problems I had were all in my head."

Jesus Christ.

A heavy silence hangs in the air as I grapple with this revelation. To know she's been through so much alone and unsupported by her own family, it's too much. I reach out, wrapping my arms around her. At this moment, I resolve to be the support she never had, to protect her at all costs. After all, she's not just my wife. She's become my world.

"Eventually, with enough savings from this job and my friend Harley's never-ending support, I left him."

I stroke her cheek, guilt eating me up like a slingshot playing with my heart.

"I'm sorry I was never there for you, even though this was happening right under my nose." She shakes her head. "Your boundaries make sense, Julius. You've built a fortress around you because of your abandonment as a child."

I tip her chin up, and she looks at me, her eyes brimming with emotions that mirror my own. "We're more alike than you may think," I say. "My beautiful, strong Bella."

As she presses herself to me, our lips crash together,

silently voicing the rising heat between us. An intense, urgent need pulls me in, feeding my craving for her.

We're two damaged souls seeking solace and sanctuary in each other. This wasn't part of the plan, but maybe, just maybe, this was the path we were always meant to take.

Our lips move in harmony as we drown in this shared need, and it's more potent, more intoxicating than anything I've ever known.

26

ISABELLA

As I dart around the house gathering Fox's necessities, my heart pounds like a kick drum. Each tick of the clock magnifies the fact that I'm not simply transferring him between homes this week. I'm leaving the country while he stays behind. It's an unprecedented leap into the unknown, and despite Julius's soothing words, anxiety gnashes at me with relentless teeth.

Every minute of the car ride to Travis's house is consumed by my mental checklist of what I might have forgotten. Amid my chaotic thoughts, Fox's plaintive voice pierces through, "Mommy, why can't I come with you?"

"Oh, honey," I murmur, my hand instinctively reaching out to curl around his tiny fingers. "I really wanted you to come. Julius did too. But it's your week with your father, remember?"

I consciously omit the details of my futile attempts to negotiate with Travis, his acidic words, and his refusal to even consider the possibility of changing the schedule. Those interactions had knocked me off the euphoric

194

bubble of my marriage, leaving me grappling with self-doubt.

Even the powerhouse Slater lawyers couldn't budge the iron-clad custody agreement despite our best efforts. This stark reality hit hard, pushing me to the precipice of a difficult choice. Stay here mired in worry for my son or travel overseas to celebrate my friend Rosie's engagement and rediscover myself alongside a man who makes everything seem brighter.

"We're here, Mrs. Slater," Carrick's voice brings me back to the present. The unfamiliar title causes me to flinch, even as the sight of Fox, preoccupied with his teddy, eases my mind a little.

"I'll see you very soon," I promise, pulling Fox into an embrace that feels like it could shatter my heart. His soft whisper, "I'll miss you, Momma," threatens to unleash the tears I've been holding back.

"No, you won't," I tell him, trying to sound more confident than I feel. "You'll have so much fun with your friends at daycare. You won't even notice I'm gone."

His eyes, the mirror image of mine, brim with innocent sadness. "When will it just be us?" he asks, the question landing like a punch to my gut.

"Soon, baby, I promise," I assure him, hugging him tightly once more. His little arms encircle me, and I drink in the feel of him, memorizing his every contour.

Carrick opens the car door, jarring us apart. As we step out of the car, Travis's home stands tall and uninviting, a stark reminder of the life I left behind and the battles still to be fought. The sight sows a seed of dread as it does every time I'm here, but I swallow it, masking my apprehension with a smile for Fox.

I watch as Fox's small frame climbs the stairs leading to

the grand entrance of Travis's home. With Carrick at my side, I follow him. His presence is a welcome comfort, albeit an odd one. When I look over at him, he shakes his head, "Mr. Slater's orders, ma'am."

We approach the door, and it swings open before we can knock. There stands Travis, arrogance etched onto his features as if it were chiseled in stone.

"What the hell do you want?" he barks out, glaring at me.

"I'm just here to drop Fox off, Travis," I say, trying to keep my voice steady.

"You've got some nerve, showing up here like this after trying to mess with the schedule. Who do you think you are?" He spits the words, his disdain palpable.

Before I can respond, Carrick interjects. "Mrs. Slater is only doing what's best for Fox. She was only trying to keep him close while she had to travel. She didn't mean any disrespect."

This only seems to fuel Travis's fury. "And who asked you?" He snarls, turning his fiery gaze to Carrick.

I put my arm around Fox, bringing his attention away from the unpleasant exchange. "Fox, why don't you pop your bag in your room, sweetheart? I'll be in shortly to tuck you in."

As Fox nods and scurries off, Travis's bitter words lash at me. "You're nothing, Isabella. A worthless piece of trash. Always were, always will be. That fake marriage won't change a thing."

I wince, his cruel words stinging more than they should. As much as I try to convince myself they hold no power over me, a small part of me wilts under the weight of his disparaging remarks. I look at Carrick, who's ready to give Travis a piece of his mind. I give him a subtle shake of the head before steeling myself to face Travis one more time.

For Fox's sake, I'll put on the bravest front, but inside, his words have left a mark.

"Listen, Travis." I muster every ounce of resolve, my voice steady, eyes refusing to back down from his intimidating glare. "This is about Fox, not us. Let's not make it harder for him."

His gaze hardens, his lips curling into a mocking smile. "Oh, dear Isabella. You've got it all wrong. It's always been about us. It was us who put him in the middle of our mess."

The words cut deep, but I don't let it show. Instead, I give him a determined look, hoping it conveys more strength than I feel. "It's not a mess if we both prioritize Fox's well-being."

His smirk doesn't falter. "Well, look who's playing the saint now. Don't forget, you were the one who ran away and ruined this family unit."

"Except you're still here, still hurting me physically and mentally." I raise my voice.

"I can't escape you, Travis!" I yell, unable to keep my anger in check.

"Well, maybe you shouldn't, sweetheart."

His words twist like acid in my stomach, and with one last look at Travis, I turn away, ready to say goodbye to Fox. Carrick clears his throat, drawing my attention. "Mrs. Slater, I'll wait here for you. Mr. Slater wants me to escort you back to the car."

His presence is comforting, a touch of civility in the midst of this chaos. I give him a grateful smile, thanking him for his discretion.

I walk into Fox's room, trying to shake off the lingering negativity. His excited chatter about the new toys waiting for him brings me back to reality. None of the grown-up problems matter in his world, and I smile at his innocence.

But as I close the door behind me, Travis's words echo in my head, their weight settling like an anchor in my stomach. Despite my brave front, his words have left a dent, reminding me of the battles I've fought and the battle scars hidden beneath the surface I can't shake.

As I slide into the back seat of the car, Travis's spiteful words hang over me, heavy and suffocating like a cold, wet blanket. It's like they've unlocked a door I've been trying hard to keep shut, letting old memories flood in.

The car speeds past familiar sights, but my mind is elsewhere. I'm back to that awful night when Travis took something from me without my consent. I remember feeling helpless, frozen in shame, too terrified to resist. Even now, those memories hit me like an electric shock, shaking me to the core.

A single tear slips down my cheek and a wave of questions surge forward, each one more cutting than the last.

How could I have married my rapist? How could I have shared my life, let alone my bed, with a man who violated me, who made me pregnant against my will?

I quickly brush away the tear, but there's no escaping the bitterness that's bubbled up. Sure, Travis is a monster, but wasn't I also at fault? Wasn't I the one who didn't put up a fight, who let shame override my anger, who agreed to marry him when I found out I was pregnant, convinced I had no other options?

But then, as I'm grappling with these harsh realities, my mind drifts to Fox, my adorable, innocent little boy. He's my rock, my beacon in the storm, my reason to keep pushing through all this darkness.

For him, I won't stop fighting.

And Julius.

He's the unexpected husband. With his support, I've found a newfound confidence, a strength I didn't know I possessed. But sometimes, the past has a way of sneaking up on me, threatening the stability I've started to build.

But I won't let it win. Not this time. For Fox, for me, I'll keep pushing forward.

And this vacation is just that.

A sense of déjà vu strikes me, climbing the steps onto the company jet. I've been on this plane once before, accompanying Julius on a brief work trip to Los Angeles, but never as an equal.

Certainly not as his wife.

Julius's family is already on board when we step in. Vincent and Rosie sit comfortably in the front two seats, with two vacant seats beside them reserved for us.

"I'm so glad you're here," Rosie exclaims, rising to pull me into a massive hug.

"So am I," I confess, my excitement bubbling now that I'm here and have left the stress of Travis behind.

"This will be a trip to remember," Vincent says, wrapping his arms around us before separating to greet Julius.

"Where's Victoria?" I ask, hoping to meet her.

"She's wrapping up her Australian tour leg and will meet us in Sardinia," Vincent fills in.

We move further into the plane, approaching Julius's mother, Tatianna. Seated in elegance, her attire impeccable as always.

"Son, Isabella," she greets warmly, and I return her smile gratefully.

Now, it's time to greet Julius's father, engrossed in his phone, barely acknowledging our presence until his wife nudges him. With a curt nod, he mutters, "Julius." His voice is cool and distant.

"Father," Julius responds with equal neutrality.

"Mr. Slater." He nods as I address him but swiftly returns his attention to his phone, dismissing us without another word.

This is going to be an interesting flight.

27

JULIUS

As Isabella and I take our seats beside Vincent and Rosie, the conversation quickly turns to our schedule in Sardinia. The second day is earmarked for the grand engagement party when the rest of our friends will be flying in.

"Victoria should arrive around the same time we do," Rosie mentions, a hint of affection in her voice for my sister.

Isabella's eyes brighten at the mention of Victoria. They haven't met yet, but I know they will get on famously.

"I've seen her music career taking off in the headlines," Isabella says with obvious enthusiasm. "She's incredibly talented, Julius."

"I'm not really into music," I admit, prompting a round of laughter from Rosie and Vincent. "But she's making headlines now for the right reasons, so she must be doing well."

We all know I'm referring to the kidnapping from a few months ago. That made news everywhere, and since then, every step she takes is on the news.

"She's not just doing well, brother," Vincent interjects,

surprising me. "She's number one in five countries with her new EP."

I raise my eyebrows in surprise, "Music, Vincent? Really? Rosie has indeed softened you," I tease, raising my champagne glass in a mock toast to him.

Rosie chuckles and turns to Isabella. "You're going to love Sardinia, Isabella. It's breathtakingly beautiful, the food is delicious, and the people are warm. We've got a lot of activities planned but also plenty of downtime to just relax and soak in the island."

"I can't wait," Isabella replies, her eyes sparkling with anticipation. And I find myself smiling, her excitement contagious. I'm looking forward to discovering Sardinia with her.

"We're all going to come back fat and puffy from all the delicious Italian food," Rosie says, which makes us all laugh aloud.

As the jet engines start to hum in preparation for our take-off, I can't help but glance over at my wife and look forward to the adventure that awaits us. This trip is not just about celebrating Vincent and Rosie's engagement, it's also an opportunity for Isabella and me to spend time together, away from our regular lives, just with each other.

After the laughter fades and the conversation shifts to Rosie and Vincent's wedding plans, my attention turns to Isabella. Our eyes meet, holding each other in silent conversation. Since we've revealed more to each other, our relationship has changed, and I can't wait to spend more time with her. The corner of my mouth tugs up in a slight smirk as I see the excitement mirrored in her eyes.

Leaning closer to Isabella, I drop my voice to a husky whisper that only she can hear. "Can't wait to taste your sweet pussy again," I murmur, my words intended to elicit a blush, and they don't disappoint. Her cheeks turn a delightful shade of pink, and her eyes sparkle with desire.

"I'll keep that in mind," she replies, her voice barely audible. Yet the anticipation in her voice is clear, mirroring my own.

The sudden burst of Rosie's laughter snaps us out of our shared secret, redirecting our attention to the group conversation. But the spark ignited between us doesn't die. Instead, it thrums beneath the surface, a relentless current that connects us.

Not long into our flight, I notice Isabella has fallen oddly quiet. Carrick filled me in about Travis and his abusive words. She never mentioned it herself, so I guess she doesn't want to talk about it. Still, I wish she trusted me enough to open up.

"Are you okay?" I ask her as she stares vacantly out the plane window.

"Yes, fine." She turns to me, and our eyes meet.

In the depths of her gaze, I see the muted anxieties, the lingering fears regarding Fox, Travis, and everything left behind. It's a glimpse into her troubled thoughts, and it stirs within me a powerful urge to shelter her, to build a wall against those fears and cast them away.

The coming days in Sardinia are not just about Rosie and Vincent or stolen moments of pleasure. It's about providing a sanctuary for Isabella, a world where she doesn't have to constantly look over her shoulder or question her worth but a world where she feels safe, cherished, and utterly adored.

I reach for her hand. I don't care if Rosie and Vincent can see, and I place it in mine. Her eyes widen, surprised yet hopeful. The anxiety in her gaze eases a fraction, replaced by a soft warmth that makes my chest tighten.

The moment we step into our hidden bungalow, I watch Isabella's eyes widen in pure amazement. The lively Pompeian red walls are dressed in glinting mosaics, their sparkle striking against the hushed hues of cream, beige, and white furniture. Beyond the living room, a spectacular view of the Mediterranean Sea unfurls, rendering the space nothing short of breathtaking.

Standing amidst this luxury, Isabella seems to shine brighter than ever. Her beauty outshines the extravagance around her and ignites a compelling urge within me to give her all the world's riches even though she's never asked for a single dime.

I wrap my arm around her waist, drawing her closer. Leaning in, I murmur into her ear, "Isabella, I want to spoil you."

She turns toward me, her eyes sparkling with a warmth that stirs something profound within me. She shakes her head gently, her smile pure and radiant. "Julius, you are all I need," she responds, her sincerity echoing in her voice.

Her words grip my heart, a powerful current of emotion flooding through me. It feels as though I'm standing on the edge of a precipice, a thrilling sensation of free falling, making my heart pound. This feels dangerously close to falling in love.

She takes my hand and leads the way further into the bungalow. When we step into the bedroom, the tension between us is palpable, charged with a yearning that negates any hint of jetlag. Her eyes meet mine, ablaze with the same raw hunger I feel coursing through my veins.

"Isabella," I tilt her chin up as I whisper her name. Our bodies crash together, lips meeting in a heated kiss that echoes our shared desire. I savor her taste and the feel of her body pressed against mine. The way she responds to me, her fingers digging into my back, sends a wave of pleasure coursing through me.

But I need more.

"I need you naked now," I manage, my voice dark with desire.

She drags her teeth across her bottom lip as we both immediately peel off our clothes, which soon join the floor, forgotten.

I draw her nearer, my hands roaming her body, mapping the curves I've become so familiar with. I hoist her lithe frame and pin her against the wall in one swift move. Then I lift her higher so her pussy is level with my mouth. A gasp escapes her lips as she shuffles her weight against the wall and her legs over my shoulders.

I take a big inhalation of her scent. "You have the most delicious pussy I've ever seen," I say and swipe my tongue over her rosy clit.

"Oh God." She gasps, her hand clenching in my hair as I focus my attention on her, my tongue maintaining a relentless rhythm. Her legs close around my head, trapping me in the sweet prison of her pleasure.

Her fingers tighten, then she's coming undone, her body trembling, every fiber alight with the aftershocks of her orgasm.

I lower her until her face is level with mine. "Kiss me and taste yourself on my tongue."

She's so aroused by my words her lips crash on mine as she moans in my mouth breathlessly.

Eventually, we pull apart, and I turn her around so her breasts are pushed up against the wall. "You make me so fucking hard, Isabella." She's hot and breathless again as my erection digs into her back. Her legs part wide for me, and I don't hesitate to sink myself into her.

I inch my cock out of her wet pussy and thrust into her again with a determination to bury myself within her. She looks over her shoulder, her gaze locked on me.

"You like me fucking you, don't you, baby?" I roll my hips, sinking deeper, harder, fully inside her.

Her eyes remain locked with mine. "Yes. Oh, yes," she echoes breathlessly.

"I want to fuck this greedy pussy harder," I tell her, her lips meeting mine in a kiss brimming with desire. Wet, breathless, our bodies radiating heat.

"Yes." She grinds against me, taking all I offer as we rise together. A wave of heat courses down my back.

"Fuck, Isabella," I growl out, thrusting harder. I'm not going to last much longer. She's got this spell over me like she's taken control of every bit of me.

Her moans get louder, then she's there, throwing her head back and coming apart. Feeling her pulse around my cock sends me over the edge, and I finish, lost in her.

She turns around, and my forehead rests against her. I'm left breathless, hot, my heart pounding.

"Is it always that good?" she asks. "With all your other women?"

Her question catches me off guard. She's never once asked about the other women in my life. The casual encounters, the one-night stands. They all pale in comparison.

I lift my head from hers, trying to decipher the look in her eyes. I see fear.

Fear of falling. Fear of making this temporary marriage real.

"Nothing compares, my love." I give her a long lingering

stare and hope she believes the truth of the words that escape my mouth. I place a palm on her cheek, guiding her to face me, her gaze unyielding. "You are my wife, Isabella. You're the only one who matters."

The sincerity in my voice fills the silence between us, and she swallows before pulling me into a long, passionate kiss that leaves me breathless.

The piercing ring of my phone interrupts our moment. Regretfully, I reach over, but a smile breaks across my face when I see my sister's name flash on the screen.

"Victoria," I greet, my hand absently caressing Isabella's cheek. She gazes up at me, her eyes tender.

"Where is everyone?" she asks.

"We're here in our suite. Are you here?

"Yes, I'm here! I'm waiting at the restaurant! Get your asses down here."

I let out a chuckle. "All right, we'll see you shortly." I hang up and turn back to Isabella, who is studying me.

"Is Victoria here?" she questions, her tone surprisingly cheerful, considering she's never met her.

"Yes, she's waiting rather impatiently in the restaurant," I reply. She gives a gleeful smile, which puzzles me even more. "What?"

"Since Rosie set up the group chat, we chat occasionally."

"Is that so?" I tease, my heart swelling at the thought of my sister and wife bonding.

"Well, I am your wife. Guess she wants to know me better," she shoots back, her grin oozing charm.

"Yes, you are, *amore mio,*" I reply, my eyes drinking in her nakedness. "But if you continue looking at me like that, I promise you will be late."

"Like what?" she teases, her eyes sparking with

mischief. I lean in and kiss her passionately, feeling my arousal grow.

She pulls away, giggling. "We have the whole weekend," she reminds me. "We should get changed and go to the restaurant."

Reluctantly, I agree, and we quickly get dressed. I can't help but wish we could spend the entire weekend alone in this room without the distraction of family.

The thought of my father's presence particularly dampens my mood.

Walking around our bungalow, I take Isabella's hand in mine, making our way through the luscious grounds. Public displays of affection aren't usually my style, but I can't pretend anymore. Taking her in, I'm hit by just how stunning she is.

Her soft pink dress ends at her knees, setting off her glowing skin. And her hair is like a river of silk cascading down. And her scent is carried on the breeze, hitting me in a wave that's downright intoxicating.

"You're so damn beautiful," I whisper into her ear as we walk through the busy foyer. Her smile makes me feel like the only man in the world.

As we enter the restaurant, the waiter greets us. "*Bonasera,* Mr. and Mrs. Slater. Can I show you to your table?"

"Thank you," I respond, squeezing Isabella's hand.

I catch sight of my father staring at us as we approach our table. And just like that, my heart drops, a sense of dread washing over me as I prepare for the dinner ahead.

28

ISABELLA

The restaurant bustles around us as we navigate through the lively venue. The aromas of authentic Italian cuisine and the warm, rustic decor create a cozy atmosphere. Still, I can't help but notice how captivating Julius is.

His black polo shirt and chinos perfectly accentuate his athletic build. His hair, tousled from our recent intimacy, gives him an irresistible charm.

Then amidst the crowd, Victoria comes into view. I'm instantly drawn to Vicky's radiant aura. She's petite yet packed with a contagious energy that fills the room.

I pull her into a tight hug. "I'm so happy to finally meet you," I exclaim, my voice brimming with unspoken emotions.

Her face lights up, reflecting my joy. "I've been looking forward to seeing you too, Isabella."

Pulling her in even closer, I let out a hushed whisper, "I'm relieved that everything turned out fine after what happened."

She quickly interjects, dismissing my concerns with an

upbeat tone. "Everything worked itself out in the end. All's well."

There's a hint of something unsaid in her voice that stirs my curiosity, but I decide it's not the right time to delve into it.

Julius, not to be left out, feigns offense at the order of our greetings. "Hold on, you greet my wife before me?"

His playful protest draws a chuckle from us, and Victoria doesn't miss a beat, "Come over here, brother." She invites him into an affectionate hug. "I didn't see you all that long ago, brother," she reminds him, her tone casual despite the grave incident she's referring to.

Tatianna greets us with a genuine warmth that contrasts sharply with her husband's frigid demeanor. Her smile softens the tension in the room somewhat, but I can't help feeling disappointed by the lack of enthusiasm from Julius's father. There's an undercurrent of detachment, a certain emotional distance in how Mr. Slater treats his son, and it's heartbreaking. His father's frosty behavior is unjustified, and I wish he would be more supportive and fatherly.

I place my hand back inside my husband's and give it a gentle squeeze. He peers back at me and smiles. It's a smile reserved just for me, his wife. When I return my attention to the table, Mrs. Slater subtly glances and smiles up at me. My gesture, it seems, speaks volumes.

Julius and I exchange pleasantries with Rosie and Vincent, and there is definitely a glow about Rosie. "You're looking extra radiant," I say to her, quietly chuckling.

She lets out a slip of laughter. "The post-orgasm glow? The one you have, you mean?" I bubble with laughter, and we both share a knowing look.

An assortment of appetizing Italian dishes is brought to

the table as the waiter announces each meal. *"Melanzane alla Sarda."*

"English, please," Mr. Slater cuts in a crass voice.

The waiter looks down at him. "Sorry, of course, sir. Eggplant, Sardinian style, baked scampi with parsley and garlic butter, whitebait fritters, zucchini flowers filled with ricotta, and carpaccio of swordfish. Enjoy."

"I'm practically drooling," Rosie admits, gazing at the feast spread before us. The waiter offers us a smile before stepping away, and Julius reaches to pull out my chair.

"No, she's with us," Rosie interrupts, gesturing to the spot between her and Victoria.

"I'm over there, apparently," I say, flashing a smile at Julius.

His eyes meet mine, and he grins back. "Of course you are," he teases, giving my hand a brief, reassuring squeeze before letting it go.

Julius sits beside Victoria and Vincent, and as starters give way to the main course, he maintains a cheerful exterior, despite his father's silent scrutiny.

There is a commotion as a waiter drops his tray and awkwardly bounces off the rugged, tattooed hulk of a man who has been standing a few meters from our table all evening. Suddenly, it clicks.

"Is that—"

"Oh yes, ma'am. That's Victoria's new bodyguard, Kingsley," Rosie chimes in, following my line of sight.

Victoria rolls her eyes, visibly irritated. "Fucking nuisance, he is."

"This is the bodyguard you've been talking about? I question, taken aback at his size and rugged muscular build.

"Yes. He's all six-foot-six of tedious, overbearing ridiculousness my brothers insist I have," Victoria explains with a grimace.

"Well, it could be worse," I suggest, trying to lighten the mood.

"Hardly," Victoria retorts, not sharing my optimism.

"Give it time. It's still new. Maybe Kingsley will grow on you," I suggest, turning to Rosie, and we share a mischievous grin.

"Like my brother is growing on you?" Victoria shoots back teasingly, and I burst into laughter, unable to deny her claim.

"Come on, it's so obvious this isn't purely a marriage of convenience anymore," Rosie adds, her eyebrows raised in amusement.

"Maybe. I don't know. We still have an expiration date on our nuptials," I add, but even I can't ignore the way I've fallen for him.

Rosie gazes at us, her eyes sparkling with mischief. "Expiration dates can be changed. I bet you two can't keep your hands off each other."

A blush creeps onto my face as I try to negate my pounding heart at the image of him throwing me against the wall and spilling into me with ecstasy., "He's my husband," I offer with a sly grin.

"Oh, I bet he is, girlfriend." Rosie giggles, her laughter infectious.

Victoria, however, rolls her eyes at us, dramatically groaning. "Okay, stop. I do not need to know about you two and my brothers. It's kinda gross. But I do love you both like sisters, you know."

We both nod, sensing the loneliness that lingers in her words. "We're both here for you, Victoria. If you ever wanted to talk about... you know," Rosie offers, referring to her kidnapping ordeal.

"Yes, we both are, anytime. It must get so lonely touring."

"I'm fine," she says, straightening. "But yes, it does get very lonely touring."

Her gaze drifts back to her bodyguard before adding, "Thank you both."

As we lounge around the dinner table, our bellies full and hearts content, the conversation shifts to tomorrow's big event—the engagement party. Our silverware clinks against the dessert plates, scooping up the scrumptious tiramisu as Rosie starts outlining her plans.

My worries melt away in the comforting presence of this family, of Julius's subtle smiles and glances my way when he doesn't think I'm looking. I notice how he has discreetly maintained a distance from his father throughout the evening, yet he seems more relaxed than before, more at peace.

We've shuffled seats for dessert, and Julius is beside me now, his fingers intertwining with mine underneath the table, and I can't help but smile, realizing that I am exactly where I want to be.

"The engagement party will start at seven tomorrow night and will be held in the Amore restaurant upstairs. It's going to be amazing," Rosie blurts out, her eyes lit up with excitement as she looks over at her fiancé.

"Cannot wait, my dear," Tatianna says, smiling.

"So, what shall we do tomorrow during the day?" Victoria asks. "It's not often I get time off, so I want to make the most of it."

Rosie turns to both Victoria and me. "Well, us girls are

going shopping, and then we have appointments to get our hair and makeup done. I've arranged it all."

Victoria and I exchange excited glances while the men across the table share bemused smiles. "And what about you guys?" I ask, chuckling as I imagine them following us around the boutiques.

Vincent grins at Rosie, wrapping an arm around her, "Don't you worry about us. We'll be just fine."

Julius's voice rises above the laughter and chatter, drawing the table's attention. "I'd like to spend the morning with my wife," he asserts, his eyes meeting mine. My heart flutters in response, an unexpected thrill coursing through me at his proclamation.

"Fine, you can have her till eleven," Rosie declares.

"Caleb and Harry are flying in tomorrow. After you spend the morning with your wife, you can join us for a game of billiards," Vincent says, staring at Julius with a wicked smile.

I turn to my husband, recalling names I've seen in his diary over the years. "Your friends?"

He nods warmly. "Yes."

"And, no getting up to mischief, I hope," Rosie quips.

"You're my only mischief," Vincent retorts, drawing his fiancée close for a kiss.

"Hard to believe my boys turned out this way," Mr. Slater finally pipes up, his words laced with a barely concealed disdain, shocking us all, given his silent presence throughout dinner.

"Isn't it lovely?" Mrs. Slater swiftly retorts, gently tapping her husband's arm.

"So lovely it makes me want to puke," Victoria jests, and the table bursts into laughter.

Julius, however, remains silent, his eyes trained on his

father. "What would you prefer, *Father?* That we remain miserable like you?" he challenges.

Mr. Slater straightens. "I am not miserable," he snaps back.

"Then why wouldn't you want us to be happy?" Julius shoots back.

"Enough. Let's go get a drink, Julius." Vincent promptly stands before their father can respond.

I squeeze Julius's leg, encouraging him. "Go," I echo, and he complies. As he moves away, I notice the silent exchange between Victoria and her mother and the tension in her father's jaw.

"Father, why can't you just be happy for Julius and Vin? They're the happiest I've ever seen them," Victoria declares.

Mr. Slater remains silent, downing his coffee while his wife looks at him disapprovingly. "Don't spoil their happiness," she scolds.

He snorts, "Happiness? You call Julius's marriage happiness? He's been caught up in a scandal. He only did this because he had to, or he'd lose his company."

I feel the sting of his words. The reality of what I feel comes crashing down in an instant. I inhale sharply, and Rosie grabs my hand from underneath the table. She gives it a gentle squeeze, and I relish the support from the blinding slap of his words.

Victoria retorts, "Clearly, this is not just a marriage of convenience. Isabella is the best thing that ever happened to Julius. Let me remind you, Father, this scandal only came about after we all discovered your involvement in our brother's murder."

"Victoria!" Tatianna's eyes widen. Then suddenly, all eyes are on me like it's some state secret Victoria just revealed.

"I, uh... Julius told me," I admit.

Mr. Slater lets out an audible groan. "Of course, he fucking did."

"Edward!!" Tatianna scolds her husband.

"Rosie is the best thing for Vincent, and Isabella and Julius's marriage... well, that seems to be thriving. The circumstances of their meeting don't matter. What matters is what makes my brothers happy. And these women beside me make them happy, Father."

Tatianna looks at both Rosie and me and nods in agreement. "I've never seen my sons happier," she asserts, staring at her husband with disdain.

Mr. Slater stands to leave. His abrupt departure effectively squashes any hopes of a father-son reunion during the day tomorrow. Victoria rolls her eyes in response while her mother tries to hold herself together. The realization of being the true outsider here settles in.

"Find that once-in-a-lifetime love and hold on to it," Tatianna murmurs.

"I guess that's not Dad, huh?" Victoria comments.

"No, it's not," her mother confirms, a note of regret in her voice. "We care for each other, but it's never been that intense connection, that spark..."

And just as her words hang in the air, the boys return. "Thank fuck he's gone," Julius declares tersely.

"Julius," his mother admonishes. "He may not be the best father, but he *is* still your father."

"Appreciate the reminder," Julius shoots back, a hint of irritation in his tone.

"Let's not allow this to spoil our evening or the weekend to come," she implores, gently steering the conversation back toward the upcoming celebrations. She shares a warm smile with Rosie and me, a silent gesture of support that eases some tension.

As Rosie's gaze meets mine, there's a flicker of shared understanding—we're the intruders here, despite our integral roles in the brothers' lives. It seems the bonds of matrimony don't immediately grant us family status, at least not in the eyes of Mr. Slater.

29
JULIUS

Isabella's lips press against mine, her arms winding around my neck as we savor our last few moments together. My hand gently traces down her back, my grip tightening slightly as I pull her closer. The taste and feel of her against me is intoxicating, making it all the harder to let go.

"Mr. Slater…" she breathes against my lips, a playful edge to her tone, "… if you do not let me go, I may never leave." I chuckle at her words, pressing one last lingering kiss to her lips before reluctantly pulling away.

We share a quiet, intimate smile, our foreheads resting together. It's a small moment of respite amidst the hustle and bustle of family affairs.

The thought of the day apart already feels like an eternity, but duty calls.

Soon, we find ourselves standing before the elevator, waiting for the doors to slide open. The silence between us is comfortable, full of unspoken words and feelings that we are both still navigating through.

As the elevator dings, the doors opening to an empty

car, I usher her inside, my hand resting lightly on the small of her back. Stepping inside, she turns back to face me, her eyes sparkling with a hint of mischief.

Caught in the moment, I press the 'hold' button to delay the elevator taking Isabella to meet the girls. In the privacy of the temporary seclusion, I pull her into my arms, dipping her slightly as I cover her lips with mine. She giggles against my mouth, her hands coming to rest on my shoulders.

We stay like this, caught in our little world until the elevator's warning ping reminds us of reality. Straightening, I press the button to release the hold, shooting her a regretful smile.

As the doors close, I squeeze her hand, whispering, "I'll see you tonight, Mrs. Slater."

The yacht, a sleek and opulent forty-foot vessel, glides effortlessly through the azure waters of the Mediterranean. Its white exterior sparkles under the sun, reflecting off the water to create a mesmerizing effect. The name 'La Dolce Vita' shimmers in gold lettering. The deck is teak, polished to a high shine, and adorned with plush lounge chairs. It's a perfect spot for sunbathing and enjoying the breathtaking views of the sea. A gleaming staircase leads down into the main cabin area, a sanctuary of opulent indulgence.

Rich mahogany panels line the walls, accentuating the nautical theme. Comfortable leather couches, a fully stocked bar, and a state-of-the-art entertainment system fill the common area. The bedrooms are akin to suites at a five-star hotel, each with private bathrooms boasting marble countertops and gold fixtures.

The yacht also has a fully-equipped kitchen, ready to serve any culinary desire and a spacious dining area set with crystal glasses and fine china. Above deck, toward the stern, is an open-air dining area, complete with a grill and bar.

Vincent stands at the helm, a broad smile plastered on his face as he steers the yacht through the water. Rosie secretly organized this surprise, and Vincent clearly swoons over his gift. I'm momentarily distracted by the constant emails on my phone, but none of them are from Gavin, my VP of Acquisitions, on my latest and most important deal.

Vincent's voice snaps me from my digital obsession. "Hey, drop the phone."

I glance up, taken aback by his sudden interjection. "Excuse me?"

He laughs, brandishing a fishing rod in my direction. "The phone. Lose it. You're on a yacht in the middle of the Mediterranean, not in the office."

I look dubiously from the rod in his hand to his face. "Fishing? Are you drunk?"

His grin widens. "Yes, fishing. A little old-school inter-action with nature. Hands-on, away from all that technology."

My skepticism remains. "Fishing. You want me to fucking fish?"

His enthusiasm is contagious despite my reservations. "Absolutely. Put down the phone and pick up a rod. Let's see if we can't catch our lunch."

With a deep chuckle, I finally place the phone down. He's right. I'm waiting for news. I can't do anything else right now.

"All right, Vin, only because I feel like a laugh."

"You will be eating your words!" He hands me a rod,

excitement dancing in his eyes. "Now, I've got no idea what we're doing, but how hard can it be?"

I hold the fishing rod, a sense of complete foreignness washing over me. We are two businessmen, about as far from seasoned fishermen as possible. We deal with contracts and board meetings, not hooks and bait. Yet, there is a charming absurdity to it all that makes me laugh.

Vincent starts fumbling with his own fishing line, and I follow suit, equally clueless. We cast the lines with all the grace of a pair of flamingos on ice skates, our clumsy movements earning us a chuckle from the crew and ourselves.

We've caught zero fish, and now I'm hungry for lunch, the Sardinia sun beating down on us.

"One more." Vincent casts out again, and the line comes back, nearly hitting him. "Fuck's sake," he says, swerving to miss it.

"Shit! Don't fucking die on me. Rosie would murder me if you didn't show up tonight."

Vincent chuckles. "Yeah, you and me both." He recasts, and this time it lands in the water.

"Did you always think Rosie would turn into love?" My question comes as he's trying to control the fishing line.

He lets out a bark of laughter. "More like hate. I couldn't stand her at first. When she threw that drink on me, I was fuming." He stares out to sea at the memory. "But then, over time, hate morphed into love. She made me feel a range of emotions I never knew I had. I'd closed myself off to anything until she came along and opened the door for me. And now, I couldn't imagine life without her."

His words reverberate through me, and my body visibly

reacts. He turns and stares at me pointedly. "I suspect you and Isabella are much the same."

As I return his stare, the realization hits me. "There is nothing that I wouldn't do for her."

He slaps me on the shoulders. "I knew it. Actually, I didn't. Rosie knew it. She suspected things were more when we had you both over for dinner."

"Is that so?" I laugh. "She's been through so much with her ex-husband and now with a custody issue with Fox, and all while this was going on, she was working for me, and I knew nothing of what she was going through."

"But that's because you have clear boundaries between business and personal life."

"I did," I say, remorse hitting me. Perhaps she would have been safer if I had shoved my strict code of conduct out the window.

He stares over at me.

"I know Isabella told you about Travis."

"She swore me to secrecy, brother," Vincent replies, a hint of protectiveness lacing his tone.

"I know."

"I confronted her the day I saw her bruise. That was when the idea of an arrangement came to me. It made sense. I knew she would be safe with you and would benefit from this arrangement, which would help her gain full custody of Fox. And by agreeing to marry her, you wouldn't get fired from the company you've built your life upon."

The truth of his words sinks in. I confess, "I think I was a coward because I knew all along something wasn't right. I would notice a few bruises crop up over the years, but my strict professionalism didn't allow me to ask her about it. I thought I'd be crossing the line. And I know that sounds so stupid to now even say it aloud, but this company means everything to me. Or it meant everything to me. I don't think I'm blinded by that anymore, by that crazy ambition."

He probes, "So things are working out perfectly then?"

"Isabella has made me want to be a better person. A better man... for her *and* Fox. I'm reading him a bedtime story and kissing his little forehead goodnight. Is it strange to think that they're my family now?"

"No, brother, it's not strange. It's wonderful," Vincent affirms, smiling. His words leave me wondering if I can be the man she needs me to be or if I will turn into my father —an adulterous, absent father.

She deserves more than that.

She deserves the world.

"What is it?" Vincent asks, noticing my withdrawal. I can't tell him my fears of abandonment. He wouldn't understand. He and Dad, their relationship isn't great either, but at least it's more than what we have.

Vincent was next in line, not me. He wasn't as abandoned as I was when my brother died. Ever since he discovered Dad's involvement, they have been estranged. Yet that was a recent occurrence. Mine has been brewing over the years.

I dismiss his concern. "It's nothing," I tell my brother.

"Holy hell, what on earth?" Vincent's eyes nearly pop out of his skull as he gazes at his wildly quivering fishing line. "What am I meant to do with this beast?"

"Pull, Vincent, pull!" I command him, laughter bubbling up uncontrollably from within me. Vincent looks like he's trying to wrestle a greased pig as he battles with the furious thrashing at the end of his line, stumbling up from his chair in the process.

"Jesus, is this a megalodon or what?" Vincent huffs, his voice laced with disbelief and amusement.

I rush to his side, trying to add my strength to his. But whatever marine creature we've hooked, it fights back with the tenacity of an enraged bull. The rod feels heavier than a lead pipe in our hands.

"Damn, this thing is titanic!" I puff, straining against the rod. We catch a glimpse of a shadowy figure growing nearer in the crystal-clear Mediterranean waters, and it appears monstrously large.

"It's gargantuan," I exclaim, my voice echoing over the open sea.

Vincent grunts through clenched teeth. But in a sudden, unexpected tug-of-war loss, the line yanks back fiercely, flinging us onto the polished deck of the boat.

"Vin, your elbow is in my ribcage!" I manage to wheeze out, squirming out from under him. Laughter erupts from both of us, ringing out into the sea air.

"What do these Italian fish eat?!" I gasp, sitting up and rubbing the small of my back.

"I have no idea. All I know is if Slater Corp. tanks, we better stick to business consultancy because our fishing careers would sink faster than the Titanic," Vincent jokes as we both laugh.

"Where's the help when you need it?" Vincent asks, looking around.

"Laughing at us, brother. I know that for sure."

Just as our laughter begins to subside, the distant hum of a speedboat motor fills the air. Our buddies, Caleb and Harry, are heading our way, surely to add more hilarity to our hopeless fishing attempts.

As the speedboat docks alongside our yacht, they both jump on board, greeting everyone with bear hugs and cheers.

The four of us sit around a table on the deck of the

boat, the salty sea breeze mixing with the aroma of a Mediterranean feast laid out. There's an undercurrent of banter and laughter as we indulge in our lunch of fresh seafood, olives, and the best local cheeses and fruits. The sunlight flickers on our glasses filled with a light, crisp white wine.

"Taken man now, eh, Vincent?" Harry teases as he takes a sip from his glass.

Vincent grins, shrugging nonchalantly. "Off the market."

Then, unexpectedly, the spotlight turns to me. Harry, with his perpetual cheeky grin, doesn't miss a beat. "Speaking of taken men, Julius, I bumped into a certain supermodel at a party recently. She was rather disappointed to hear about your shotgun wedding. Seems you've dashed many a hope."

The laughter around the table continues, but I sense an undertone that wasn't there before. Caleb, ever the astute observer, leans in. "Well, considering the circumstances, I reckon it won't be long before you're back in the game, Julius."

His words hang in the air like a misplaced note in a melody. A marriage of convenience, that's what everyone thinks of my union with Isabella. I can't help but bristle at the casual dismissal of my commitment.

"Wait, what?" Harry looks genuinely taken aback, his eyes widening in surprise. "Don't tell me you're falling for the single mom?"

I shift uncomfortably in my seat at his words. "Don't talk about Isabella like that," I warn, my voice low, yet it carries a tone of severity.

They all look at me, their expressions shifting from surprise to dawning comprehension.

"You are?" Caleb ventures after a moment, his voice barely more than a whisper.

Harry's eyes widen as he takes in my silent affirmation, his fork clattering onto his plate. "What the actual fuck?" he sputters out, his shocked exclamation hanging in the air like tangible proof of my confession.

"She's not perfect, but she's my kind of perfect," I concede, downing an oyster with a swift swallow.

Harry looks at Caleb, smirking. "Just you and me now. Our dicks are free agents."

Caleb retorts smoothly, "Free to Carlena Robinson, who just happened to savor mine midflight."

I recoil, nearly choking on my oyster. "What the fuck?" I sputter, taken aback by his casual name-drop of the Hollywood star who, apparently, had quite the enticing run-in with my shameless buddy.

"She hitched a flight with me. She was going to Milan for a film premiere. Things just... worked out, you know?"

Caleb grimaces. "Not exactly. I had to hear you two. Private planes are one thing, but you'd think they could soundproof the bedroom from the cabin?"

"Or the cabin from the bedroom," Harry shoots back, grinning widely.

Caleb gives him a look of mock surprise. "Please, I know you fucked Brianna. I recognized the sound of her moans."

"You two are animals," Vincent interjects, taking a sip from his Evian.

"Fucking manwhores!" I chime in.

"You just miss it," Caleb fires back at me.

"On the contrary, I don't miss it one bit," I retort, smirking in defiance.

"But how long do you have left of your marriage term?"

Harry asks, lowering his polarized sunglasses down his nose.

"I'm not keeping track anymore." And that's mainly the truth. It's something looming that, in my eyes, doesn't matter now.

"So what's next then?" Harry probes further.

"We haven't exactly discussed the future. We are happy with the arrangement we are in now," I admit, my voice dropping to a murmur.

"She has a kid. Women like that need plans. They need to know what the future holds," Harry insists, and I glance at Vincent, who nods in agreement.

"He's right. If it's not on your mind, it probably should be."

Caleb adds, his voice certain, "I guarantee you, it's definitely on her mind."

Their words echo in my ears. *Could Isabella imagine a future with me beyond the time stamp of our nuptials?*

"But since your balls are tied up in a vice, tell me, boys, who have you invited to the party tonight?" Harry grins wickedly, changing the topic abruptly.

"Can you keep your dick in your pants for twenty-four hours?" Vincent retorts, rolling his eyes.

30

ISABELLA

Rosie and Vincent's engagement party is a dazzling spectacle. Rosie's absolutely radiant in her golden floor-length gown, and the love-struck way Vincent looks at her is strangely similar to how Julius gazes at me. Fairy lights twinkle against the night sky, creating an enchanting canopy from the sky down to the Mediterranean Sea.

Every flower arrangement, champagne flute, and piece of décor has been meticulously curated while maintaining an intimate, familiar warmth.

After having a drink with Rosie and Vincent, I'm back at Julius's side, his firm and comforting presence like a light-house in a crowd full of friendly strangers and fresh faces. He lifts our entwined fingers and kisses my hand. "Mrs. Slater, you are the most beautiful woman here," he compliments.

I smile up at him, the sincerity in his blue eyes piercing the walls around my heart. It's then I'm reminded of the strange duality of my reality—bound to Julius by the terms of our agreement, yet not in the way Rosie is to Vincent. Our circumstances are as unique as they come with an end date I cannot forget.

When Victoria finally escapes from the throngs of people fangirling her, she spots us over the crowd and bumbles toward us. She looks fucking fabulous. Her auburn hair is set in monstrous Hollywood curls and hovers around her waist. She's wearing a striking red dress that hugs her slim figure.

Close behind her, a towering figure follows—her ever-present bodyguard. His tailored suit does little to hide the bulk of muscle underneath, and his hawk-like gaze never leaves Victoria. He has the air of a silent protector, his watchful eyes scanning the room, taking in every detail, every movement.

"Julius, Isabella! What are you both doing over here alone?" Victoria exclaims, her arms wide open as she reaches us. She envelops us in a warm embrace, her laughter ringing clear and infectious in the buzz of the party.

Stepping back, she nearly topples onto Kingsley. He catches her before her high heels can betray her. Her brows knot in annoyance. "Shit, Kingsley, must you hover so close? It's just a party!" she scolds, rolling her eyes.

Kingsley maintains a poker face. "It's my job, Miss Slater," he responds in his deep baritone voice, his eyes locking onto hers.

Victoria huffs in exasperation, folding her arms over her chest. "See what I have to deal with?" She sighs dramatically, her cheeks flushing from the whole encounter.

Soon enough, two men break away from the crowd,

their matching grins as wide as their confident strides. Both are gorgeous, and I get the feeling, like the Slater brothers, women flock to them. Julius's face lights up as two strapping men walk toward us.

"Oh God. Fabio one and two have arrived. That's my cue to get another drink," Victoria says, spotting the men approaching.

"Who?" I inquire.

"I'll tell you later. Bye!" She leaves as does her shadow.

"Julius!" He shakes both men's hands then his hand slips back into mine comfortably. "Isabella, meet Harry and Caleb," he says, his voice laced with affection. "We boarded together at school."

With his rakish charm and devilish smile, Harry takes my free hand, his eyes shining with mischief. "A pleasure, Isabella. And may I say, you look absolutely enchanting tonight."

"Stop flirting with my wife," Julius says firmly, piercing him with a stare.

He puts his hands up in surrender. "Touchy, Slater, " he admonishes, earning a wry grin from Julius.

"Thank you, Harry. Don't mind my jealous husband," I quip back, earning a surprised chuckle from him. Julius's tantric blue eyes wash over me, and I feel on fire, so wanted and adored in just one glance.

Caleb clears his throat, breaking the moment between us. "Indeed, Isabella. You've certainly managed to outshine us all."

"Why thank you, Caleb," I playfully retort, and their laughter rings out, genuine and warm. I immediately like these guys and see why Julius feels they're family.

"So you all went to boarding school together?" I ask, intrigued about my husband's formative years.

"Sure did. I've known Julius since he was just out of nappies," Caleb adds.

"Why haven't we met until tonight?" I turn to my husband, curiosity piqued.

"Believe me... it's for the best," Julius retorts playfully.

"He's likely right," Harry chimes in with a wink. "We're dreadful influences."

"Don't mind them. We've been in Puerto Rico, Isabella," Caleb interjects, diffusing the playful banter.

"Damn, is that Camilla Pleno?" Harry's voice slices through our chat.

"Who?" Julius asks, and we all trail Harry's gaze.

"The Italian actress with the stunning—"

"Harry, for God's sake," Julius interjects.

Only then does Harry realize I'm present. "Apologies, Isabella."

I chuckle in response.

"I think it's time to save my wife from your disastrous influence," Julius announces and gently tugs me by the arm, steering us toward the heart of the outdoor area while I can't help but burst into laughter.

We arrive at a beautiful black and white checkered floor lit by lights and projections as if we're dancing on water. Julius wraps me in his arms, my hands circling his neck. "They're intolerable," he says playfully.

"They're *your* friends," I retort, "And I can see why you like them."

"Can you remind me? I seem to have forgotten," Julius teases, and I laugh again.

Julius pulls me closer. "Damn, I love hearing you laugh," he murmurs, cradling me, tilting my chin to meet his gaze. "I don't want to be anywhere else in the world right now as long as I'm with you."

His heartfelt words puncture my defenses, seizing my heart. The intensity in his gaze solidifies the moment's reality.

Yet, waves of doubt actively surge through my veins, drowning me in a sea of emotion.

"Um... just... give me a sec," I stammer, pulling free from his hold. With a swift pivot, I melt into the crowd, looking for an escape.

My heart races as I beeline for the elevator, jabbing the button with urgency. As the doors open, I lean against the cold wall, gasping for breath. Just as the doors close, they judder open again, and my eyes fly open. Julius rushes to stand beside me, his face close to mine.

"Julius, go!" I beg, but he only pins me to the wall as the elevator doors shut behind him.

"What is it, Isabella? Tell me," he insists, desperation lacing his voice.

Struggling to express myself, I'm swamped by a rush of emotions and insecurities, years of abuse and self-doubt suffocating my voice.

"What's going on between us, Julius?" I question, the words heavy on my tongue. "Is any of this real, or is it just a performance?" He looks at me, a mix of shock and confusion on his face as if I've physically slapped him. "I'm not sure I can keep up with this," I admit, avoiding his eyes as the elevator rises.

I feel his hand gently lift my chin, guiding my gaze back to his.

"This is real," he breathes out, his forehead pressing against mine. "It's always been real. I just didn't want to admit it," he confesses. "Isabella, I love everything about you. I love you."

His admission catches me off guard, overwhelming me in the most wonderful way. "Why?" I manage to whisper.

"Why?" he echoes. ""Because you complete me, Isabella. You fill the parts of me I didn't even know were empty," he tells me, looking at me with such intensity I can feel the depth of his emotions.

I'm totally swept up in his magic, but then my rational side kicks in. "There's more than just me you've got to love."

"Nado? He's closer to my heart than you could possibly understand."

The echo of his words soothes me, penetrating the walls I've built, kindling a soft warmth that floods through me, melting my defenses from the inside out. "I... I love you too."

His smile is all the answer I need. Our lips meet in a slow, sizzling kiss that sends an exhilarating jolt of electricity coursing through me.

The moment the elevator doors slide open, he scoops me into his strong arms. "What are you doing?" I gasp out in surprise.

"I'm carrying my wife over the threshold," he declares, grinning from ear to ear.

31
JULIUS

Somewhat awestruck, I scoop Isabella up in my arms. She runs her fingers up my neck, staring at me with eyes full of trust and love.

She's light, like a feather, and fits so perfectly against me. I carry her through the bungalow to our bedroom, my heart pounding with anticipation. Once inside, I set her down gently.

The room is quiet, just the muffled sounds of our breaths and the soft rustling of clothes. My fingers brush against the fabric of her dress. It's smooth, slipping off easily as I pull it down.

My breath catches as I take her in. She's beautiful, her body glowing in the soft moonlight.

"You're my wife," I tell her, my voice barely above a whisper. "You... your body... it's all for me."

Her cheeks turn a little red, but she doesn't look away. "I'm yours, Julius."

Hearing her words, I'm unable to resist her any longer. I pull her closer. Our lips meet in a searing kiss, our bodies pressed against each other. I can't get enough of her. The

234

feel of her against me, the taste of her lips, it's all so intoxicating.

I continue to undress her, my heart pounding as she
responds to my touch—the way she shivers slightly, the
soft sounds she makes.

Damn.

She reaches for my shirt, fumbling with the buttons. I
chuckle, her eagerness stoking the fire inside me. I help her,
my fingers quickly undoing the rest of them, and the fabric
slides off my shoulders, falling to the floor in a forgotten
heap.

She runs her fingers over my chest, tracing the defined
lines of my muscles. The feeling sends sparks shooting
down my spine, making me shiver. Her gaze meets mine
again, a challenge gleaming in her eyes.

I quickly kick off my shoes and step out of my pants,
leaving me in my boxers. She giggles, her eyes roving over
me appreciatively. It makes me feel desired, wanted.

"Impatient?" I tease, pulling her closer.

She nods, wrapping her arms around my neck. The
taste of her lips is sweet and intoxicating, and I lose myself
in the sensation.

With the rest of our clothes on the floor, we fall onto the
bed, and the world outside ceases to exist. It's just us here
and now—Isabella's body against mine, her laughter in my
ears, the taste of her on my lips. This moment with her is all
I've ever wanted. The reality is even better than any fantasy
because she's real, she's here, and she's mine.

"Make love to me," she says, pulling me on top of her.
Her voice is breathy, filled with need. "Make love to me,
Julius."

The sound of my name on her lips is sweet, sending
waves of desire coursing through me. I pull her closer,

pressing my forehead against hers. Her fingers trail down my chest, making my heart race.

"You are my fucking world, Isabella." With that affirmation, I lose myself in her and claim her lips in a kiss.

Our kiss turns deeper as we explore each other. Every gasp she makes, every shiver that runs through her body, stokes my desire. I explore her with my lips and fingers, sliding two inside her drenched pussy.

Her hands clutch at my back, her nails digging into my skin as things heat up.

"I need all of you," I whisper as I remove my fingers and climb on top of her, spreading her legs widely, then sink my hard cock inside her.

"Oh God, yes." She moans, and I watch her head tip back in ecstasy.

"Fuck, I could live inside you," I urge out on a moan.

We move together in a rhythm only we understand. Isabella's legs wrap around me, pulling me closer. I kiss her slowly and deeply, conveying my love, desire, and need for her.

The pressure is building within me, every nerve in my body screaming for release. But I hold back, focusing on her and her pleasure.

"Isabella," I whisper against her lips, my voice hoarse with emotion.

She pulls me down, her eyes glossy with emotion as she dusts her lips across mine. Her lips part as she reaches her peak, her body convulsing with waves of pleasure. Seeing her like this, putting all her trust in me and loving me, pushes me over the edge, and I find my release, pouring myself into her completely.

We collapse together, a tangled mess of limbs and sheets, and I pull her closer, wrapping my arms around her.

She snuggles into me, her head resting on my chest, her fingers tracing lazy patterns on my skin.

We lie there in silence. The only sounds are our ragged breaths and the occasional whisper of the sheets. Her heart beats against mine, the rhythm soothing, grounding.

This is what love feels like—overwhelming, intense, all-consuming. It's incredibly wonderful and utterly terrifying at the same time.

A warm hand on my stomach has me opening my eyes. She is staring at me, her eyes warm and wide as she kisses me gently on my lips.

I let out a groan as her hand snakes down my front to my cock..

"I dreamed about you last night and woke up dripping wet," she murmurs, pulling away from our kiss. Her body glides down mine, her fingertips leaving a trail of fire in their wake. When she's level with my already-thickening cock, she grins up at me, her eyes sparkling with mischief.

"Do you want a taste, Isabella?" I ask, my voice rough with desire. I reach down, gently tilting her face upward with a hand at the back of her hair.

She nods, her eyes never leaving mine. Her fingers lightly trace along the length of my cock, causing a shudder to roll down my spine. Then, she wraps her lips around me, her eyes closing in pleasure.

She's all warm and wet. "Fuck, take me in, just like that... such a good girl."

The sensation is intense and overwhelming. I grip her hair tighter, my other hand clutching at the sheets.

"Jesus. Fucking. Christ."

Watching her, seeing the pleasure on her face as she takes me in her mouth, makes me impossibly harder.

I'm on the brink, her movements pushing me close to the edge. But I need more.

I need her.

With a groan, I pull her up, guiding her body over mine.

"Isabella." I pant, my voice filled with desire. "I need to be inside you."

Her eyes meet mine, dark and full of need. She's so goddamn beautiful with her lips around my cock. She understands, her body moving to align with mine. As she sinks onto me, she lets out a strangled moan. Then she rocks back and forth, rubbing herself on my shaft as she moves, in full control.

"Tell me how good that feels, baby." I hold her close, my hands on her hips, guiding her movements.

"Oh God. Yes. So fucking good."

I watch her, my wife, the most beautiful woman I've ever known, riding me with abandon. The sight of her, the feel of her around me, brings me closer and closer to the edge.

And as she cries out, her body clenching around me, I follow her over the edge, our bodies convulsing together in our shared climax.

Finally, we collapse together, spent and satisfied. I pull Isabella closer, her body flush against mine.

As our breathing slowly returns to normal, I kiss her forehead softly, whispering, "I love you."

She smiles, her hand reaching up to stroke my cheek. "I love you more."

~

We eventually make it out of bed and start our day exploring the captivating beauty of Sardinia. Isabella's eyes gleam with excitement as we wander, hand in hand, through the pebbled streets.

The bustling Mercato di San Benedetto is an indoor market the size of a city block with individually run stalls selling meat, cheese, produce, baked goods, and bread, just to name a few.

A local cheese merchant steps forward with a platter of cheese. "*Vuoi provare un po' di formaggio?*" <Want to try some cheese?>

"Thank you," Isabella says, taking a wedge.

Her fingers tighten around mine as she relishes a taste of the local cheese.

"Julius, you need to try this!" She passes the remaining piece to me, and I take a bite.

"Damn, that's good. We'll take the lot." After indulging in all these mouthwatering dishes, I can't help but think about the extra gym sessions I'll need.

Our journey continues toward the marina, where the sea greets us with its endless expanse of blue. Boats bob gently in the water, their white sails painted against the sky. As we watch, Isabella's fingers trace patterns on my hand, her touch as soothing as the gentle waves.

After a sweet interlude with gelato, we venture to Nora's ancient ruins. Isabella's fascination with the past lights up her eyes as she studies the Roman amphitheater. "Can you imagine the stories these stones could tell?" she murmurs, tracing her fingers over the weather-beaten rocks.

Our day culminates on the shimmering beach. As the sun dips low, casting a warm glow on the turquoise water,

Isabella tugs off her shoes and pulls me toward the sea. It's as if she's finally freed herself and found her happiness.

"The water's perfect, Julius!" she calls out over her shoulder, her laughter carrying on the salty sea breeze.

I step into the water, the cool waves a refreshing balm against my dewy skin. I swim toward her and pull her close, the rhythm of the waves echoing in my chest.

"Sardinia is beautiful," she whispers, her gaze on the stunning horizon.

"Not nearly as beautiful as you," I return, kissing her temple gently. I glance at the time, the evening already slipping away from us. "Regrettably, we have dinner with the family," I state, looking back at her.

"I like your family," she admits, then seems to reconsider. "Well, everyone except for one," she amends, drawing a knowing sigh from me.

The warmth of the Sardinian sun is a stark contrast to the cold scene that greets us back at the hotel. In the sprawling lobby is my father, charming a beautiful woman with an all-too-familiar ease. It's a sight I've dreaded, one I've seen replayed countless times. It makes me sick. He can at least have the decency to fuck around without family present.

Isabella's voice pierces through my rising anger. "Julius," she murmurs, her fingers tightening around mine, an understanding in her tone.

Summoning my resolve, I stride over to my father, a hard edge in my voice. "Father."

He looks up, his practiced smile faltering under my icy glare. "Julius. How was your day?"

He attempts to mask his surprise with an insincere question.

Ignoring his attempt to divert the conversation, I cut right to the chase. "What's going on here, Father?"

His response is as dismissive as his demeanor. "Just a friendly chat."

A lump forms in my throat as I think of my mother, likely oblivious, in her bungalow.

I force my voice to stay steady. "Just like all you other 'friendly chats' throughout my life?" The woman glares at my father as I let the bitterness seep into my voice. "I will never let myself become you."

His confident veneer cracks at my words before recovering swiftly. "We are not magnanimous creatures, son."

The fury surges within me, making my nostrils flare. "Don't you dare call me that," I spit, spinning on my heel and marching away before the urge to strike him again becomes too strong to resist.

As Isabella and I leave the tainted atmosphere of the lobby behind, a chill of dread follows me—the fear of repeating my father's mistakes and betraying Isabella's trust. But as I squeeze her hand, I reinforce my silent vow.

I will never become my father.

I can't.

32

ISABELLA

Sardinia, right now, it's like the backdrop of a dream. We're just walking around the old streets of Cagliari, then laughing our way through the hustle and bustle of the *Mercato di San Benedetto*.

But it's not just about the gorgeous scenery. It's about us. It's about this connection, this *marriage*. It feels so damn real. Being with Julius is like opening my heart up to the sun and learning to trust again. Except this time, it's like nothing I've ever felt before.

It's in the way he looks at me, a silent love letter. The shared glances, the quick hand squeezes. They're simple, sure, but they're ours. It's in the way he holds me, promising a thousand times over to keep me safe. It's in the words he speaks to me, solidifying that promise, making it tangible. He makes me feel like the only woman in the world by showering me with sincerity and love. Julius has penetrated the walls I've built around myself for fear of being hurt again.

As much as I tried to think this was just an arrangement, I know in my heart it is not. It's so much more, and

Julius has awakened in me a love so deep, so protective, it's coursing through my veins, pounding with each beat of my heart.

When he stood up to his father in the hotel lobby, my heart practically bursts with love. Julius, my protector, standing firm, defending us.

As he promises never to become like his father, I see his commitment—a man willing to protect us against any odds. There's no point hiding how we feel about one another. We're both all in, and although I'm still terrified that one day he'll wake up and realize I'm not from his world, I'm pushing that fear to the farthest part of my mind.

Julius is holed up in the study, attending to an urgent matter before dinner. I find myself with some free time and decide to check in on Fox.

Travis picks up the phone after just a single ring. His voice comes over the line, smug and self-satisfied. "Well, well, if it isn't my slutty ex dialing in from her European vacation."

His words hit me like a freight train, as they always do. Except this time, I steady myself and stand a little taller.

"Put my son on the phone," I demand, doing my best to push away his hurtful words.

"Our son," he corrects, the possessive pronoun a stab reminding me of the violent circumstances of Fox's conception. My eyes momentarily close as the image of him violating me enters my mind.

"Put him on the phone now," I demand, this time louder and more authoritative in my tone.

He laughs, shocked by my confidence. "Oh, I will. But just you wait. You wait for what's coming to you. You're nothing. Sooner or later, Julius will see you for who you are."

I take a steady breath. "So help me God, Travis, put my son on the phone or—"

"Fox, come in here!" Travis yells, cutting me off before I finish. Then, amidst the chaos, a sound washes over me, healing and grounding.

"Momma!" he calls.

"Sweetheart. How are you?" I ask, trying to keep the tremble out of my voice.

"I miss you, Momma," Fox says, his voice so innocent and sweet.

"Oh, darling, I miss you too," I reply, swallowing back tears.

I hear Travis's voice in the background, snarling at our son. "Ungrateful little shit!"

"No, Dad, I like it here too," Fox replies. My boy is so smart for his age. When he should be a four-year-old, he knows when to placate his father to avoid triggering his explosive temper.

"When are you coming home, Mommy?" It's hard to ignore the plea of an undertone in his voice. He never likes spending time with his father.

"Tomorrow, sweetheart. I can't wait to give you the biggest hug and kiss you from head to toe!"

"Me too, Mommy."

"Hey, kiddo, I got you something while I was out today," I say, glancing at the gift I've picked from a local store.

"What is it?" Fox asks, his voice filled with childlike excitement.

"It's a surprise," I tell him, giggling into the phone.

"I love surprises," Fox exclaims, his excitement contagious.

"Your dad will drop you off at daycare in the morning, and I'll pick you up. I can't wait to see you," I promise him.

"Does Jules miss me too?" Fox asks, his voice hopeful. His question melts my heart. I just want him to be loved and have a stable father figure in his life, unlike the tumultuous relationship he has witnessed between Travis and me.

"He sure does," I reply, with a knowing nod. Even if Julius hasn't spelled it out, he often talks about Fox. And his name, Nado, has become a pet name now, not just a funny story about that time when Fox splattered ketchup all over his rug.

When Julius finally resurfaces from the office in our suite, I'm dressed and ready for dinner.

"Hey, beautiful," he drawls, sauntering toward me with that confident swagger of his. A satisfied grin dances across his face as he reaches out, cupping my cheek with a tender hand. Then he leans in, pressing a fierce kiss onto my lips.

His kiss pulls me in, and damn, I missed him. He's been wrapped up in work all afternoon. I can't help but wonder if he is purposely keeping me at arm's length? But no, I don't want to push it.

I pull away from the electrifying kiss that's left me all aflutter and look at him. "Everything okay?" I ask.

"Never better." He grins, his eyes dark with mischief. It feels like a little promise of the good things to come.

"Let's go to dinner," he suggests, intertwining his fingers with mine.

～

Our final dinner in Sardinia is a riot. Rosie and Vincent, now engaged, can't stop gushing over the events from the previous night. "Is this real life?" Rosie exclaims. "Feels like I'm still dreaming!"

Vincent reaches out, capturing Rosie's hand and bringing it to his lips for a tender kiss. My eyes dart to Julius as he turns toward me, his gaze mirroring the same profound affection Vincent is showering on Rosie. The sight of it, the depth of love in his eyes, sends the butterflies in my stomach into a wild frenzy.

But then, from across the room, I catch Julius's dad casting us a long, stern look. His face, usually so inscrutable, seems tinged with disdain. It hits me like a splash of cold water.

It's clear he doesn't think we belong together.

As Julius's hand finds mine, I feel a sense of ease wash over me. It doesn't matter what his father thinks. It only matters what Julius and I know.

After we finish dessert, we move on to espresso, the air buzzing with animated conversation, mostly around the wedding.

"A Tuscan vineyard would be perfect," Rosie suggests enthusiastically, her eyes reflecting the dreamy Italian landscape. "Imagine the pictures. We'd be surrounded by rows of grapevines under the Italian sun."

"But don't dismiss the Hamptons too quickly," Victoria chimes in, a playful smile dancing on her lips. "There's something magical about springtime there. The blooming flowers, the ocean breeze, it could be straight out of a fairy tale."

"The wine alone in Tuscany would be worth it," Rosie continues, her eyes lighting up at the thought. "Plus, the rolling hills, the rustic charm... it's the stuff of movies."

"Yes, but the Hamptons is classic elegance. The pristine beaches, the luxury estates, it's like a perfect picture post-card," Victoria counters with a teasing grin.

Then Julius's mother jumps in, her tone light but assertive, "Why not both? A ceremony in Italy and a reception in the Hamptons."

"You can't be serious, Tatianna?" Mr. Slater says in a dismissing tone.

"I think I like that idea," Vincent chimes in, and I'm pretty sure it's just to ruffle his father's feathers.

"I'm on board with it too," Julius concurs, giving my hand a comforting squeeze on his sturdy thigh.

The vibrant chatter comes to an abrupt halt, shattered by a sudden, ear-splitting clatter that jolts everyone's attention. Victoria's body tenses, her eyes quickly darting toward her bodyguard, searching for reassurance. In an instant, his entire demeanor shifts, assuming a protective and alert stance as if instinctively responding to an unseen threat. But within the blink of an eye, they both realize it's nothing more than a dropped dish.

As the cacophony of noise gradually subsides, giving way to the sweet symphony of laughter, I can't help but feel a twinge of sadness for Victoria. Despite the joy and excitement swirling around her, she carries an unwavering sense of vigilance—a hidden shadow that stubbornly clings to her after her ordeal.

It's a feeling I know all too well.

33

JULIUS

The private jet descends, revealing the towering skyscrapers of Manhattan. I can't help but marvel at the incredible woman by my side. *How did I become so fortunate to have Isabella fall for me and care for me?*

Once we land and step off the plane, Rosie quickly corners Isabella, looping arms with her and Victoria, engaging in animated discussions about wedding plans. "Just going to steal your wife for a moment to talk plans," Rosie says with a mischievous grin. Isabella bites her lower lip, and I reluctantly release her hand, my fingers lingering as they unravel.

The excitement radiating from Isabella is infectious, and I find myself determined to do whatever it takes to permanently see that smile on her face.

"Thanks for coming," Vincent says, slapping me on the back.

"I wouldn't miss it," I respond with sincerity. "You and Rosie are perfect together."

He looks at me, raising an eyebrow as we enter the

terminal. "Nearly as perfect as you and Isabella?" he questions, a wholehearted smile gracing his face.

A trace of a smile appears, and my brother nods, seemingly satisfied. "You can thank me later," Vincent adds.

I chuckle deeply, recognizing the truth in his words. The prospect of marrying Isabella initially seemed like the worst idea imaginable.

"And by later, I mean now," Vincent adds pointedly.

I laugh again, genuine gratitude in my voice. "Thank you," I say, my tone reflecting the seriousness of my appreciation.

"Now that we're alone, tell me, is everything ready?" Vincent lowers his voice, and I understand precisely what he's referring to.

I make sure Isabella is out of sight before answering him. "Yes, I got the call last night just before dinner. "Everything was handed over to Detective Tascott at the NYPD yesterday," I confirm.

Ever since Isabella disclosed the truth about her abuse, I've been dedicated to a singular objective—bringing him the fuck down.

As my investigative team delved deeper into his life, an alarming pattern emerged—a series of women had been victims of his non-consensual advances. The realization of the pain he had inflicted upon not only Isabella but more innocent women ignited a burning rage within me, fueling my unwavering determination to bring him down.

Following the money trail, I uncovered a disturbing pattern of payoffs—an insidious attempt to silence those who dared to speak their truth. Travis had wielded his wealth and influence to bury their stories, perpetuating his vile acts and denying them the justice they deserved.

I wanted to investigate him to try and use something for Isabella to claim sole custody of her son. But what we uncovered was much more sinister, and it was clear that justice could no longer be evaded.

"Son of a bitch won't know what hit him," Vincent says, his voice filled with satisfaction.

As Isabella and I ride together, her excitement about picking up Fox from daycare is palpable. I miss the little guy too, and I can't wait to see his reaction when Isabella gives him his gift. Arriving at the daycare, I accompany Isabella to the gate, our hands entwined.

"Do you think he's going to like his present?" Isabella asks, her voice filled with anticipation. I squeeze her hand gently, filled with pride for her thoughtfulness.

"Of course," I reassure her.

As we approach the daycare, I notice the woman at the gate staring at Isabella, her demeanor lacking the warm pleasantries one would expect. It becomes apparent that this place is not up to par, and I make a mental note to find a new daycare or even consider getting a nanny for Fox.

"He's not here," the woman states bluntly, not even bothering with the usual niceties. Isabella's face falls, confusion clouding her features. "You must have gotten your days mixed up because Travis came and got him already," the woman adds, delivering the news without an ounce of sympathy.

A mix of disappointment and concern washes over Isabella, and I tighten my grip on her hand, offering comfort and support.

"He seemed different," the woman at the daycare says, her voice tinged with concern. My brows furrow in confusion as I try to make sense of her words. "What do you mean?" I inquire, my own worry creeping into my voice.

The woman takes a moment before responding, her gaze searching for the right words. "He was angry, very edgy. Fox was crying. He didn't want to go with him," she finally explains.

"And you just handed over my son?" Isabella's voice is laced with concern.

"He threatened to call the police if we didn't."

Isabella's face falls, a mixture of shock and worry crossing her features. Panic begins to rise within me as I grasp the severity of the situation.

"Oh my God," Isabella murmurs. "Why did you let him go with him?" Isabella's voice rises, her frustration evident as she trembles with anger and concern.

"He's his father," the woman replies with a dismissive tone, throwing her hands up in the air as if it's a trivial matter.

My anger simmers beneath the surface as I witness the lackluster response. "Where are your procedures, your check measures?" I interject firmly, my voice resolute. "He may be his father, but he was definitely not scheduled to pick him up today." I watch Isabella move away from the woman and quickly grab her phone from her purse. "Your actions will have consequences," I caution her.

"Travis, where is he?" Isabella's pain pierces her voice, inflicting its cuts on me.

There's a long pause as I watch her worried features morph into horror. He says something to her, and she puts the phone on speaker.

"Julius is here," she says as I clamor around the phone in her hands.

"Where is Fox, Travis?" I demand into the receiver.

"You did this," he says, his voice dripping with venom. Isabella pierces me with a stare that breaks my entire heart.

"You didn't think I'd find out what you were up to?"

"You raped women, Travis. You must be held account- able." I look at Isabella. This is not meant to be happening. The DA's office assured me they would inform me before an arrest was to be made.

"How dare you fucking interfere in my life."

"You will go to jail for what you did to not only Isabella but to the countless other women you paid off. Your time is up, Travis."

Isabella stares at me in disbelief.

"On the contrary, it's just beginning. What, you didn't think I'd find out? You didn't think at least one of the women your team was investigating wouldn't be on my side?"

I find myself in the depths of despair, grappling with an unforeseen turn of events. I never anticipated that Isabel- la's ex-husband would stoop so low as to threaten one of the brave women who had come forward to expose him. Somehow, he managed to manipulate her, breaking through the safeguards I had put in place. I'm left stunned, questioning how he could have possibly reached her and why she succumbed to his pressure.

"Travis, stop this," Isabella pleads, cutting through the back and forth.

"Once you break them down, they can do anything you want, even manipulate them into telling you who is coercing them to come forward."

No, this can't be happening. Who would want to do that after what a monster he was to some of these women?

"Travis, tell me where my son is now." Tears stream down Isabella's face like a river bank overflowed.

He sniggers into the phone. "Far away from you, Bella. I'm taking our son so you never see him again. That is your punishment for ruining my life. "

"Travis," she screams into the phone, but the line goes dead.

Her eyes find mine wide with horror and fear, then she collapses. I barely manage to catch her as she crumbles, her entire weight in my hands. I hold her close as the magnitude of the situation settles in. My mind races, mapping out every possible move we could make, every avenue we could explore.

"Isabella," I say, keeping my voice steady. "Isabella, look at me."

It takes a while, but eventually, she lifts her tear-stained face. Her eyes are wild, shining with fear and pain. I've never seen her so terrified before.

"We will find Fox. I promise you," I reassure her, my voice echoing with a determination I can't afford to lose. "Travis won't get away with this."

I help her to sit down, her legs shaky. She clings to my hand, her grip tightening in a desperate plea for comfort.

"Dial 911," I instruct the woman who's now fearing for her job.

Isabella moves to finally stand, and her face morphs into anger. "How could you have done this, Julius? My son is missing. I can never forgive you for this."

Her painful glare renders me speechless as the realization of my careless actions dawns upon me. She put her trust in me, and I shattered it.

She picks up her phone off the floor and makes a call as my mind churns with possibilities. I couldn't have foreseen this twist or predicted that Travis would stoop this low. But now that it's happened, I have to face the harsh reality. He had the means, the motive, and, more importantly, he had Fox.

34

ISABELLA

W e've scoured the city, the police are relentless, but my son, my Fox, is still missing. His name echoes across media outlets. Every update is a sharp stab to my heart, but there's still no sight of him. I'm drowning in despair, unsure of how I'm managing to keep it together.

Rosie, Harley, and Victoria keep me grounded at home after the police send me back. They give me tasks to focus on, to distract me from the unbearable reality. Vincent and Julius are at police headquarters, immersed in intense discussions with their investigative teams. They relay updates every half an hour, working with the police to piece together the puzzle that has become my life.

Despite their combined efforts, the outcome remains unchanged. Fox isn't here. He's not safe at home where he belongs.

The world around me buzzes with activity, the news playing in the background, conversations ebbing and flowing. I block out the noise, retreating into my mind.

Where would he have taken him?

His car was last seen heading north on the highway.

Fox, my sweet little boy. The image of his terrified face sitting in the passenger seat next to Travis sends a shiver down my spine. I tremble at the thought of what Travis could possibly do to our son out of revenge. Revenge for me, for what Julius did.

Julius. *How am I to forgive him for hiding this from me?* Even if he meant well, I can't bring myself to look at him. The hurt in his eyes pales compared to the anguish tearing me apart from losing my son.

"Here, drink this," Victoria suggests, holding out a steaming mug. The aroma of coffee wafts from it, instantly nauseating me.

"I can't," I confess, pushing the mug away gently. The scent of the brew churns my stomach, stirring up the rising bile in my throat. It's a sensation of revulsion I've never felt for coffee before, but everything is different now. The world starkly contrasts with what it used to be only hours ago.

"Maybe some water, then?" Victoria offers, her eyes fill with worry. Despite my despair, I manage a small nod.

Somehow, water seems bearable.

Victoria returns with Rosie, who has her phone to her ear, an unreadable expression on her face.

"They spotted him," Victoria blurts out, her eyes filled with a mix of hope and concern. "Camera recognition software near Maine."

"Maine?" Why Maine? I search my memory, ransacking every conversation, every memory for a hint, but come up empty. *Why would Travis go there?*

"Julius wants to talk to you," Rosie adds, handing me her phone. I take it with trembling hands, pressing it to my ear.

"Isabella," Julius's voice is low, filled with urgency.

"He's been spotted on the I95 leaving a gas station in Waterville near Maine. It looks like he is fleeing the country to Canada. The jet's being refueled as we speak. Meet me at the airport."

My heart pounds in my chest. A lead. It's not much, but it's something. It's hope.

"Okay," I say, my voice shaky. "I'll be there."

I hear the line go dead and see Rosie has gathered my things.

"I'm coming too," Victoria interjects, her determined voice breaking through my conversation.

"We all are," Harley says.

"We're all in this together," Rosie says, taking my hand in hers as we wait for the elevator doors to open.

I don't waste time disputing. There isn't any to spare. With a knot in my stomach, we set off to Maine to bring my son back.

35

JULIUS

I failed her.

I failed Fox.

Despite my best efforts and all my careful planning, he has unveiled my involvement in bringing him down. The truth remains that these women have suffered, subjected to Travis's heinous acts of rape and assault, with the majority enduring the horrors during his marriage to Isabella.

It sickens me to the core.

But now, the consequences of my actions have come crashing down upon us. Fox is missing, kidnapped by his father as a twisted act of revenge.

I am consumed by guilt, knowing that my attempts to seek justice have led to this unthinkable outcome.

The two people most important to me, and I failed to anticipate the lengths he would go to protect himself and the innocent lives he would put at risk. My heart is heavy with regret and sorrow as I understand that my actions have inadvertently caused more pain and suffering for the ones I vowed to protect.

I've tried talking to her, but how she looks at me is like a knife twisting in my gut. We're about to touch ground, and I'm at the end of my rope. Vincent tries to take my mind off things, going on and on about some work mess, but it's no good.

Every time I steal a glance at her, she's either pretending I don't exist or when our eyes lock, she hits me with this poisonous glare that tears my heart in half.

I get it. I messed up. I should've told her. But all I wanted was to shield her from all of this.

"So, the board wants to have a chat when we return about the Smith merger." Vincent is yapping away, but I'm not listening. I can't really focus on anything he's saying.

"Julius," he tries again. "Give her some space. The whole situation's got her messed up."

"No," I counter, my voice slicing through the chit-chat. It's enough to make her look up. I unbuckle my seat belt and move to her side. The girls, Victoria, Rosie, and Harley, are watching me, but I don't bother meeting their gaze.

"Isabella, can we talk?" I almost beg her, standing over her, looking down. She looks shattered, dark circles hanging heavy under her usually vibrant eyes, tear stains marring her face. It's like I'm staring at a ghost. And it kills me to know I caused this. It's like someone is reaching in and yanking my heart out.

She doesn't respond, just gazes at me, completely lost. "Please," I plead, stepping back to make room for her to stand. I gesture to the plane's back bedroom, hoping for a moment of privacy. Victoria gives Isabella a gentle nod, and Isabella unbuckles her seat belt, reluctantly following me.

I swing open the polished mahogany doors, and she brushes past me, keeping her distance. How I long to reach out, to hold her, to comfort her. But we're miles apart, even in this confined space. She's closed off, distancing herself as she enters the room.

I close the door behind us and take a deep breath. "Isabella, you need to understand. I'm doing everything I can to find Fox," I say, but she can't even look at me. *God, what have I done?*

"I believe you," she whispers, her voice barely audible.

"Look at me," I plead, and reluctantly, she raises her eyes to meet mine. Once, her gaze was filled with love that completed me. Now, it's replaced by a chilling indifference.

I can't stand the distance between us. I step forward, but she recoils, pressing herself against the wall.

"Don't," she warns, holding up a hand.

"I never imagined this would happen," I admit, running a hand through my hair in frustration.

"You kept this from me our entire marriage. Just how long were you digging up dirt on Travis?"

"I started the investigation a month into our marriage," I admit, deciding to come clean.

No more secrets.

She shakes her head in disbelief. "How could you?"

"I did it for you," I confess. "I never expected to find what I did. The media doesn't do justice to the monster he is."

"Don't you think I know that?" She's screaming now, her voice high-pitched. "I was his victim every day of our marriage. He violated me, and I was too scared to fight back."

My stomach churns at her emotion, but I try and steady myself. "My only intention was to help you get sole custody of Fox," I say, trying to explain myself. "I had my team start digging. What they found was more horrifying than we could have ever imagined."

"But why didn't you tell me?" she demands, her voice a raw whisper.

"I wanted to protect you," I answer, repeating my excuse, though it sounds weak even to my ears.

"Protect me?" She's practically shrieking now, the sound scraping at my already wounded heart. "He's taken Fox, the only person I've ever loved!"

"I never anticipated one of the women confiding in him about our investigation before we could make an arrest," I admit, the weight of my miscalculation pressing down on me.

"That's not good enough! You should have told me everything. I thought I knew you. I thought I could trust you."

"You do know me," I say, reaching out to touch her.

"I don't know you at all, Julius," she counters, pushing me away. "I wish we'd never married. I wish I'd never met you." She tries to move past me, but I reach out to stop her.

"You don't mean that," I protest.

She stares up at me, "I do."

Her words hit me like a sucker punch, leaving me winded and heartbroken. My father's words suddenly echo in my head. *We are not magnanimous creatures.*

What the hell have I done?

36

ISABELLA

Feeling the sting of betrayal, I can't bear to be near him. His eyes reflect the same pain that's tearing at my own heart. I know he didn't mean for things to turn out this way, but my son, my innocent Fox, is missing because of Julius's actions.

As the plane jerks to a stop, I grip the sides of my plush leather seat, forcing myself to push the heartache aside. Now is not the time to wallow in it, not when my son is missing. I can't afford the distraction of worrying about Julius's feelings when I need to focus on finding Fox, on ensuring his safety.

Around me, people start to chat as we disembark, but their words are just a low hum in my ears. My gaze is fixed on the scene below, a police car and two black Suburbans parked haphazardly. Julius strides toward a uniformed officer, but I don't hesitate to push past him. After all, it's his actions that have brought us to this point. I can't trust him to handle this alone.

"Mr. and Mrs. Slater, I'm Detective Tascott," the man greets us with a curt nod. I fight the urge to correct him and tell him I'd rather use my maiden name, but my son is all that matters right now.

"Have you found my son?" My voice trembles with desperation, but I don't care.

"We just received word, ma'am, that they checked into a hotel using a false credit card we've tracked," the officer explains.

"Where?" Julius interjects, his voice sharp with worry.

"About thirty miles from here." The detective points toward the west.

"All right. Isabella, you'll come with me and Vincent. The girls can wait at the hotel." Julius tries to take charge of the situation, but I barely hear him over the pounding in my ears.

"Like hell!" Victoria erupts. "I'm coming with you."

"No, you're not," Kingsley counters. Her bodyguard has been practically invisible this entire trip, blending into the background so effectively I'd almost forgotten he was with us.

"Victoria, it's fine," I try to soothe her. "Listen to him." I see the relief in his eyes as she finally backs down.

"She's right," Vincent concurs. "We'll see you at the hotel later."

Victoria sends me one last worried look before retreating to the other Suburban. The detective motions for Julius and me to follow him toward the police car.

"We'll ride with you," he says, "My team will follow. We're sending another team to the hotel as we speak."

"I don't want them to make any moves without me there," I say quickly, my mind filled with nightmarish images of what my son could be going through.

My knees feel weak, and a sudden wave of nausea sweeps over me. *What if we can't get him back? What if Travis has a weapon?* The man is capable of anything. I knew he was cheating on me during our marriage. It was a welcome reprieve from the nights of forced intimacy. But the person being painted by the media now is a monster who abused multiple women while we were married.

How could I not have known? How could I have left my son with him?

Sliding into the back seat of the car, I fasten my seat belt and try to quell the sickness churning in my stomach. But it's no use. I unclip my belt and lean out the car door, vomiting up my meager breakfast of coffee.

"Isabella!" Julius is there, holding me steady. His hand sweeps my hair back from my face.

Vincent hands me a tissue from the front seat as I wipe my mouth, attempting to regain my composure.

"I'm fine," I state firmly, pushing away Julius's hand as it hovers near mine. "Drive," I command, slamming the car door with a definitive click.

As the car starts moving, Vincent turns to Detective Tascott, seated in the front. "What are we walking into, detective?" His voice is laced with an urgency that mirrors my feelings.

As we head to the location, Detective Tascott tells us everything he knows. "Travis is alone with your son in the hotel room. We've viewed some brief footage from security cameras at a gas station and the hotel lobby. It's clear that Fox is upset. He was seen crying, but he seems to be in good physical health, Mrs. Slater."

"Oh God." I gasp, my hands flying to my face as the reality of the situation hits me once again.

"He's in good health," Julius echoes beside me, his tone deliberately steady. "Let's focus on that." He reaches over and places his hand on mine. Despite the anger and hurt still fresh between us, I can't deny the comforting warmth it provides. For a moment, I allow myself to lean into it, to draw strength from his presence.

The atmosphere in the car is as tense as a taut string, filled with a flurry of voices discussing the plan of action. It's an intense back-and-forth between Detective Tascott, Vincent, and Julius. But for me, the solution seems crystal clear.

Detective Tascott lays out his perspective. "We need to get Fox back immediately. My team is waiting in the wings, stationed discreetly around the hotel perimeter."

"I'm with you on that," Julius chimes in. "We have to reclaim Fox, no matter what it takes."

Hearing them, I can't hold my silence anymore. "No," I state firmly, making my disagreement evident. "Absolutely not." I see surprise flash across their faces as I question their plan. "What's the next step? Charging in, guns blazing? What if Travis has a weapon? What if something happens to Fox in the chaos?"

As we pass the somewhat shady Motel Laguna, an involuntary shiver races down my spine. The sight of the motel fills me with cold dread, making me more resolute.

"Isabella, I think the detective's plan is the way to go," Vincent tries to convince me.

"No," I stand my ground, placing trust in my instincts for once. "We need to think of another strategy."

Julius finally joins the conversation, "She's right. We cannot gamble with Fox's safety." I feel a flutter of relief that he's siding with me on this, even though I don't need his support to hold firm.

"Is there an alternative, detective?" Julius asks, his voice echoing my hope.

Detective Tascott pauses. "There is, but it's risky."

"What is it?" I urge as our vehicle comes to a discreet stop, hidden from view at the rear of the motel.

He kills the engine and turns to face Julius and me. "It's a waiting game, Mrs. Slater," he says, his eyes serious. "We hold our ground until Travis leaves the room. He's bound to come out sooner or later. When he does, that's our moment. We apprehend him off-guard, secure Fox, and make the arrest."

"Yes," I agree without hesitation.

"The longer we leave Fox with him, the more harm he can inflict. I need you to understand the risks," Detective Tascott implores.

I shake my head, holding firm in my decision. "We wait," I assert. "The risks are too high otherwise. I know Travis. If cornered, he could act recklessly, do something desperate. As of now, he believes he's escaped. He's free. Let's let him keep thinking that. But the moment he steps out of that room, you better have your team ready to take him down and bring my son back to me."

I turn to Julius, who's visibly drained. "We will get him back, Isabella," he promises.

"Don't make promises you can't keep, Julius," I warn.

His face is a mask of regret and remorse. "Isabella," Julius pleads, his voice a low murmur.

He looks like a man walking on the razor's edge, trying to balance regret and resolve in the same breath. And as much as it pains me to see the anguish in his eyes, I divert my gaze. Instead, my eyes are glued to the grimy motel in the distance. It's as if I can almost see through the walls, envisioning the nightmare my son might be living.

Meanwhile, Detective Tascott takes his role seriously. He repeats the plan over his radio, making sure every officer on his team understands the critical nature of the operation. His voice is firm and authoritative, outlining the strategy we had agreed on.

The waiting game.

"All units, stand by," he instructs, his eyes on the rearview mirror. "Subject is inside the motel room. We wait for him to exit. Do not engage until subject is in plain sight."

The radio crackles with confirmations, giving me a sense of strange comfort hearing the different teams stand by.

Julius finally breaks the silence, "We're doing the right thing, Isabella."

I keep my gaze fixed on the motel, my hands clasping each other tightly in my lap. "We better be, Julius," I reply, my voice barely above a whisper. "For Fox's sake, we better be."

37

JULIUS

Every time the detective's radio crackles, Isabella jerks in anticipation next to me, our shared adrenaline jacked up, expecting that Travis might have finally left the motel room. Maybe this is the moment we're going to get Fox back.

We've spent three hours in this car caught in this agonizing wait. All the while, my mind is spinning like a hamster on a wheel, churning out a reel of nightmarish scenarios.

Poor Fox, he doesn't deserve any of this. He's just a kid caught in a mess, thanks to his piece-of-work father and me, who indirectly set off this chain of disasters.

And Isabella, she's just as much a victim in all this. If I could change things for her, repaint our reality, hell, I would. But we can't. All we can do is sit here and wait, feeling pretty damn helpless.

Tick. Tick. Tick.

. . .

Time's a taunting metronome. Every now and then, I hear her trying to muffle a sob, and it's killing me. I want so much to reach out, pull her close to reassure her with my touch, envelop her in my arms, and whisper that everything is going to be okay, even if I'm not entirely sure of it myself. I yearn to wipe away her tears, kiss the furrows of worry etched on her beautiful face, hold her close, and give her the comfort she desperately needs.

But I can't. I'm the cause of this fuckup, and my guilt is a thick wall separating us. My hands feel bound like I've lost the right to offer her comfort. To touch her feels like overstepping like I'd be crossing a line I have no right to anymore. I can practically feel the heavy cloud of regret that hovers over me.

The silence between us is stifling, filled with a million unspoken words and unaccepted apologies. Then, the radio crackles again. It's like a jolt of electricity, a tangible current of hope that surges through us. I see her body tense, her eyes wide and filled with a mixture of fear and anticipation. I can feel my heart leaping into my throat, a response to her silent plea for this to be the moment we've been waiting for.

"Alpha team four checking in."

All sorts of emotions play out on her face—fear, anxiety, a glimmer of hope, and a stubborn kind of determination. She looks like she's been through the wringer. It's clear she's putting on a brave front, but I can see right through it.

And the guilt twists like a knife in my gut.

Every time she jumps at the sound of the radio crackling to life, it feels like my heart jumps with her. My eyes flicker to her hand, clenched so tightly on her jeans that her knuckles turn white. An almost overwhelming urge to reach out and comfort her hits me. But then, the reality of our situation lands like a sucker punch to the gut.

My gaze travels to the tense set of her jaw, the way her shoulders hunch over as if she's carrying the weight of the world. The last thing she needs is empty comfort, especially from me, the root of her distress.

The silence in the car is interrupted again by the radio, and the four of us jerk in response. The crackle of static fills the vehicle before a voice comes through, laced with the urgency that has my heart leaping into my throat. Isabella stiffens beside me, her breath hitching as we both wait for the news we've been dreading and hoping for at the same time.

The next words have the power to either alleviate our fears or amplify them, and for a moment, that seems to stretch into eternity, stuck in a limbo of suspense.

"We have movement," the voice says.

Detective Tascott is immediately on the radio as he exits the vehicle. "Do you have a visual?"

"Oh my God." Isabella gasps, her face etched with dread.

"We have visual," the voice from the radio relays, causing a rush of relief to flood through me. I let out a breath I didn't realize I'd been holding. "Subject has opened the door exiting the motel, moving north toward the parking lot."

Suddenly, the tone of the voice over the radio changes, causing my heart to plummet back down to my stomach. "Stand by... he is holding the boy."

At that, Isabella gasps, her hand flying to her mouth. Her eyes, already wide with fear, grow even wider.

She's terrified.

We all are.

"Stand down, stand down. Wait for my signal," Detective Tascott commands over the radio. We all watch as a group of officers carefully maneuver around the motel from the vantage point of our parked car.

From a safe distance, we see Travis, oblivious to their movements, leading Fox by the hand. My heart aches for Fox. He's so small and appears so scared. Travis, however, seems calm, even nonchalant, as if he isn't a wanted man walking right into a trap.

"Don't move in until they're separated," Detective Tascott instructs, his voice firm but strained.

Isabella's hand squeezes mine tightly, her nails digging into my skin, but I don't even notice the pain. All I can focus on is the unfolding operation.

Suddenly, Travis lets go of Fox's hand, stepping away to talk on his phone. This is it. The moment we've been waiting for.

"Go, go, go," Detective Tascott barks into the radio.

The team springs into action. They move with a swiftness and precision that's jaw-dropping. Two officers break away from the group, heading straight for Fox. He looks startled, but he doesn't move, paralyzed by fear.

At the same time, four of the team close in on Travis. He drops his phone as he finally notices what's happening, but it's too late. They're on him, wrestling him to the ground and cuffing his hands behind his back.

Isabella gasps beside me, her hand clamping over her mouth. Her eyes are wide, brimming with tears, as we watch the officers scoop up Fox and whisk him away to safety. "Oh, my boy," she yells out, her voice choked with emotion.

Without a second thought, Isabella is out of the car. Her movements are a blur, fueled by a mother's desperate need to be with her child. The slam of the car door echoes behind her, but she doesn't hear it.

"Fox!" she screams out, her voice a mixture of relief and terror. Her words are swallowed by the distance and the chaos of activity around them, but it doesn't matter. She's moving, her feet pounding against the rough asphalt as she races toward her son.

I hastily shove the car door open, my feet hitting the gravel with a crunch.

She's already way ahead of me. Isabella is swift, her panic is fueling energy I'm not sure I could match.

"Isabella!" I call out, but she doesn't slow down or look back. Her silhouette continues to grow smaller, her determination propelling her toward Fox faster than I've ever seen her move.

Each stride she takes is filled with a mother's love and desperation. She's unstoppable.

I give chase, my breath hitching as the cool evening air fills my lungs. The adrenaline pumping through my veins drowns out the noise around us.

Every fiber of my being wants to be there when she reaches Fox, to share in the relief and joy of having him back.

My eyes don't leave the sight unfolding in front of me. Wide-eyed and disheveled, Fox is being walked out by a police officer. He seems dazed, his small shoulders slumped, a stark contrast to the lively boy I know.

And then, Fox's eyes meet his mother's. There is an immediate shift in his posture. His eyes widen, not in fear this time, but in disbelief and then recognition. His movements become frantic, his little body struggling against the officer's grip.

Just as Isabella reaches him, she collapses to her knees

in front of him, her breaths coming out in choked sobs. Fox pulls away from the officer and stumbles into his mother's waiting arms.

"Mommy!" he cries out, his small voice filled with relief and desperation.

Isabella's arms wrap around him tighter, pulling him close to her. Fox buries his face into her shoulder, his body shaking with sobs. His tiny hands clutch at her, holding on as if afraid she might disappear.

The sight is both heartbreaking and beautiful. Their shared relief fills the space between them, and the love in Isabella's eyes as she holds her son is enough to make a grown man emotional.

I take a few steps forward, the lump in my throat making it hard to swallow. My heart feels like it's being squeezed, relief and regret washing over me in waves. I watch as Isabella showers Fox with kisses, her trembling hands caressing his face and ruffling his hair, reacquainting herself with the feel of him.

"Baby," she chokes out, her voice a whisper against his ear. "I'm so sorry. I'm so sorry." Her voice cracks on the last word, and she buries her face in his hair, her body shaking with her sobs.

Fox clings to her, his small body trembling in her arms. "It's okay, Mommy," he whispers, a maturity in his voice that no child his age should possess. "I'm okay."

Slowly, I make my way over to them. My heart clenches when Fox spots me, his tear-filled eyes widening. "Jules!"

Isabella looks up at me, her eyes welling up with fresh tears. There's no malice in her gaze, no blame, just a deep-seated sadness and relief. Silently, she shifts Fox to make room for me, and I drop to my knees beside them.

Reaching out, I wrap my arms around them, pulling

them into a tight embrace. Our shared tears soak each other's clothes. Our broken family, pieced together in this moment of relief and love, right here in the middle of the chaotic scene.

"It's over," I whisper into their hair. "It's all over."

38

ISABELLA

The world shifts under me as Julius wraps his arms around Fox and me. I blink away the tears that threaten to obscure my vision, my heart pounding with relief so intense it's almost painful. My baby is back. Safe. Alive.

"M-Mommy," Fox stammers, the words muffled as he buries his face against my shoulder. "I was so scared."

My heart breaks, the sound loud in my ears. "I know, sweetheart. I know." My voice is raw, the words coming out as more of a whisper. "But you're safe now. We've got you."

Julius's hand is on my back, steady and warm. I meet his eyes over Fox's head, and something unspoken passes between us. A shared relief. A shared dread for what Fox had to go through. A shared resolve to make it right.

"It's over," he whispers, his gaze never leaving mine.

I nod, more for myself than for him. The nightmare is over. My son is back.

Suddenly, I feel a tugging at my sleeve. I look down to see Fox's wide, tear-filled eyes staring back at me. He looks from me to Julius, then back at me again. His small hand reaches out, his fingers brushing against mine. I grasp his hand, squeezing gently, a silent promise of the security he so desperately needs.

"I want to go home, Mommy," Fox whispers, his voice barely audible over the chaos around us.

I pull him tighter against me, whispering words of comfort into his ear. "We will, sweetheart. We're going home."

As I look back up, I meet Julius's gaze once more. His eyes hold a promise, a vow to make things right.

For Fox.

For us.

Despite the exhaustion pulling at me, a tiny spark of hope ignites within me. Perhaps, after all, we can find a way through this together.

But for now, we just need to get Fox home, where he belongs.

The sound of a struggle distracts me from the small bubble of peace we'd found. Twisting around, Travis is being wrestled to the ground by police officers. "Get the fuck off me," Travis yells, but the officer pins his head harder to the ground.

In the midst of my relief, a sudden fury rises within me. I gently pass Fox over to Julius, my gaze never leaving Travis. Julius seems to understand and steps back with Fox, giving me a clear path.

"Stay with Julius, sweetheart," I whisper to Fox, who clings tighter to Julius, his small face pinched with fear.

I promise myself that Travis will never hurt him again.

With each step I take toward Travis, the rage within me grows. He's surrounded by police officers, on his knees, his rights being read to him. But I don't care. I march straight up to him, my heels digging into the gravel.

His eyes meet mine, and they're filled with surprise and a hint of the arrogance I've come to detest. He tries to say something, but I'm quicker. My hand swings through the air, connecting with his cheek in a stinging slap that echoes around the lot. Travis recoils, his cheek red and eyes wide.

"Fuck you, Isabella," he spews.

"You will never touch my son again," I hiss, standing tall despite the trembling in my knees.

Travis responds with a scoff, a smirk marring his face. "I'll get the best attorney on the planet to get me off."

The audacity of his jest stokes the already furious flame within me. I step closer to him, close enough to see the defiance in his eyes. It does nothing but fuel my anger.

"You will die in jail, Travis," I spit out, my words laced with an icy venom I hope cuts him as deeply as his actions have cut us. "There is a lifetime of evidence stacked against you. You're going to rot in there like the monster you are."

The satisfaction of seeing his smirk falter, replaced by a flash of fear, is more gratifying than I would have expected. It doesn't ease the pain entirely but offers a small glimmer of justice for what he's put us through.

Suddenly, the satisfaction I'm feeling is replaced with a wave of nausea, the reality of the situation hitting me like a tidal wave. This man, this monster, has hurt us—my son and me—in unthinkable ways. But this is the end.

His eyes flicker from my face to something behind me, his expression hardening. "He's my son too, Isabella," he growls, his voice desperate, his plea falling on deaf ears. I realize he's scrambling to find something, anything, to cling onto. To justify his actions. But it's too late. He's lost everything.

"I should have protected him from you the moment I realized what you were," I admit, my voice barely more than a whisper. I am overwhelmed by regret for my past mistakes. But no more. "He was never truly yours, Travis. You might be his father, but you were never his dad."

There is a silence so profound it drowns out the chaos around us. I leave him with that, turning my back to him for the last time.

I have to return to my son, to hold him close, to assure him that this nightmare is finally over.

39

JULIUS

Fox is dozing in the back seat of the car, curled in a small ball against the vast space of the seat. Isabella is focused on him, her fingertips lightly grazing his hair as he sleeps soundly.

"We should bring him upstairs," I suggest gently, my voice barely above a whisper. She gives a single nod, her gaze never leaving Fox.

We carefully lift him from the car and carry him into the penthouse.

Isabella is a pillar of strength as we tuck Fox into bed. Her hand sweeps tenderly through his hair, and she gently kisses his forehead before snuffling the blanket around him. She settles herself next to him, her body curving protectively around his.

"Of course, you're sleeping here," I reply instantly, swallowing the lump in my throat.

She replies with a swift nod, then closes her eyes. A part of me longs to join them, to assure them with my presence that they're safe. But I know better. This is their moment, a time for mother and son to find comfort in each other after a harrowing day.

As I walk away, heading to my room, my mind is crowded with thoughts. I can't shake off the guilt spreading like a poison in my veins. Today's events replay in a merciless loop in my mind. Isabella, in her bravery and determination, and Fox, innocent yet so resilient.

The guilt seems to intensify in the silence of the night. I was the one who brought Isabella back into a world filled with fear, a world she had tried so hard to escape. And because of my actions, she had to face her worst nightmare. Fox also had to endure something no child should ever experience, and the long-term effects of his ordeal are yet to be seen.

I spend the night in restless contemplation, unable to escape the fear that Isabella is distancing herself. Her protective hold on Fox, the way she positioned herself next to him, felt like a barricade, a safeguard for her child. And I'm left on the outside looking in.

As the night stretches on, my decision becomes clear. I need to talk to Isabella. I need to reassure her, to convince her I will do everything in my power to protect them. And perhaps, she might let her guard down and let me back into their world.

The morning light streaming through the floor-to-ceiling windows of the penthouse paints a beautiful, serene picture. But the calm exterior belies the tension that has enveloped us since we've come back from the distressing events of the previous day.

~

I find Isabella in the kitchen, brewing a fresh pot of coffee. She's dressed casually, her hair pulled back into a neat bun, the dark circles under her eyes a stark reminder of all I need to atone for.

"Morning," I greet her, trying to keep my voice light and casual. She glances up at me and offers a small, strained smile. I can see the weight of the world resting heavily on her shoulders, but she stands tall, her determination unwavering.

The day passes in a blur of activity with Isabella attending to Fox, making his meals, soothing him when he wakes up from a nightmare, and comforting him when he clings to her, his small body shaking. She barely leaves his side, her focus solely on her son.

My heart clenches as I watch them from a distance. The guilt, the regret, and the fear are all mingled with a profound sense of longing. More than anything, I want to be back in their world, but I feel like an outsider relegated to the sidelines.

Late in the afternoon, I receive a call from the Human Resources department of our company. They inform me that Isabella has applied for an indefinite leave of absence, and the news hits me like a sledgehammer.

"Why didn't you tell me?" I ask her when I find her sitting on the sofa, Fox's head cradled in her lap. She looks up at me, surprise flashing across her face.

"It's for the best, Julius," she says, her voice barely above a whisper. "Fox needs me."

"I understand," I reply, even though a part of me feels

slighted that she didn't discuss it with me. "Just... don't shut me out, Isabella."

She holds my gaze, her eyes reflecting a myriad of emotions. "I'm not shutting you out, Julius. I'm just... I'm just trying to protect my son."

Her words hang in the air between us. We're both trying to navigate the aftermath of a storm, trying to pick up the pieces and put them back together. But it's clear we're handling it in different ways. For now, I can only respect her decision and hope that in time, she'll let me back in, but I have my doubts.

The penthouse feels different these days. It's still brimming with life, yet a haunting silence lingers in every room. Days morph into weeks, and the rhythm of my life has altered entirely. I wake up, get ready, and go to work, but the spark that used to accompany my mornings is missing.

Isabella isn't there.

The office, once our shared sanctuary, is cold and impersonal without her. I can't shake off the sensation of her absence. It's like a ghost that haunts every corner. The soft hum of her voice, the smell of her perfume, and the sound of her laughter all vanished, leaving an echo that teases and torments.

And when I return home, it's the same story. Isabella is there, but she's not really there. Not for me, at least. She's entirely consumed by Fox, by his needs and his healing. It's understandable, of course, but it's also undeniable that she's drifting away, constructing a wall around herself and Fox, one that I can't seem to break through.

Some nights, after Fox is tucked into bed, we sit on the

sofa, separated by a space wider than the entire city spread out below our penthouse. Our conversations are minimal, restricted to Fox's well-being, household needs, and mundane logistics. The warmth, the intimacy, and the shared laughter that used to color our evenings all seem to belong to another lifetime.

With each passing day, I feel her slipping further away. And the worst part is, I can't even blame her. After all, everything that happened was entirely my fault. The guilt gnaws at me every waking moment, reminding me I'm responsible for her and Fox's pain.

But I'm at a loss. I don't know how to bridge the gap or break down the walls she's meticulously constructing around her heart.

I find her in the kitchen once more, brewing another cup of tea. The silence is crushing, smothering me from within.

"Hey," I try.

"Hey," she replies, her gaze fixed on the tea, hardly acknowledging my presence.

I can't bear it any longer.

"Isabella." The tone of my voice forces her to look up.

"We haven't shared a bed in over a month. I get that you needed to look after Fox, but he's doing great now. He's back to his old self."

She looks at me guiltily, "You're right. He is," she concedes.

"Then why are you still pushing me away?"

She lets out a sigh. "This was temporary, Julius. That's all it was. I think it's time I move out."

"What? No!" I protest. "You don't believe that."

My mind races. This is not what I want to hear.

"I need to focus on my son and my own healing. As hard

as it is, I think we both need to move on, forget this ever happened."

Her words slam into me like a punch, leaving me reeling. I can only stare at her, my mind wrestling with her words. "You... you found a place?" I manage to stutter out.

"I have," she responds simply, her eyes reflecting a firm resolve I've rarely seen before. "Fox and I are moving next week."

"Isabella..." I start, but my words trail off into nothingness. I don't know what to say. I don't know how to convince her to stay when I've failed to show her how much she means to me.

I feel my heart shattering in my chest. The realization that she's leaving and thinks our marriage is merely a 'convenience' and nothing more is too much to bear.

"But... we are so much more than a contract, Isabella," I insist, desperately hoping she sees the truth in my words. "Yes, it started like that, but... it's become so much more. Can't you see that?"

She avoids my gaze, her eyes brimming with an emotion I can't quite discern.

"I'm not the playboy of Manhattan anymore," I argue. "I haven't been that man since... since you. And as for you being a single mom, you're the strongest, most amazing woman I've ever known. You're... you're everything to me, Isabella. You and Fox."

I reach out to her, wanting to pull her into my arms, but she steps back, creating a physical distance that mirrors the emotional one. It's like a punch in the gut. I drop my hand, a feeling of defeat washing over me.

"Isabella," I say softly, my voice pleading. "Please... don't leave."

"Julius," Isabella's voice is steady, but I catch a hint of

softness in her gaze. It's not enough to quell the fear gnawing at my insides, but it offers a sliver of hope. "I need to do what's best for Fox and me. It's time we found our own space."

"But this is your space too," I protest, looking around the penthouse that suddenly feels empty, even with all its grandeur. "*Our* space. We've built a life here."

She shakes her head, a sad smile tugging at her lips. "No, Julius, you've built a life here. I just tagged along. And as for Fox... he needs a stable home, not a penthouse with memories of a man who almost destroyed his life."

I flinch at her words. I can't deny the truth in them. My reckless actions put Fox in danger and almost tore our family apart. And now, it seems they're tearing Isabella away from me too.

Her words sting, a harsh reality I'm not ready to face. But I see the determination in her eyes and the unwavering certainty that her decision is right. I want to argue, plead, and promise I'll become the man she needs me to be. But the words die in my throat. Instead, I can only nod, respecting her decision even though it tears me apart.

With those final words, she turns and walks away, leaving me alone in the echoing silence of the penthouse. I watch her go, my heart aching with a sense of loss that's all too familiar. I thought I'd found a family, a purpose, a sense of belonging.

But as I watch Isabella walk away, I realize I have lost it all.

40

ISABELLA

I need to heal.

And it begins with resuming therapy sessions with my therapist, Prudence, who I haven't seen for many years. The buzz of my phone cuts through the silence of the waiting room. *Julius.* Again. The pang I feel at the sight of his name on my screen is a familiar one now—a mixture of pain, disappointment, and an ache that I refuse to name.

I quickly silence the call, plunging my surroundings back into quiet. Staring at the screen, I can't help but replay the conversation we had.

Betrayal, that's the bitter taste lingering in my mouth. Julius knew my history, knew my struggles with trust, and yet, he chose to dive headfirst into his investigation of Travis without a word to me.

Discovering the monstrous truth about Travis was one thing, but Julius keeping it from me was another blow altogether. I keep coming back to my insecurities. Maybe we could have had a chance if I wasn't so damaged by them.

With a sigh, I shake my head, trying to focus on something else.

"Isabella, come in." I lift my head and see Prudence's warm smile. She still looks the same— short black bob and red frames halfway down her nose. Her warm and refreshing smile makes me feel like I'm doing the right thing for myself.

It all feels too familiar as I get up and make my way into the office.

"Thank you," I say, sitting in the armchair opposite where she sits.

She sits down across from me. "It's so nice to see you again."

"Yes," I admit rather nervously.

She checks the folder in front of her. "Last time I saw you, you had just separated from Travis and were sharing custody of Fox. Then you stopped coming."

"I... uh... yes. Being a single mom, I had no time to go to therapy sessions."

She sighs. "Well, I'm glad you are here, Isabella. We always have to make time for ourselves to make the space to take care of ourselves before anyone else."

I nod, feeling the meeting overwhelm me.

She closes the folder and looks at me with concern as a tear spills from my eyes. "Tell me what's been going on?"

For the next fifty minutes, I tell her about the continued abuse Travis has inflicted, the marriage of convenience with Julius, and our trip. Then the kidnapping of my son.

It's cathartic just to share. When I finish, she hands me a tissue which I take gratefully.

"Isabella, you have endured what no woman or mother should ever have to. And you have come out the other end."

"It doesn't feel like I have," I say, sniffing through tears. "Come out the other end, that is."

"Why do you think that?" she asks, but I feel like she already knows the answer.

"I just can't let go of the past."

"And do you blame Julius for what happened with Fox?"

"I know this is Travis's fault. Logically, I know this..."

"But..." she interjects.

"But he should have told me he was investigating him."

"And what difference would that have made? Do you think if Travis wanted to kidnap Fox, he would have stopped if you had known?"

"No." I take a deep breath.

"Do you love Julius?"

"Yes," I reply. "But sometimes love is not enough. I need to think about my son, his healing, and my own."

Prudence nods in agreement. "Your healing is paramount. And by your own account, Fox is doing very well."

"He is," I admit, astonished at how well he has been doing considering his ordeal.

"I just wonder if you need to rewrite a new chapter for yourself."

"That's what I'm trying to do for us both."

"I see that. But in order to move forward, we need to accept the past. We know we can't escape it, and it's futile to try and do so. By doing so, we can learn to love ourselves and eventually love others."

Tonight, against my better judgment, I agree to a dinner out with the girls. They've been persistently urging me to take a breather, step out, and regain some semblance of normalcy after the storm.

Then there's Fox. Sweet, resilient Fox. Julius convinced me with a touch of guilt, a dash of persuasion to leave him under his care for the night. I can tell that he's trying, trying to mend fences, trying to assure me he won't mess up again. The session with Prudence has helped me see that.

Still, I can't deny that Fox needs him. Despite everything, Julius has been a constant in Fox's life—a supportive presence, a protective figure. Fox needs that right now. He needs to feel safe, loved.

As I dress for dinner, I allow myself a moment to hope. Hope for a night of laughter and a few hours of respite from the constant worry gnawing at me. But as I look in the mirror, the face staring back at me seems unfamiliar. The woman in the reflection is stronger, harder, tougher somehow. She's a survivor. I recognize her, but I also don't. I guess we all change and evolve with the challenges life throws our way. And I've had my fair share of them.

The car halts outside the restaurant, and I walk inside, spotting the girls immediately.

"She's arrived," Rosie declares, welcoming me with a warm embrace as I approach the table.

"I have," I respond, mustering a faint smile. "Thank you for coaxing me out of my retreat."

Victoria's bright eyes lock with mine, then she draws me into a firm hug, holding me close.

"Hey, release her. It's my turn now," Harley jests, her tone mirroring the bear hug she wraps me in. I allow her to embrace me, finding solace in her warmth.

"Come sit," Rosie invites, gesturing to the spare seat beside her. The table is loaded with an array of dishes. "This looks amazing," I say. They've ordered everything from garlic bread to three different pizzas and bruschetta, and I'm chomping at the bit. I notice a green salad in front of Victoria but say nothing.

"I love how you girls love food," Harley comments, reaching for the garlic bread.

"I adore food," Rosie shrugs, "As long as I don't indulge in pizza daily, why worry about being a size zero?"

"She's got a point," I concur, grabbing a slice of garlic bread. As I bite into it, the melted butter, coupled with the warm bread, is overwhelmingly comforting. "And it's simply too delicious to resist."

Victoria shoots me a scowl, but it lacks true malice, merely a grunt of envy.

"Well, I'd like to resist this fucking salad!" Victoria interjects as she pokes a random lettuce leaf in frustration.

We all erupt into laughter.

"Do it!" I say.

"The online world can be brutal if you show even a hint of cellulite," Victoria argues, trying to defend her vanity. "And after Italy, I feel like I've ballooned."

"Oh, come off it!" Harley stresses.

"Enough about food." Rosie turns to me. "It's wonderful having you back with us, Isabella," Rosie says, her smile soft and welcoming.

"Thank you for not giving up on me," I reply. Despite my silence and unreturned phone calls, they persevered, and that's why I'm here now.

"How's Fox holding up?" Harley asks, picking up a slice of pepperoni pizza.

"He's fine," I assure her. "He's actually doing quite well. He doesn't fully comprehend what transpired but understands he's secure and won't see his father for a considerable while. I've opted to enroll him in weekly counseling sessions, and so far, the feedback has been positive."

"Oh, that must bring you such relief," Victoria says, picking at a lone pine nut atop a spinach leaf.

"You have no idea," I concede. "It's miraculous he wasn't harmed or worse." The idea of potentially never discovering my son is chilling.

Rosie places a comforting hand on mine, squeezing it reassuringly. "But he wasn't," she soothes. "And you can't continually dwell on that."

"I know, but still," I reply.

"I understand, Isabella," Rosie comforts. "But you can't hold Julius responsible. You must realize he had no inkling his probe into your ex-husband would lead to Fox's abduction."

"He withheld it from me when he shouldn't have," I argue.

"Do you think maybe he was endeavoring to safeguard you?" Harley intervenes.

"Perhaps," I acknowledge.

"This is rubbish," Victoria abruptly proclaims, placing her fork down with a clatter.

Everyone gazes at her as she grabs a slice of pizza and bites into it. Her face lights up as she relishes the flavors.

"Trauma can alter everything," Victoria begins. "It changes how you perceive life, how you connect with others. All I know is that my brother, Julius, adores you and would have gone to great lengths to shield you from the monstrosity that is your ex-husband."

"He admitted that to you?" I ask.

She shakes her head. "No, Julius is like a sealed book. But the way he looks at you... you're his sun, and he'd shift the earth for you."

I lean back in my chair, trying to push away the depth of feelings we have for one another to focus on Fox and me. "Fox and I are moving out next week," I declare, the weight of my decision settling around the table.

There's a beat of silence, then Harley clears her throat. "Are you sure about this, Bella?"

"I have to be," I admit, attempting to steady my voice, "We need a fresh start. Time to heal and focus on myself and my son."

Rosie reaches across the table, her hand finding mine. "We're here for you, Isabella. You and Fox."

Victoria's eyes meet mine, intense and understanding. "And if you ever need to rant or just let off steam, you know we're only a phone call away, right?"

"Or a girl's night away," Harley adds, attempting to lighten the mood.

A warm, grateful smile curls up on my lips. "Thanks, girls," I express, feeling the love from around the table. "You're my family now."

The chatter around the table shifts to wedding discussions, and I find myself mentally drifting away. The enormity of my decision settles in, and an inexplicable sadness tugs at my heart. Julius and I are no longer together.

Moving out is one thing, but the thought of eventually finding a new job and being completely disconnected from him is another level of heartbreak.

With the meal drawing to an end, we make our way out of the restaurant. Just as we step outside, we are met with an enthusiastic crowd, fans who recognize Victoria. Immediately, Victoria's bodyguard moves protectively in front of her, blocking the surging fans.

"Ugh, would you just move?" Victoria tells Kingsley, nudging him aside while radiating an air of command. He immediately spins around, his gaze locking intensely onto hers. Sparks seem to fly in the air between them. "Don't make me repeat myself," she adds, her tone playful but firm.

He steps back with a nod that's so subtle it's almost missed. But he remains vigilant, keeping a watchful eye on the enthusiastic crowd from a short distance.

"Is it just me, or does her bodyguard want to kill her," Rosie teases.

"Or kiss her," Harley interjects.

41

JULIUS

God, I miss her.

I can't concentrate. It's useless. I shoot a glance toward her desk. It is now filled with some fresh-faced assistant who looks like he's barely managed to keep his head above water.

Calls come in, one after another, and I watch him struggle with managing them, juggling between picking up and transferring.

"Dammit, Tarrant, get your act together!" I holler from my office.

"S-sorry, sir," he stammers, clearly flustered, but I couldn't care less. I miss her. He's not supposed to be here.

I grudgingly take a call he's finally transferred while seeing my mother approach from the foyer. I'm wrapping up the phone call, and she is already eyeing me, tapping her wristwatch pointedly. Yes, I did agree to have lunch with her. Do I want to go? Hell no. But when it comes to my mother, options are scarce. She's the glue barely holding this family together.

I push my chair back, ending the call. "Hello, Mother. You're early," I say, trying to keep my irritation in check.

"Tarrant, I need the board notes from this morning," I demand.

She watches the sorry excuse for an assistant I have now as he flusters around his desk, trying to locate the document.

"For God's sake, is it that hard to stay organized?" I mutter in disbelief.

My mother shoots me a look, but I choose to ignore her silent reprimand.

"Are you ready?" My mother's voice cuts through my thoughts, demanding my attention.

"Just a moment," I reply, my patience wearing thin. My attention flickers back to my useless employee now fumbling with a stack of papers, his face flushing a deep shade of red. "Where are the notes?"

"I... I don't know, sir," he stammers, looking more terrified by the second.

I exhale loudly. "For fuck's sake! Move, I'll find them," I snap, storming over to the desk to take matters into my own hands.

I can practically feel my mother's disapproving gaze burning into my back.

Tarrant abruptly shuffles out of my way, wide-eyed and horrified. I don't blame him, but at this point, I don't give a fuck. All I can think about is how everything seems to be spiraling out of control since Isabella's departure.

I finally locate the elusive notes hidden under a mess of irrelevant documents. Snatching them up, I flap them in front of Tarrant with a scowl.

"Let's go," I tell my mother, my tone curt. Without

waiting for a reply, I march toward the door, leaving the chaos of the office behind.

We make our way to the restaurant's busy dining room on Park Avenue. Seated at our usual table by the window, we peruse the menu in silence. Despite the room being filled with hushed conversations and the delicate clinking of cutlery, an unspoken tension looms between us—a sort of dance around topics we know are too raw to discuss openly.

"So," my mother begins, breaking the silence. Her eyes are fixed on the wine list, but I can tell she's miles away, lost in her thoughts. "How are things at work without Isabella?"

"Managing," I reply curtly. We both know that's not entirely true, but she lets it slide.

"And... Fox?" she ventures, her voice barely above a whisper. The mere mention of his name stirs a whirlwind of emotions within me. Fear, anger, guilt—a potent cocktail that's become my constant companion these past few weeks.

"He's okay. They're both okay," I answer, avoiding Mother's gaze. I'm not ready to delve into that subject, not yet.

We navigate through our meal, discussing a variety of mundane topics. It isn't until she orders her coffee that she lets out a heavy sigh. There's a certain weight behind it, a silent plea for honesty that shreds through the wall of pretenses we've built around ourselves.

"Julius, please talk to me," she pleads, her voice barely above a whisper. Her eyes hold a desperate need for understanding, a longing to bridge the growing chasm between us.

"About what, Mother?" I retort, the bitterness in my

voice sharper than I intend. "The part where my wife wants nothing to do with me anymore? The part where I blame myself for all of this, for putting her son's life in danger?"

I pause, my anger simmering beneath the surface, the tide of resentments I've been holding back threatening to crash over. "Or should we start from the very beginning? Why you left me at the boarding school and never wanted to see me, never cared to bring me home for the holidays. Take your pick."

The words hang heavy in the air between us, a sharp departure from the superficial niceties normally exchanged. But it needed to be said. The unsaid truths we've been skirting around for so long needed to be acknowledged.

Delicately, she raises a napkin to her mouth, dabbing it with a politeness that sharply contrasts the intensity of our conversation. "Don't you think I wanted to bring you home?" she responds, her voice cracking with the weight of the question. "Don't you think I yearned to see you more than anything?"

"Stop it, Mother. You could have. You chose not to," I respond, my voice laden with a bitter resentment that's been simmering for years.

"You're right," she concedes, her gaze dropping to the table momentarily before meeting mine again. "I chose to protect you. I chose to shield you from the chaos at home. If that makes me a bad mother, then I'm guilty of that."

"What are you talking about?" I ask, my curiosity piqued despite the resentment.

"Your father, his women," she starts, her voice shaking slightly as she continues. "It was a volatile period. He was having affairs."

"I knew that. We all knew that," I admit into my glass.

The mere notion of my playboy ways was founded on my parents' dysfunctional relationship.

"You were oblivious to it all when you were a little boy. So young, so innocent," she continues, her voice trembling slightly. "You idolized your father, aspired to be successful like him. It would have shattered you to discover it was all a lie."

I remain silent, digesting her revelation, struggling to reconcile the image I had of my father with the truth my mother was now revealing.

"His mistresses lived in the guest wing," she finishes, a hint of disdain creeping into her voice. "He was audacious enough to have them living under our roof."

Rage surges through my veins. I knew my father was unfaithful, but to imagine him housing his mistresses in our home, under our roof. "And Vincent was aware of this? What about Victoria?" I manage to grind out through clenched teeth.

"Yes, Vincent was aware," she confirms, her gaze never leaving mine. "As for Victoria, I'm not certain. It's never been a topic she's broached, and naturally, it's not a subject I'd care to introduce. She was far too young to be sent to boarding school when all this was happening."

I shake my head, struggling to process this new information. My own father's deceit suddenly paints my childhood in a different light. "How did you endure it all, Mother?"

"With grace and patience," she says, her voice barely a whisper. "It wasn't easy, Julius. But at the end of the day, I had to consider what was best for my children. I thought I was protecting you, sparing you from the harsh reality of our home life by keeping you at boarding school. But you know what, Julius?" she continues, looking at me with a resolve that surprises me. "You're strong, stronger than I ever was. You're dealing with a situation far more complicated than mine ever was. And I believe you will pull through."

Her words provide a strange sort of comfort. But then reality comes crashing down, and the image of Isabella shutting me out over the last few weeks springs to mind. I shake my head. "She hates me, Mother. She blames me for it all. And I blame myself."

"Sure, this didn't turn out like you expected, but Travis is no longer a threat to Isabella or Fox, and that was because of you. He never will be again. That was your doing. Don't forget that." She leans forward, pushing away her coffee. "You are not your father, Julius. Stop living in his shadow," she advises, her voice a low murmur amidst the ambient noise of the restaurant.

I exhale deeply into my espresso, taking it in one swift gulp as the weight of her words settle in.

"Then again, what do I know about love?" she says, casting me a sideways glance. "Rosie and Isabella are both women not from our world, not women I thought my sons would end up with. But maybe they are the best things that happened to both my boys. If you had followed in my footsteps and married for mere convenience or married one of those awful socialites with predetermined motives to get the Slater name... God, I couldn't think of anything worse. It's a dead end to a black hole into a loveless marriage. Don't let your past destroy your future. Go to her if you love her."

Her words resonate within me, stirring something deep inside. There is no question my love for her.

"I think it's too late," I say, finally meeting her gaze.

She reaches across the table, her hand coming to rest

over mine. "You're a Slater. It's never too late. You just need to believe you're worthy of her love too," she insists, her eyes locked on mine, filled with a rare warmth.

Her words start to sink in, warming the coldness that has embedded itself in my heart. For the first time since Isabella turned her back on me, I begin to consider the possibility that our love might still stand a chance. Maybe there's a way forward for us, a path I've been too blinded by guilt and regret to acknowledge.

But can I find the strength to have faith in us again and, more importantly, in myself?

42

ISABELLA

As I'm halfway across the expansive living room of the penthouse, madly packing, when a firm, familiar hand halts me. Spinning around, I find myself almost colliding with Julius. His close proximity brings a rush of familiarity. His scent, a combination of refined cologne and his distinct aroma, envelops me, reviving a flood of memories. His presence is heady, and for a brief moment, I forget about the turmoil and why I'm leaving tomorrow.

The intimacy of this moment feels so distant yet so present. Part of me wants to reach out, meld into his embrace, and reassure him that I'm not going anywhere. Yet, I restrain myself, my resolve intensifying with each ticking second.

"I'm so sorry, Isabella," he murmurs, his gaze never straying from mine, his eyes brimming with remorse and desperation.

His apology, like the many before it, is genuine. That much is obvious, but the trust that was once there is now shattered. While a part of me wishes to forget about everything that has happened, to offer him a second chance, I realize I can't. I can't disregard the pain, the fright, and the betrayal. His sorry can't mend the past.

"So am I, Julius... but I just can't..." I whisper, my eyes welling up with tears desperate to fall.

"I'm not him, Isabella. I'm not like your ex. I am a good man who will stand by you, be there for you to lean on, and keep your secrets safe. Let me be the man you fell for once again," he pleads, the sincerity in his voice tearing at my heartstrings.

There's a moment, just a brief one, where I feel myself taking a step toward him. The need to lean on him, to find comfort in his embrace, is overwhelming. But the reality sets in, breaking through the haze of longing. I pull back, creating a physical distance that mirrors the emotional one.

"I'm sorry... I just can't," I choke out, tears threatening to spill from my eyes. Turning my back to him, I leave him standing alone in the expansive living room.

I've got a multitude of boxes awaiting my attention and a heart that needs mending, but for now, I focus on the former.

"Isabella, wait." I hear him call and slow down. "Will you let me say goodbye to Fox? I can't be here tomorrow when you leave."

I spin around quickly. In the chaos of the moment, I didn't even consider the goodbyes between Julius and Fox. "Of course," I say, almost a whisper, the guilt creeping in. "Yes, of course, he's in his room playing with his Legos," I add, gesturing for him to follow me.

I watch as Julius swallows hard, and I pivot again, hearing his footsteps echo behind me. With a heavy heart, I move toward Fox's room, the sight of boxes being packed up, tugging at my emotions. The lingering scent of Julius nearby is hard to ignore, but I push it aside.

"Fox, sweetheart, we need to say goodbye to Julius and thank him for..." I hesitate. For opening my heart, for bringing me back to life. I shake my head, trying to dispel the intrusive thoughts. "For letting us stay with him in this beautiful home," I manage to say, forcing a smile and catching a glimpse of Julius shifting uncomfortably beside me.

"No, I don't want to go!" Fox's scream cuts through the tension in the room.

Ignoring the involuntary shiver that trails down my spine as Julius walks past me, I watch as Fox leaps off his carpeted play area and into Julius's arms.

"Jules, I want to stay here." Fox's plea hits me like a punch to the gut. I watch Julius run a hand through his hair, his other arm securing Fox to him. He lowers to his knees, and the sight in the mirror catches me off guard—his eyes filled with emotion.

I can't watch this. I hadn't considered the impact this would have on Julius. It's not just us I'm tearing apart. It's Fox's relationship with Julius too. A man who, apart from the initial shock of having a child whirl through his penthouse, has only ever been kind to my son.

"Now, kiddo, you've got to listen to your mom. You can visit anytime. And I'd love to come see you play soccer if that's okay with your mom," I hear Julius negotiate, his voice wavering. I peer back into the room, meeting Julius's eyes as he looks up to find me in the doorway.

"Oh, please, Mommy, please!" Fox begs, looking at me with hopeful eyes.

"Of course, Fox, whatever you want, sweetheart," I relent.

His cheer echoes through the room, and his excitement is palpable. "I wouldn't miss it, buddy. Now, what are you building here?" Julius asks, diving into Fox's world with an ease that tugs at my heartstrings.

I watch as Julius gives Fox his full attention, his patience with him so clear. It's painful. He's everything I've ever wanted for my son, a nurturing, attentive father figure. He ticks all the right boxes, but I know what I have to do.

I have to let him go.

Fox is sound asleep, and I have no idea where Julius is after hearing him leave. It's probably for the best if he's not here tomorrow when the U-Haul truck comes. A tear escapes my eye, moist from earlier tears and rolls down my cheek.

I'm exhausted.

I know I'm making the right decision, but I'm constantly second-guessing myself. For Fox, for me, for our future. I can't let my heart lead me down this path again. It's my head I have to trust now, even if it feels like my heart is breaking into a million pieces.

As morning breaks, the day of the move arrives. The U-Haul truck sits idly in the parking garage, ready to transport our lives to a new beginning—the one-bedroom in upstate New York, near Harley, where I can start over.

We exchange goodbyes with the maids and staff, who've become like family to us over the ten months we've been living here. Even Fox, who adores Julius and initially protested, is surprisingly comfortable with the move.

Perhaps it's Julius's promise to continue visiting him, a promise I'm okay with.

Despite everything, Julius is a far better role model for my son than many men out there.

I call the elevator and stare down at Fox beside me. "Ready?" I ask.

He clings to his beloved blue teddy bear, a memento we purchased in Sardinia. It hasn't left his grasp since we gifted it to him following the ordeal.

"I'm hungry," Fox declares, causing me to let out a groan. I've thought of everything but completely forgot about food. With a drive of around an hour, I know we need to eat something.

"We can ask Paola to make us a sandwich," I suggest, beginning to turn around to see if I can find her.

"I want a hot dog, Mommy!"

I let out a nostalgic laugh, remembering the ketchup-stained rug from the first day we moved here and the look on Julius's face. It seems only fitting we have one on our last day too. Despite the heaviness of the day, I can't help but feel a pang of bittersweetness.

"All right, one last hot dog from the stand," I agree, chuckling at the excited look on his face. This simple ritual, created during our time in the penthouse, has become a comforting tradition, one that I know we'll both miss.

We exit the elevator and step out into the bright sunlight. A car horn blares loudly, a jarring reminder that we're leaving this place behind.

We amble up the street toward the hot dog stand, the sizzling scent of grilled dogs wafting our way and causing my stomach to rumble in anticipation.

The familiar street vendor lights up as we approach, recognizing Fox instantly.

"Back again, little man." He chuckles, already preparing Fox's usual order.

"This is the last time," Fox announces, a hint of sorrow in his voice. "We are moving today."

"Oh. Well, young man, even though we may move, we'll always have our memories. And your smile is one I'll never forget." The man laughs heartily.

Memories.

A wave of them crashes over me, starting from the day we first arrived at Julius's house. I remember the ketchup-stained rug and the leaps and bounds we've made since then. The memory of Julius playing with Fox, not out of obligation but because he genuinely cherished the moments with him. The way he defended Fox at the kid's birthday party, the bond between them mirroring that of a father and son.

My mind shifts back to my terrifying nightmare and how Julius was there for me and supported me after realizing I'd been hurt again. I recall him opening up about his childhood and fears. I then realize he's become the man he is today for me, and I am utterly, irrevocably in love with him.

I can't let all of that go.

"Miss?"

Snapping back to the present, I hurriedly hand the man some cash. He looks at me in confusion, but I ignore it, taking Fox's free hand and leading him away.

"Wrong way, Mommy," Fox comments trying to keep up.

"No, sweetheart," I correct him. "This is the way."

43
JULIUS

I can't stand being here.

Knowing she's walking away from me, I leave early, before anyone awakes, scared of completely losing control.

Honestly, if I have to see Tarrant bungle one more call or flail around aimlessly, I'll fire him on the spot.

Frustrated, I rise and slam my office door shut. Tarrant's voice grates on me like nails on a chalkboard. But it's no use. Even with the door closed, I can't concentrate.

I sink into my chair, cradling my head in my hands. *What else could I have done?* I replay everything in my mind. Could I have done anything differently to convince her that I'm the right man for her, that we're perfect for each other?

I shake my head, coming up empty-handed.

My thoughts shift to Fox. I'm going to miss that whirl-wind tearing through my living room. I'll miss his clutter, his shrieks, and even his tantrums. Yes, even those.

My penthouse will feel like a deserted town, devoid of their presence, their warmth. It will be hauntingly empty without them.

I must be hallucinating as I hear his squeal as if he's here. But then it rings out again. I lift my head from my hands and look up. Fox dashes into my office with a flustered Tarrant trailing behind him.

But then I see her, hot on the heels of her son.

Isabella is here.

"Stop right there, Mr.!" Tarrant has finally found his authoritative voice. The absolute fool.

"Tarrant, fuck off," I retort, and he quickly withdraws.

I circle my desk and drop to my knees as a small child runs into my open arms.

"Julius!" Fox squeals, wrapping his little arms around my neck.

"Fox, what are you doing here?"

"Did you just say 'fuck?' " He giggles, and I can't help but join in.

Isabella steps into the room, her demeanor carrying a sense of nervous anticipation. However, her gaze has an undercurrent—a glimmer that sparks a flicker of hope in me. Brimming with uncertainty, her eyes lock onto the sight of Fox and me wrapped in a heartfelt hug.

"Rosie!" Fox's exclamation resounds in my ear, his youthful excitement startling me.

Promptly, Rosie materializes in my office, instantly aware of the palpable tension coiling between Isabella and me. "Fox!" she calls out, her tone a blend of surprise and delight.

"What's the occasion? What brings you two here?" Rosie inquires, curiosity piquing.

My gaze lingers on Isabella. She seems caught in a silent dialogue, her eyes darting between Fox and me, contemplating an unspoken question.

"Fox, how about a little adventure? Let's raid the

kitchen! I'm certain we could unearth some cookies hidden there. What do you say?"

"Oh yes!!" His ecstatic squeal resonates through the room as he disentangles from my embrace, his small form dashing toward Rosie's outstretched hands.

Rosie gives Isabella one last look as she mouths out *thank you* to her.

"Isabella, I don't know why you are here, but I know I don't want you to leave." I take a step closer so the gap between us is smaller. "I love you," I declare, my voice clear and unwavering. "I love you so damn much, Isabella. And I will do whatever it takes to prove it to you. I want Fox to be my son, and you, Isabella, to be my wife. I want us to be a family again, to create our own cherished memories."

Her sobs echo through the office, and my heart constricts. In recent weeks, she's pulled away, blaming me for everything. Yet, reality hints that the blame is shared. She's shut down at the slightest misstep, her fears of repeating the past causing her to retreat. I can't handle being this far away from her as I close the gap between us and wipe away the tear sliding down her cheek.

"I want that too," she says, offering me a smile.

"You do?" A wave of relief washes over me, her words igniting a spark of hope. Illuminated with joy, her face imprints a memory that will stay with me forever.

"I do. You have taught me how to not only love you but how to love myself again," she utters, her voice thick with sincerity.

Closing the distance, I wrap her in a tight hug. "Isabella, you and Fox are not just part of my world. You both *are* my world," I whisper, my voice heavy with emotion.

As I hold her close, a sense of warmth and protection radiates from me. Our eyes meet, sharing an unspoken depth of love. I gently lift her face, aligning our gazes, before I claim her lips in a kiss that words can't capture.

Fox's voice rings out. "Eww, gross!" His mock disgust breaks the intensity of the moment as he bursts through the door with Rosie just behind him.

"Can I eat these cookies, Julius?" Fox chimes in, holding up two cookies with a wide grin.

Isabella laughs as I wipe away her wet cheek. "Oh, course, kiddo. You can have whatever you want."

Fox scampers off excitedly, and Rosie tosses us both a broad smile.

"Take your time, lovebirds." She winks, then closes the door shut behind her.

"Does that apply to me too?" Isabella asks on a purr that has my cock on full alert.

"What's that?" I ask, dragging my thumb across her bottom lip.

"Having whatever I want..." Desire coats her blue eyes as her tongue glides over the pad of my thumb.

A pang of desire surges within me, my heart full of longing. "That depends on how soaked you are for me."

44

EPILOGUE

O NE MONTH LATER

"Go, Fox, go!" Julius shouts enthusiastically from the sidelines.

This is only Fox's third soccer game, yet Julius's fervor makes it feel like the World Cup.

His genuine excitement is absolutely endearing, and I find myself unfazed by Marianne and another woman's disapproving looks at his passion and our affectionate exchanges.

Instead, I meet their condescending stares with a smile and nod. Life is too short to concern oneself with those who bring you down rather than lift you up.

"Go, Fox, go!" I join in, cheering as Fox artfully maneuvers around the opposition, heading straight for the goal.

We chant in unison, our voices full of anticipation. I

watch my son line up for the shot, but the ball whizzes past the left of the goal.

"Ah, never mind!" Julius commends, clapping enthusiastically. "Good job, Fox! Now, hustle back!"

"Someone should get him some lessons," Marianne's biting comment rings out.

Usually, I'd brush off her negativity. But when it comes to my son, that's a different story.

As I whirl around to confront her, Julius mirrors my action, but I quickly put a hand on his chest to stop him from intervening.

"Marianne, are you all right?" I ask genuinely.

"What?" she retorts, taken aback by my sincere question. The other parents hush their chatter, their attention now focused on us. "Of course, I'm fine," she exclaims, looking around at the gathering crowd.

"I only ask because harboring such resentment toward others isn't healthy. Constantly complaining and putting others down, it gets old. You're wearing us all out. Why not try something different for a change? Take the high road, perhaps?"

Her eyes widen in disbelief, and her friend beside her can't help but chuckle.

"Go, Isabella!" a supportive voice chimes in from behind, accompanied by a smattering of cheers and agreement.

Marianne huffs indignantly before storming off in a huff.

Julius pulls me into his embrace just as the final buzzer sounds. "My, my, woman, you sure know how to turn me on when you're fierce like that," he murmurs.

"Oh, is that so, Mr. Slater?" I respond, teasingly biting my lower lip.

"Good Lord, woman, I'm like a rod of iron."

I burst into laughter as he captures my lips in a searing, toe-curling kiss.

"Did you see it?" Fox asks Julius excitedly, interrupting our embrace.

"See what?" I query, looking perplexed between them.

"I saw it, buddy. You did exactly as I taught you," Julius replies, tousling Fox's hair and handing him his water bottle.

"Am I the only one out of the loop here?" I ask as we begin to walk back toward the car.

"The sidestep ball flick," Fox explains as if I should inherently understand what he's referring to.

"Oh?" I reply, a question mark still etched on my face.

"Come on, Mom, Julius will explain it in the car on our way to the hotdog stand," Fox chimes in.

I shoot Julius a curious look, to which he responds with a playful wink.

Fox is already tucked into bed, and I'm in the middle of reviewing the list of charities that Slater Corp. will be supporting this year.

Having returned to work, not as Julius's secretary, I've been training Tarrant for that, and he's gradually getting there. I now serve as the Head of Philanthropy for Slater Corp. My focus primarily involves supporting charities for women affected by domestic violence and those offering mental health assistance. So far, we have distributed hundreds of thousands of dollars in donations.

Next week, I'm due to give a speech at a luncheon for one of the charities we've helped fund. With Travis behind bars for an indefinite period, the fear I used to carry around has dissipated. Over the past month, I've started to heal and regain my confidence. It's not an easy journey, but with Julius's support and guidance from my therapist, I know I'll be okay. In fact, I don't think I've ever felt happier in my life.

As I sit, absorbed in my thoughts, Julius walks in. Wearing low-slung gray sweats and shirtless, his toned physique distracts me from my work.

"You're always working," he observes as he approaches me in the armchair.

"I want to ensure we're giving where it's needed most," I respond, leaning in to share a quick kiss.

"And I want to ensure you're always loved and adored, becoming a part of my life by taking my name as your own."

My heart skips a beat as I watch him get down on one knee.

"What?" I whisper, tears welling up in my eyes. He opens a blue velvet box to reveal a massive, teardrop-shaped pink diamond that steals my breath away.

"Mrs. Slater," he begins. "Will you be my wife for real?"

Overwhelmed with emotion, I let out a laugh through my tears. "Yes, Julius! Of course, I will," I exclaim. He places the stunning ring on my finger, then sweeps me into his arms and seals our promise with a passionate kiss.

Our moment is interrupted by a small, jubilant voice. "Yay," Fox exclaims, pulling us out of our intimate moment.

"And there's something else," Julius continues, "I'd like to formally adopt Fox. I know I'll never replace his father, but I'll always love him and be there for him uncondi-tionally."

My vision blurs with tears of joy.

"Yes, Mommy, please!" Fox rushes in, grabbing our hands in his small ones.

"Is this what you want, Fox?" I ask, needing to hear it from him but already knowing the answer.

"Yes, Mommy, I love Julius."

I see Julius visibly affected by his declaration.

"I love you too, kiddo," he says, pulling him in for a hug.

"Yes!" I agree, my emotions overwhelming me.

"Yes?" Julius repeats, his eyes sparkling with emotion.

I nod my affirmation, and he pulls us both into a tight hug. "You two are my world, and I promise to share the rest of my days with you."

Never before in my life have I felt so loved, protected, and so damn happy.

THE END.

WANT MORE?

Interested in the next instalment of the Slater Siblings Series?

A protective bodyguard clashes with a fiery pop star with a HEA. Preorder Victoria's book on Amazon or from Missy direct on www.authormissywalker.com

ALSO BY MISSY WALKER

SLATER SIBLINGS SERIES

Hungry Heart

Chained Heart

Iron Heart - coming soon

ELITE MEN OF MANHATTAN SERIES

Forbidden Lust

Forbidden Love

Lost Love

Missing Love

SMALL TOWN DESIRES SERIES

Trusting the Rockstar

Trusting the Ex

Trusting the Player

Forbidden Lust/Love are a duet and to be read in order.

Lost Love and Missing Love are standalone books.

Small Town Desires series are standalone books.

Join Missy's Club

Hear about exclusive book releases, teasers and box sets before anyone else.

Sign up to her newsletter here:

www.authormissywalker.com

Become part of Missy's Book Babes - the exclusive reader group for Missy's fans.

https://www.facebook.com/groups/
missywalkersbookbabes

Acknowledgments

I enjoyed writing this book and delving into the wounds of both characters. I couldn't have done it without the help of my team.

Thanks to my Beta readers, Lauren, Chayde, and Ella. You make me push myself harder, and I'm so grateful you do.

To the readers and fans who have reached out to me, knowing I was touching on the topic of domestic violence in this book. Thank you for trusting me with your stories. I hope that each and every one of you who have experienced abuse from another can heal in time from your own wounds and not only survive but thrive.

To my amazing editors, Chantell and Nicki, I couldn't do this without you!

To the fans: all I hope is to take you to a place where you can escape from reality and hibernate in a good book. That is my mission, and I thank you for joining me on this crazy ride.

You have no idea how much it means to me that I get to do what I love each and every day. It's all because of you.

Missy xxx

About the Author

Missy is an Australian author who writes kissing books with equal parts angst and steam. She loves writing stories about billionaires, playboys & forbidden romance – just to name a few.

When she's not writing, she's taking care of her two daughters and doting husband and conjuring up her next saucy plot.

Inspired by the acreage she lives on, Missy regularly distracts herself by visiting her orchard, baking naughty but delicious foods, and socialising with her girl squad.

Then there's her overweight cat—Charlie, dog—Benji, chickens, and bees if she needed another excuse to pass the time.

If you like Missy Walker's books, consider leaving a review and following her here:

tiktok.com/@authormissywalker
instagram.com/missywalkerauthor
facebook.com/AuthorMissyWalker
amazon.com.au/Missy-Walker
bookbub.com/profile/missy-walker

Printed in Great Britain
by Amazon

48151235R00189